ENERGY

Michael Ikevos

ISBN 978-0-9936182-1-5

Published by Mihail Kosev

Contact info: michaelikevos@gmail.com

First edition

Table of Contents

Mark   1

"Global Energy -18"   20

How?   53

Exceptions   92

Stage 1   99

Back in the game   124

Jennifer   144

Are you ready for this?   168

Unequal equality   174

Inconspicuous terrorism   200

Escape   210

New World Order   224

Tumor   233

"Technological progress is like an axe in the hands of a pathological criminal?"

Albert Einstein

Mark

The alarm clock was about to produce its usual wicked sound, when a hand heavily landed on the oversized STOP-button. Mark was truly grateful for the selfless and loyal wake-up service this priceless artefact had always provided for him, but there were times, when he felt annoyed with it. He got up slowly with eyes still half-closed. Mark knew the layout of his rented den like the back of his hand, so he confidently headed towards the bathroom – he could do this blindfolded. Often he had to open his eyes unexpectedly on his way, forced by the debris on the floor, left over from his midnight pursuits. This morning, he managed to trip over a geography map, which had probably rolled off the table in the night. Despite the hitch-start of the day, he got himself ready in less than ten minutes and headed towards the accountancy office, where he worked. He intended to divert and stop to fetch a sandwich. Well, he rarely had breakfast so he could give it a miss this time. His brain might have been fully awake, whereas the same applied, a little later, for his stomach – just before lunchtime.

Out on the street, Mark walked towards the nearest bus stop. He had never owned a car and hoped that one day he would be able to afford one. His salary did not agree with the idea of buying a vehicle and it was not going to, even after hundred years, unless his dull and low-paid job as an accountant suddenly did not become a lucrative and well-respected occupation. The public transport service was not always that punctual, as it was believed. Although, the bus was five minutes

1

late and the traffic was quite heavy as usual, Mark got to work on time, i.e. 5 minutes before 8 o'clock.

His work-colleagues avoided him and would just about say "Good morning" to him should they meet his eyes accidentally. His boss also disliked him very much. The reason was not because Mark was not doing his job well. On the contrary, he was one of the most efficient employees. However, there was something off-putting about him and his personality, and most people discovered this at the first instance of talking to him. Mark had been a dreamer since early childhood. He would speak his thoughts aloud to himself and talk about all the things that had impressed him. Well, the stuff that was going on in his mind was and would sound rather strange to any other normal person. At school, he was often mocked by his classmates, who would take every opportunity to laugh at him as soon as he uttered another of his unwise statements. Years later, at the mature age of 35, nothing really had changed that much. The only difference was that the ridicules were less open. Asociality had become his second nature.

Mark performed his duties at work so effortlessly, unlike anybody else. His natural vocation for Mathematics had taught him to develop the ability to actually rest while working. The real heavy problems to solve awaited him at home. There was his kingdom, overburdened with strenuous tasks. The current project, he was working on, if successful, it would resolve one of the most pressing problems that mankind had been confronted with. For four years, every single day after work, including weekends and nights, Mark was trying to find a solution of a problem that it should not have been any of his business, really, nor should he has had any knowledge and expertise about. The more information he gathered, the more he felt how close he was getting to the right answer.

Last night, Mark went to bed just after 3 o'clock pass midnight and fell asleep, feeling the happiest man on Earth. At last, he had finished completely his research project. He had substantiated his argument scientifically, down to the tiniest detail. Despite his personal great achievement, nothing changed in his behaviour at work and he did not give out any signs that something big and important had happened. It meant a great deal only to him, for now. The time just flew that day. Mark could not wait to go home and check again the fruits of his several-year efforts he had spent on his project. The realization of it was next and this was the hard part. The anonymous accountant had to find a way to present his plan somehow to the public and then straight away, he had to strive towards putting it into practice. There was a great shortage. The crisis was spreading slowly but surely, even to regions, which were not considered to be having energy problems until recently. The situation was worsening by the day.

Timor was one of the few people, who Mark could call a friend. He was a former colleague of his, from Mark's previous job, where he had worked, again, as an accountant. Timor was his boss and was always ready to listen to him. He had heard about Mark's interesting research pursuits and findings. Their friendship was, maybe, possible and based primarily on their mutual interests in science and unexplored possibilities. Timor, however, made no efforts to discover things for himself, but would happily listen to Mark – the "fascinating talking book". In reality, he felt sorry for Mark and that was the main reason he befriended him. He felt about him as if he was a vulnerable and helpless child without parents, who, on the other hand, was just full of ideas. Some of them were truly unrealistic, where others – plausible and worth a second thought. Their ways parted, when Timor accepted one of too many lucrative job offers and left for the capital, which was not far from town. He was now a company's executive director. Mark also got a new job but not of his own accord. He was fired only because there was no one to stick up for him, when a couple of his colleagues very accidentally dropped by their boss and suggested that this 'basket case', over there, should just pack up his stuff and go. He apparently did not make any sense whenever asked about something. The spiteful and united co-workers had made out that Mark was not only a bit of a lunatic, but they had also expressed their concerns that he was not doing his job properly and that he always tried to skive. Despite that this was a big lie, the boss believed them. He was new on the job and he was still not quite sure who was who amongst his employees.

Mark, the oddball, hardly made any contact with his friend during the last five years and now, out of the blue, he decided to ask him if they could meet up. Timor was, to say the least, very surprised and agreed straight away to see Mark, completely unaware about what he might want from him. People would rarely make an attempt to see an old friend, unless there was something they needed.

Mark would finish work at 17.30 every day, from Monday to Friday. He did not have to do any overtime. He always completed his tasks on time, despite his boss giving him some extra work recently. The executive director, on the other hand, could pop out from work whenever he felt like it and for as long as he wished, however, Timor was far too conscientious to leave his office any earlier than 5 o'clock. He agreed to meet his former employee in the town he also used to work a few years ago. After all, Mark did not have a car and disliked traveling. The pleasant small town was very pretty and quiet. This could be said about any similar town; yet, it was very true about this one. The streets ran parallel and straight and it was almost impossible for one to get lost. Plenty of parks and pretty gardens made the town feel less urban but more countryside like. There was just one tall building in the centre of town, which housed the Courts and the Council. Only seven of the twelve floors were being used and this was a known fact to all the locals. One of the tourist attractions that visitors were advised to see was the birthplace house of a mediocre writer, which stood on 47th Street and was turned into a museum. He was one of many that had "enriched" so much the cultural history of the country. The dull feel of the town thoroughly fulfilled Mark's requirements for what he would consider a comfortable place to live. He hardly ever noticed his immediate environment, nor did he care so much about the town, as he was always engaged in his strange and eccentric pursuits and ideas.

4

It was getting towards dark and Mark was waiting for his old friend in one of the three decent restaurants in town. Despite the good air-con system, he was sweating profusely, feeling very stressed out. Timor arrived a minute later than the arranged time. The traffic cops had stopped him on his way to town. Far from being busy, they clearly loved bothering drivers, whose registration plates gave out that the person behind the steering wheel was not local.

"Hey, you, nutcase!" Timor belted out as he was entering the place. This was not said in any offensive way and just brought a smile on Mark's face. He got up to shake hands with his former boss, who was wearing a smart suit. Timor looked a little tired and his eyes were slightly red. This was certainly down to the hour of driving with headlights. In this moment, Mark, in his plain unseemly clothes, looked as if he was the visitor and not Timor.

"Eh-r-r, well, hello, Timor! I'm glad to see you. I didn't... you know, expect you'd agree to come and I thought that you might not come... And I'm sitting here, wondering about whether you're going to come and..."

"You are still the same chatterbox!" Timor cut him short, while settling down at the rectangular table. "Of course, I'll come! Guys like you are rare species. There's no one at work, now, to talk to me about how to build a base on the Moon, achieve time jumps or whether human teleportation is ever possible. Only you can come up with ideas like this."

"Well, actually, that's not possible. It turns out that teleportation is not feasible in our dimension. One vital link is missing – a certain attribute of matter cannot manifest itself in neither natural, nor artificial environment. Well, for now, that's how it is..."

"Ha-ha-ha, sorry, Mark, but you always amaze me! You haven't changed, the same old same! Don't tell me that you are sill living in that bed-sit of yours! And you believe it's a decent place!"

"Well, I like it. It's not bad at all. You know I'm not that fussy..."

"But you should be! You should always try to better your life! Now, if you tell me that you are still working as an accountant at the same place we toiled together, I'll just get up and leave…" Timor's threat was not serious. He just could not get his head round about how little his friend's life had changed in the last five years.

"Well, I'm not. Got a different job now, but…"

"Oh, thank God!"

"Well, you see, Timor, the pay is a bit better and it's nearer to where I live. Eh-r-r, it's maybe the same distance as the old job, but it takes me less time to get to work…"

"And what's your job?"

"Well, I'm an accountant again."

"No way! Really? Hey, man, aren't you fed up with this boring occupation or you're still getting kicks out of it? Numbers… all your life… Yak!" Timor cringed, looking as if he's just eaten a lemon, mixed with shit. He really detested Mathematics. This important and practical science was the most foreign subject for him than anything else.

"Well, Timor, you know I'm fond of numbers and I find it easy to do this sort of job. The new manager, he always keeps me busy, but as it's not a problem for me… and as I'm used to it, and because I'm not bothered…"

"I know, I know. You are a living calculator. I'm only joking, don't listen to me. You remember, like the good old times – I'm kidding with you and you don't care or take offence."

"Eh-r-r, well, I think, everyone, then, was making fun of me, but you." Mark replied and was beginning to feel helpless like in those days.

"They were all idiots, Mark, whereas you were just different and still are as I see."

"Well, I may be different, but folks think of me as an oddball. Only you see me as …"

"Forget about that. What are we getting? I'm starving."

"Eh-r-r, well, but we have to choose what to order, first. I'm not sure what I feel like eating now…"

"Mark, you pick! This place seems cool. It's new; I don't remember it from when I used to live here. They must have some great dish, I should try!"

"Well, I've never been here before and I'm not sure what's good and..."

"But why? Don't you come here on a date, have a meal and a drink with a girl, and try to seduce her?" Timor was joking again. He was famous for his great sense of humour, which had often helped him in life, at work and at home with his wife.

"Eh-r-r, well, I don't go out on dates." Mark blushed. "I don't get the time to find a girlfriend." He never felt uncomfortable around Timor, but after so many years, he needed some time to feel at ease.

"Believe me, Mark, there should be always time for a pretty woman, and not just one..."

"Well, I don't get the time..."

At this moment, the waitress came to take their order, which consisted of roast beef stake, medium done, garnished with mushroom risotto and chilli sauce. Mark, who had a chocolate doughnut on the way back from work, ordered only a salad. Timor was leering at the young woman, without trying to hide his lecherous thoughts, whereas Mark was just wondering about why she had come to their table so late, when the restaurant was not so busy.

"Well, Timor, aren't you still married?" Mark asked. He imagined that something must have happened between his best friend and his wife if he stared so openly at other women.

"You mean to Ella? Oh, yes, we are married. She's such a nag! If I'd known she would become like this, I would've thought twice before I got into this." Timor opened up and there was not a trace of irony in his words. Suddenly, his good mood disappeared.

"Well, I wasn't prying or anything, just asking and I didn't want to..."

"It's alright, Mark. It's just when things aren't going well, there's nothing I can do about it. We are trying to start again and be happy like before but it doesn't work. We'll see what happens, but until then, I shall be looking at the other dollies and think about all the naughty things we could do together if I was single." Timor said and he smiled again as soon as he saw the provocatively dressed waitress, who was bringing their soft drinks. "Go on, now, tell me why you dragged me here?" The guest changed the subject and leaned towards Mark in a threateningly friendly way.

"Well, I thought, we haven't seen each other for ages... It got a bit dull when you left work, because I had no one to talk to. My colleagues never really liked me. Now, at my new job I talk to no one, well, almost. And I thought about how much we used to talk, you and me, and that's the reason I called you and..."

"Oh, don't give me this, now!"

"Well, Timor, I don't mean..."

"Common, spit it out! What has your dreamy head got into this time and how can I help you? And by the way, what happened to the Moon base project you were working on? Last time when you bent my ears about it, you were nearly finished working on it! What's up with it now, five years later?" Timor was quite interested in this venture of Mark's, mainly because he had heard about it at least hundred times.

"Well, I finished it, and... well, I sent it to the International Space Agency and they've probably got it..."

"But what happened after?"

"Well, not much. I thought they would call me and possibly ask me to work for them, or become interested if they could use my idea, but I never heard from them. I did such a good job of describing everything and I doubt that the Moon bases in the future would be any better than mine."

"Oh, I'm sorry to hear that, my friend! I know how much this meant to you, developing the best Moon base project ever!"

"Well, my project was really good and it would have worked, and I'm not saying this because it was my idea..."

8

"I'm sure you've done a good job, Mark. These idiots from the Agency, they should have, at least, said <Thanks> in a letter or something!" Timor felt slightly angry at the fact that they have not taken Mark seriously, although he knew very well that no one ever took his former employee seriously. Even he thought of Mark as a dreamer first and then he considered him as being someone, who had something to do with science.

"Well, that is if they've bothered to read it all, my project!"

"Oh, they've read it, I'm sure they have! But there's no way to know whether it's in the hands of some half-witted underling now. These agencies are full of nobodies! You should've got in touch directly with someone high in the rank, someone in charge." Timor's suggestion fell into place with the reason why he was asked to come to this meeting.

"Well, Timor, actually, this is why I wanted to talk to you. I feel a bit awkward…" The accountant did not try to pretend and hide it.

"Look, Mark, don't! You and I go a long way back now. Go ahead!"

"Well, I heard, well… actually, I know for sure that your company, eh-r-r, it's not YOUR company, I know, but you're the executive director, aren't you? So I heard that you are one of the organizers of the summit about the energy problem that is part of the Global Energy Project… And I was wondering if there's any way, only if possible, of course, and it doesn't cause you any problems…"

"Common, Mark, say it!"

"Well, I'd really like to be there. So if you could get some sort of pass or an invitation…"

"Hey, it wasn't that hard, was it?" Timor said with a sigh of relief, looking as if he had just taken a heavy weight off his shoulders.

"I'm sorry! I just didn't want to bother you in any way…"

"And why do you want to go to this conference?"

"Well, you know I'm interested in Physics and in the power industry and energy, and also I quite like Chemistry and Geography…"

"Mark, you have interests in every subject, so there's no need to list them all now!"

"Well, everything to do with science… I was going to mention only the most important subjects, but anyway… I want to be present at the meeting, so I could get an insight into the latest tendencies and developments, regarding how to overcome the energy crisis and then, take up and get involved in my own research. I've just finished quite an important project of mine and now, I'm kind of looking for something new and interesting." Mark did not mention that he had been doing a research on the subject for the last four years and that he had a breakthrough and had found a solution to the world energy shortage. He believed his request would be turned down if he shared this with Timor.

"Is that all?"

"Well, I'd like to learn a little bit more about this. I've been hearing that some of the scientists, who are going to the conference, have already come up with an answer to this problem and can provide enough energy for the entire world. And I'm just interested to see if their findings are experimentally new or they'll be talking about some already known technology that's been revised and improved. Also, it's good to see, how they intent to apply their discovery time wise! As you very well know, the renewable energy resources research is always legging behind. The energy shortage is a dooming certainty and if the world doesn't take radical measures, soon we'll all be forced to have our supper in daylight!"

In the last few years, most people, living in the temperate zones, were having their dinner while it was still light outside. Governments in these regions had introduced special saving energy programs, which encouraged the population to use less of precious energy after dark, as well as to promote the healthy living habits of eating supper earlier. All households, supporting the initiative, had their energy quota increased.

"To be honest, Mark, I didn't get any of this! But the main thing is that you know what you're talking about. My company is one of the organizers and I can get you a pass for the conference. It's not a problem. The problem will come from all these activists, who are expected to turn up and protest in front of the building. There will be a very strict admission policy but as soon as you show your pass and you're in!" Timor clapped his hand as if to illustrate how easy everything is, as long as one has an entry pass.

"Well, thanks! I really appreciate this! It's very important to me and interesting to… well, get a bit more information on this issue. It seems they're not quite aware of how bad things are, and if I could be there, it'll be just grand!"

"Mark, I might be wrong, but it feels like you have another reason for wanting to go to the conference?" Timor had got wind of something. Mark's face was so transparent. He just needed to be a bit more persistent now and the diffident accountant, who was totally incapable of lying, was going to spill the beans.

"Well… Timor, I could always read the shorthand records after, they make them public. Also I imagine, the coverage in the media will be quite extensive, but well, you know I don't watch television… and I just wanted to see everything in person and if I have a chance to actually talk to some of the scientists there…"

"I knew it! You'll try to elaborate on your genius plans! Please, don't do this, Mark, or I'm not going to get you a pass! You'll get me, too, into trouble if you start going on about your mad theories!"

"Eh-r-r, well, Timor, I won't… I'm just going to mention some of the things I've been thinking about quite a lot lately and give them a couple of ideas, all based on my scientific knowledge, about how to overcome the energy crisis. I've worked extensively on the subject recently and I know, well, I'm not certain, that's not possible but I think I'm right. I know it!" The accountant sounded confident rather than naïve. However, Timor knew him very well, so he "laid" a couple of undeniable facts before him.

"Mark, you are not a scientist! You haven't even got a Science Degree. Accountancy doesn't count as science. I know you love this subject and it's very important to you, but can't you take it less seriously? You're an accountant. Have you ever made any money out of your research projects? Ever?"

"Well, I haven't, but…"

"Exactly! I totally understand your keen interest in science. You, like many others, want to find a solution to the global energy crisis, but leave this business to those, who have devoted their entire life to this cause!" Timor was speaking his mind and simply wanted to bring Mark down to earth. He was just an accountant, after all.

"Well, you're right Timor, but I think, this time is different and I…"

"What do you mean by "different"? It's always the same story with you! Time has stopped for you. Listen, Mark, it's great to see you tonight! You're my friend but you really need to leave this duff science business alone! You're single; find a woman and just move from this town. Here, even a Main Street restaurant is never busy! Where are all the working folks having dinner? Where? At home, of course, because this is just an apology for a town! There's plenty of electricity until 11pm but every redneck in town has gone home, instead of taking an advantage of the light power restrictions."

"Eh-r-r, well I like it here. Are you getting me a pass, then?" Mark asked again still unsure that he would get an affirmative answer. Timor's annoyance might have changed his mind to a "No".

"Fine, but promise me that you won't be playing the clown, trying to chase the greatest present-day scientists, so you could share with them your amazing ideas!"

"Well, I won't be chasing them, but at least…"

"Mark, when we worked together, you never caused any problems at work, although our colleagues began to dislike me a bit, too, because of you! I don't want you causing any problems at the conference!"

"Well, Timor, I wasn't the reason for them to hate you! You were just quite stern with them but, maybe, a little bit because of me, too, but I…"

12

"Mark," His former boss raised his voice and gave him the index finger warning gesture with his right hand "promise me!"

"Well… I promise." Mark gave his word hesitantly. He did not see much point to go to the conference if he could not speak to any of the key figures there and share his research project with them.

"Good. I'll get you the pass and post it to you next week, since you're not going to play up. I doubt that we'll meet up at the conference, as I'm going to be very busy but we can catch up after and talk about what you think and whether the smart heads have come up with some solution as to where to get energy from. There hasn't been much optimism in any of the comments on the subject, lately. Also, things are getting serious with all this fear from terrorist attacks and the nuclear power plants!"

"Well, there's nothing wrong with them. The situation is not that bad as it's pictured in the media."

"What are you talking about?"

"Well, about the nuclear power plants, they are not dangerous. The terrorists are just making a bad image of them. They are not nuclear bombs and they could never explode! This statement is just silly. People, who are not working in the field of Nuclear Physics, they simply don't know anything!"

"I've heard that, too, Mark. There's no reason to worry, though, it's easy to say it. In reality, no one would ever want to live next to a nuclear power plant. What they've turned them into now, they look like some military zones. It's kind of scary!"

"Well, that's a standard security measure, as there are residential areas right next to them but all this could change. Timor, can I ask you something? I don't want to bother you but when I go to the conference, I don't have a place to stay… And I'll need a hotel room, and if you could help me with this and tell me how much it'll cost…"

"There are plenty of hotels around but it's best if you stay at my place. Ella and I, we bought a very nice house and it's quite spacious."

"Well, I surely couldn't take an offer like this, take advantage…"

13

"Don't be silly! This will be a good chance for my wife to get off my case. But there's nothing for free, Mark, so you'll have to pay me."

"Well, of course, Timor, whatever you say. I don't want to intrude, but if I could stay the night at your house, I'll pay for it…"

"Ha-ha-ha! I'm kidding, Mark! It's free, at my expense! It's priceless the way you make me laugh! Come on, let's eat I'm absolutely starving. This waitress has completely forgotten about us. I'll just go to the 'Gents' and you, if you spot her just pinch her bum and tell her to bring in the food quick!"

"Well, I won't pinch her, I can't…" Mark said, unable to understand the joke, while Timor got up off his chair and headed towards the restroom.

Left alone at the table, Mark tried to recall what Ella, Timor's wife, looked like. She had come to see him a couple of times at work but Mark could not make a clear picture of her face now. He was glad that Timor was going to assist him in attending the conference and he was truly pleased that there was still someone out there, who treated him like a friend. At this moment, the waitress appeared out of the blue and served the ordered dishes. On a second thought, it was very possible that she intentionally delayed completing the order. She was probably waiting for Timor, who brazenly stared at her figure, to go somewhere, so she did not have to put up with his sexist ogle but attend to her duties that she was getting paid for.

Hungry Timor emptied his plate in less than five minutes. Mark was not far long behind. When they finished their dinner, it felt the meeting was coming to an end. It was getting towards nine o'clock and the visitor had to drive back home. The journey was going to take at least 50 minutes and Timor, who was tired from his long day, did not want to go to bed any later than 11.00 pm. In reality, it was his wife, who always made him go to bed early so he got a good night sleep. She believed that her husband's insufficient sleep contributed to their marital problems at the moment. He was very short-tempered with her every time when he got home from work. The truth, however, was that

Timor could not bear being around her for more than 10 minutes even if he had a 12-hour sleep.

"Right then, Mark, I have to go, it's getting late."

"Well, Timor, if you have to… I could tell you about so many other things but if you need to go… You've got work tomorrow, and you have to drive back in the dark, and I'm working, too, so…"

"Don't worry about me. With this car, I have no problems. I'll press on the gas and I'll be home in no time." Timor replied and left money on the table to cover the bill. Then he put his leather wallet in the inner pocket of his jacket. Mark figured out why Timor did that just then and hurried up to correct his crude error.

"Well, I'll pay. Put your money back, you are my guest and you've driven here just to meet me and now I'm not letting you pay. I will get this, I'm doing the honours, well, we're not at my house but…" Mark fired away without taking a breath.

"Hey, calm down, man! If you're that keen, I'm not stopping you. By the way, I've got the mortgage now, and the car lease…also the energy battery is half way down." Timor's sense of humour was there as always, sharing with his friend about all the commodities he had on credit. Mark could never get the joke, as usual, so he quickly offered his help.

"Well, Timor, if you need money I can lend you some. I have savings in the bank and I don't spend a lot, my rent is cheap because I've been here seven years now, so I get some sort of a reduction and I can…"

"Thank you, my friend, but if I get to the point of borrowing money off an accountant, I better kill myself!"

"Well, but I have and if you need some I can give you!"

"I know, Mark. I really have to go now, because my wife will get on my case. It was great to see you."

They left the restaurant at the same time. Timor's stylish car was parked just a few steps from the entrance. Mark thanked him again for

15

the conference pass and wished him a safe journey home. The two old friends parted after their first meeting in ages.

The executive director was a very capable man and totally deserved his position at work. Timor was born to be in charge. He was a big man and had a deep voice, which made every order sound like a must. His sense of humour also helped him managing over his staff. He applied the following tactics. First, he would always ask an employee very calmly to do something, without displaying any of his bossy side. On successful completion of the task, Timor would let one of his so called "working" jokes slip out, however, if the outcome was unfavourable, he would often raise his voice and criticize the poor worker quite badly. This would make even the most carefree amongst his staff feel like nobodies. When Mark was working for Timor, the latter never shouted at him. The reason for this was that Mark would sit at lunch breaks, opposite his boss, and tell him about all sorts of scientific accounts and facts, while the rest of the personnel avoided eating with the high ranks. Timor even made the effort to read "Fundamental laws of Physics and Chemistry" and the reason for it was his strange employee. Soon, though, he found all the formulas in the book totally incomprehensible.

Timor did not think about today's meeting on his way home, driving along the highway. He would not have any difficulties finding a personalized pass for Mark Eos. One of his assistants would get it first thing tomorrow. He was more apprehensive about getting home in a minute. Unlike most people, who could not wait to finish work at the end of the day, for the big boss, this meant the start of another family argument. He doubted he would ever discover what sparked them, really. Ella, his beautiful wife, had changed tremendously since they first got together. From a kind and considerate girlfriend, who took care of her other half, she had now turned into a miserable woman, who was feeling rather neglected. She had a point about the second, because the executive director often had to finish off his work after hours, back at home. However, she had no right to feel discontented. One could say that Ella was probably the most contented woman in the whole neighbourhood, well, with a few exceptions. They bought the house because of her; the old one was too small apparently, despite its area of 300 sq. m, excluding the garages. Her habit of going shopping for clothes was not a hobby; it was more like a sport activity, in which she invested huge sums of money on a regular basis each month. It did not matter whether she needed any new clothes or not. Her rich husband made sure she had everything. And like any fool in love, he would give her his last penny, as long as this made her happy. Over the years, her happiness became far too costly and the arguments started. The first major row between them was a year and a half ago. Timor, who was giving to his wife 90% of his earnings, then, hinted at her that she should maybe get a job and start contributing to the family budget. Her typical accusations: "You don't love me anymore! Why are you doing this to me?" accompanied by whining and sobbing, just won over Timor's wish for Ella to start work, too. She stopped cooking for him and he was not allowed to sleep in their bedroom. Several times she helped herself to his credit cards without his consent. Timor decided to counter strike and bought himself a flash car. He hoped that by spending significant amount of money for it every month, Ella would realize that she had to start bringing in money, as well. His attempt to bring Ella to earth was not only stupid but it had adverse consequences for Timor. His wife did not miss a day to make a nasty remark about his ego and lavish act.

At the doorstep of his family nightmare, just outside the door of his house, purchased out of his own money, Timor thought about Mark and how fortunate he was to be living alone, without some woman, who embittered his life. He confidently unlocked the door and went in. The moment he came in, Ella was already waiting for him in the entry, demanding an explanation about him being so late. She had called the office, where she was told that he left work four hours ago. Another row was just eminent.

The fact that Timor was openly mocking Mark about his occupation did not worry him or offend him in the slightest. All bean counters had always had this sort of reputation for a long time. Accountants were not ranked any higher than cleaners, well, maybe just a bit. The meeting with Timor went very well and Mark could not wait to go back to his small cluttered bed-sit. There were 12 days left until the conference and he had to get ready for it. The preparation, really, consisted of him placing the entire research project papers on overcoming the world energy crisis in one folder. Mark, being so disorganized was as typical for him as his vocation for science. This characteristic of his did not help him at all and it was very possible that he might not be able to find everything he was looking for. There were hundreds of pages, scattered on the table, a few were down on the floor. He would pick them up several times only to find that gravity, together with the light draft, produced every time he opened the door, played a funny trick on him and they always ended up under the table again. There were numerous hand-drawn plans, but even Mark could hardly make any sense out of them. Yes, he was mad about science and was probably more knowledgeable than most leading university scientists but when it came to drawing, he was absolutely useless. Some of the models he had cobbled and glued together from thick cupboard only proved that he was not very good at this, either. And the walls, they were quite dreadful, indeed. Acting like wallpaper, a variety of geographical maps covered every vertical inch. Well, one could learn something from this wallpaper by scanning it briefly while sipping from their morning coffee, of course. However, Mark did not just look at them in attempt to discover different locations around the world - he loved jotting notes, too. The entire room was scribbled all over with different color-pens, whereas the badly hanged maps were as if begging for their "bodies" to be taken off and freed from the numerous drawing pins. Almost half of them were damaged and had pieces missing here and there. When Mark hanged them, he obviously had not cared whether they overlapped or not. Despite all the peculiar features in his bed-sit, he liked it exactly as it was. The chaotic accountant, who had ventured to provide energy for the world, spent a few hours until midnight, looking for bits and pieces, so he could compile his research project. He collected what he could find and went to sleep in his short, narrow bed, which he also liked.

"Global Energy-18"

One of the basic roles, the media had, was to present the world people lived in, in the way it actually was. More often than not, the media exaggerated events, even when they were insignificant and concerned relatively small groups, and aimed at creating big news, which were supposedly of great importance to the public. Probably, the only global news, which the media never overstated and on the contrary, they had tried to play down for many years, was that, regarding the energy shortage. The population had never been misled to such extent. When in some of the world megalopolises there was a 6-hour power restriction policy initiated, it was excused with some government preventive scheme, so that the national grid did not get overloaded. Apparently, there was an eminent danger of shortcuts, which could result in possible household fires. No mention of any power crisis whatsoever! All articles that featured the energy batteries were produced on the principle: "say something good or nothing at all", and thus, hiding the truth about them. The crisis had deepened in the last few years and the media was coming up with more and more nonsense just to pull the wool over people's eyes. Most citizens were indifferent to the naïvely presented news that reflected the current energy status quo. The public had been constantly convinced that the restrictions would soon be remembered as some short spell of inconvenience from the past. The persistent announcements that scientists were on the brink of a breakthrough, which will secure unlimited energy resources to all, were pure charade. In reality, they did not have the slightest idea of how to resolve the problem, which was growing deeper. There were plenty of ideas but their realization was practically impossible for a number of reasons: it could bring on a huge wave of discontent, cause riots, or even wars. It could also deem unfeasible because of the astronomical costs or because of the political grounds of the world leaders and chief players in the energy industry.

The conference, Mark was going to attend, was the 18th of series of seminars, which were all part of the Global Energy Project. Some of the world's leading scientists were partaking in this mission. They were all burdened with the unattainable task of finding a solution to the energy crisis. The first few seminars were considered a success, when it was unanimously agreed to concentrate on obtaining energy from the hydroelectric power plants by increasing their number. This was not a solution on its own, as it would not satiate the persistently increasing energy consumption due to the growing number of energy batteries, which meant that any positive change in the situation would be insignificant. The media, complaisant as ever, did not think in this way. They viewed the ideas of the energy wizards as an outstanding triumph. At the last couple of conferences, the discussions emphasized on solar energy resources. The detailed but ineffective plan that was drawn up encouraged investing in as many solar panels as possible, which had to be positioned in close proximity to cities and large towns. The regular citizen, of course, did not think much about some obvious facts. Firstly, there were times when the sun was not shining in the sky and secondly, solar energy was ten times more expensive to produce than, say, the energy from nuclear power plants.

Lately, that regular citizen had enjoyed having electricity for maximum of 8 to 10 hours per day, depending on their geographical locale. Well, this turned out not to be a bigger deal, because people learned to adapt quickly, when they had no choice. They started to believe that this was more than sufficient, forgetting the times, when they had constant power in their power sockets.

During these summits, the attention was very often drawn to the events, occurring outside the building rather than to what was going on inside, with the scientists. This was because more and more intelligent people, had realized that the entire world population, which had been living under energy restrictions for two decades, was heading towards a grim and inevitable future, where the light could never break through again. They also knew that the optimistic solutions, announced after each conference, did not improve the situation and had no practical value. The fanatical activists were determined to demonstrate that the scientists had come to a dead-end and were simply lying. Despite that the protestors had a point, they were arrested and fast track sentenced every time, no matter what continent the summit took place. The media, in compliance with the Law of the respective country, always condemned "these drugged up criminals". Unfortunately, totally innocent people would often get locked behind bars.

As soon as Mark heard about the conference, he knew that this might be his only chance to present his plan to someone influential, like the six members of the Project. It was really convenient that the meeting was taking place not that far from his town, in his own country, so he didn't need to travel abroad. What was more, he knew someone, who can secure his entry. While working on his research for four years, Mark never thought too seriously about how he would manage to get to one of these international meetings. It all seemed to be pure and lucky coincidence for him. It was the perfect timing for the world to hear how one accountant had discovered energy for all.

Mark did not like to travel whatsoever. He preferred to stay where he was and had no desire to visit any parts of his own country, let along go to other foreign places. He was born in a town, smaller than the one he currently lived in and worked. In his 35-year life, he had visited just 6 places. He had been to the Capital only twice - both visits took place, when he was under 10, together with his parents, who were still living in his hometown.

It was Saturday morning and Mark was all set up to go. He had prepared his suitcase, kindly lent to him by his landlady, from the night before. His luggage had everything he needed for two days. On the previous day, he bought a black folder from a near-by stationary shop, in which he placed his important project notes and a few dozens of badly drawn plans. He got on the right bus and arrived at the bus station just before 10 am. Timor had given Mark his business card with the exact house address, written on it. The accountant fetched the first cab he came across and grinning contentedly, told the driver the directions.

Timor's two-storey house was located in one of the newest neighbourhoods, where the residents enjoyed a better quality of life in terms of their electric power supply. To be precise, the electrical network was new, hence reliable, although dwellers were subjected to the same power restrictions. The perfectly manicured lawns in front of the properties proved that the occupants applied meticulous efforts, so the green areas looked flawless. Mark had phoned Timor as early as on Thursday to thank for his conference pass and to confirm the exact time of his arrival. The expected guest rang the doorbell twice and waited. Timor was at work, so Ella had to meet Mark and welcome him into their home. Although, she had agreed to do her husband this great favour, she seemed to be in no rush to open the front door. She did not really care, so she took her time to get down to the entrance.

"Well, hello! I'm Mark. He… Timor, I mean, invited me and I've come for the conference… and Timor's assured me I could stay at your place. And I know that he is at work now but he told me that he'd let you know that I was coming…" The visitor was talking away in the manner he always did. His words failed to impress Ella or affect the indifferent look she had on her face.

"Come in!" She ordered, cutting short his rant. Mark followed her in, where she showed him to the guest room. "This is your room. I'm going out shopping in a minute. The key is under the door mat."

"Eh-r-r, well, thank you very much! I doubt that I'll be going anywhere before the start of the conference, but thanks for telling me, just in case if I have to…" Ella did not hear him, as she was already outside, just closing the door. Her stunning appearance was obviously the only good thing about her. Mark did not even think about having a good look at her, like any other male would have done. He was not the type to stare at other people's wives, no matter how irresistible they looked.

The room was very nice and neat, something that Mark was definitely not used to. This, of course, did not mean that he would turn it into a pigsty, too. He had plenty of time to unpack his suitcase and to look through the contents of the black folder for the nth time. It was almost lunchtime but Mark did not consider having something to eat like most people would usually do. The nearer the time it was getting before the conference, the more his anxiety grew. He was fidgety and was sweating profusely. He could just not stay still for more than ten seconds.

The second taxi he had to hire that day, took him one crossing away from the Hall, where the world's energy future was being at stake. The street in close proximity to the building was blocked by the Police, so 'no driving through' had been enforced. Dressed in his best black suit, very different from his usual accountant's apparel, Mark went up the stairs that led to the main entrance. The only way for one to get access to the inner part of the building was to show a special pass with their name on, together with an ID card. Mark did exactly that. After the Pass-Control, he headed towards the hall, where the conference was going to start shortly. Most of the special guests were already there, calmly waiting for the scientists to appear. The conference agenda featured the usual introductory part, which outlined the main pressing problems. Attention was always drawn to the regions, experiencing the worse energy shortages. Then, a discussion followed with proposals and ideas on how the situation could be improved as soon as possible. Any of these celebrated meetings concluded with some elaboration on the energy status worldwide, as well as with a summary of the tendencies for the future.

The scientists, all six, arrived and took their seats, behind the respective table name cards. One of them, the chairman of the Global

24

Energy Project, announced the start of the 18th conference and delivered a short welcoming introduction. The audience, which included no more than 100 people, hailed the beginning with a short round of applause, very much in tune with the protocol. Mark, however, failed to applaud. He noticed a slight problem. There was a strong police presence around the long table, where all that he needed to get to were sitting. Moreover, there were two security guards, positioned in front of each exit. His sense of logic, being an accountant, was giving him some alarm bells. If the scientists left the premises the same way that they came from at the end of the meeting, he would not stand a chance to gain access to them any closer than 5m.

Usually, conferences were characterized with plenty of generic talk. This one was not any different. Some obvious lies were applauded, only Mark and the security guards abstained. The guards did not, because they just weren't allowed to, whereas for Mark, he simply knew that none of it is true. The first day of the meeting was coming to an end. Half of the forum's agenda had been already covered after three hours of nonsensical discussions. The conference was going to continue on the following day. Mark was still wondering about what to do, so he could have at least a couple of minutes in private with one of the participants. He wanted to give them a brief account of his project and give them the folder, containing all the information in support of his idea. He could not come up with anything and just followed the other guests towards the nearest exit. On his way out, he noticed one of the corridors that the scientists took after they left the conference room. The short and plain looking accountant headed in this direction, trying his best to suppress his anxiety. He had never broken the Law and had never done anything dangerous or illegal. It seemed that the security were very attentive to who left the building, so they did not even looked at the man, who was walking inwards. At the end of the corridor, there were three guards, standing in front of a big two-leaved door, who were looking gravely at Mark. The largest of them, who weighed about 130 kg, made a few steps with the intent to help the lost guest and show him the right direction as quickly as possible. Mark went stiff. There was no way he could hide the drops of sweat on his forehead. His gait also spoke of his nervousness.

"Sir, it looks like you've lost your way. The exit is in the opposite direction." The big strong man was surprisingly polite. Mark did not answer straight away and just stood there, unable to speak. He felt he had to say something soon or the three hefty guys could, and were definitely going to, apply physical force.

"E-r-r, I'm… well, I've come to see my uncle, he's here at the conference and he told me to come and see him as we haven't seen each other for a long time… I'm his nephew, aren't I? We're not that close, but we are still relatives…" This was the only thing he could come up with in this nerve-racking moment. Mark could not act, so he was dreadful at playing the nephew. The guards, on the other hand, were not drama critics in any way or form, so they saw sense in his explanation.

"Who is your uncle, so we could tell him you are here?" The guard asked, consistent in his courteous manners. Mark did not expect that the security would so easily believe him. The accountant truly thought they were going to kick him out at once.

He delayed his reply again, carefully thinking about whom to choose from the leading scientists to be related to. He knew their names, and so he picked prof. Rice.

"Well, it's Mr. Rice." Mark uttered, almost convinced that he was related to the scientist. The stocky guard turned his head and announced the name to his colleagues behind him, who were obviously his assistants. The situation was taking a bad turn again. In just a couple of minutes, it would become clear that Mr. Rice did not have a nephew or even if he had, there was no way he would have come to the conference. Mark had even stopped sweating, as if there was no water left in him. He carried on with his lies. He looked up again, where he met the guard's eyes and said:

"Well, I've brought something for my uncle and I'd like to be a surprise, so if it's possible for me to give it to him in person… By letting him know, you'll give it away, and I have, here, some research papers, connected to his latest project. He's working on it in his lab and it's very important to him…" The man, babbling away, clearly did not impress the professional guard. However, the latter knew that sometimes, one had to allow for exceptions on the job, especially when working for such important people. He quickly called back his assistant on the radio so to avoid saying anything to the 'uncle'. It would be a huge blow to any guard's reputation should they made a mistake that involved a close relative of the client. If the nephew complained later to his famous uncle, the best the guard could hope for was to work for some local B-list celebrities or even worse – get a job as a security of some industrial warehouse for the rest of his life.

"Please, go ahead!" the big man kindly opened the solid wooden door.

"E-r-r, well, thank you!" said Mark and slowly entered into a room, which was around three times smaller than the conference hall and much cosier. Any visitor here felt like they were in their own living room. What contributed to this impression was possibly the bright thick carpet that covered the floor from one end to the other, as well as the fascinating figures, engraved in the suspended wooden ceiling. Mark did not feel the softness under his feet, nor did he look up. He turned his eyes towards the centre of the room. He could see three long tables, which were loaded with lavish dishes, buffet-style, and surrounded by starving vultures in human disguise. There were also two improvised bars, situated at both ends of the room, where the swift-handed barmen took their pretentious customers' orders for alcoholic and soft drinks. This so called buffet and cocktail party was not announced at any point on the conference agenda. Apart of the key participants, the rest of the guests included just a few politicians and the odd super rich businessman. Mark quickly came out of the initial shock of being so near to these people. It was action time. Who should he approach, though, for a little chat and give him the folder? Why not talk to 'uncle'? He headed towards Alex Rice, who was just in the middle of a heated discussion about the energy problem with another prominent scientist. It was apparent that no one noticed the uninvited newcomer and probably none of the staff, or the official guests would have been aware of his presence, unless Mark did not draw attention consciously to himself.

"Well, Mr. Rice, how do you do? My name is Mark Eos and I've been doing a research, working on a project… well, I can say I've completed it. I think, I've discovered how to solve the energy shortage once and for all. Everything's here in this folder… The technical side is lacking a bit, but I'm not an engineer, aren't I, despite the fact that I've got quite aplenty of literature on this topic. May I ask you if you could have a look and see what it's all about? I think… I, maybe, really… if my project works, there'll be energy for all and…"

"Who are you?" 'Uncle' asked and raised his eyebrows grumpily. "And how did you get in here?"

"Eh-r-r, well, they let me in, the guys outside. It's very important, Mr. Rice! If you could just read a bit from it and you will see that there is an answer to the problem and it's not that hard… There's no point to try to look for some non-existent technological solutions! We've already discovered the method but only need to modify its geographical parameters…"

"Security!" Rice shouted, cutting short Mark's endless sentence.

Although there were not any guards inside the hall, four appeared from nowhere and surrounded the troublemaker with their guns, pointed at him. Mark was startled. He kept turning his head, looking like an animal that was just being encircled to get shot. The last thing he managed to do before he was brought heavily to the floor was to stick the folder into Rice's hands. A blow to his head, by someone's knee, sent him into unconsciousness.

There was no record of a breach of security like this before at past conference meetings, although a few protesters had managed to sneak in and throw some eggs at the scientists during the 7th forum. After the incident, all invited to these meetings, had to go through a body search procedure, where every object in possession, which was as big as or bigger than an egg, received vigorous checks. At the last two forums, there was some turmoil, where stones and other dangerous objects were thrown; however, it all took place outside the building and around the venue, at a safe distance from the members of the Global Energy Project event.

Mark, the attacker and audacious activist, did not have a clue that he had become world news number one on the following day of the conference. His unconscious body, handcuffed, was carried out through one of the back doors of the building, where some defiant paparazzi happened to be waiting in the narrow back street. A few snapshots, showing how three guards were loading a 'corpse' in a police van, went around the world media in less than an hour. The key question was: "Who was this man and why was he handcuffed?" When the forum finished, the police chief inspector gave a special press conference, which featured Mark as the main topic. According to the authorities, one of the protesters outside the building had managed to enter somehow and when discovered by the security, he did not comply with their orders so force had been implemented in this case. The arrested man was facing prosecution and if convicted, a possible ten-year prison sentence. In addition, a huge fine was to be determined by the Court. The high rank policeman also added that all those, responsible for this act of security breach, were going down, too. He was personally going to carry out the investigation within the force. Leading media, however, did not applaud this statement. The chief inspector was openly attacked for the guards' obvious misconduct: the man had been handcuffed in a moment when he was completely immobilized. There were accusations of torture by some of the more intrepid journalists at the press conference. There were also some elaborations on the Human Rights Act as the security guards had deprived the arrested from his intrinsic right to be treated humanely even if he had committed a crime.

The human rights subject was long time journalists' favourite! There was always someone violating others' rights somewhere, and society had to know about it! Hundreds of campaigners at the energy conference now were furious and demanded Mark's immediate release, although unaware of the fact that he was not one of them. They insisted the state should reimburse him for the damages and for the injustices he had endured. The building, in which Mark was kept, was blockaded by crowds of people, where more and more were joining in the protest. Some of them did not object the conference but could not accept what had been shown on the pictures. "Poor guy" was commonly heard amongst those who had gathered. The hatred towards the Police was growing, threatening to turn into a riot. A little before midnight, the chief inspector held a second press conference. It was clear by the look of him that more than one or two high-powered politicians had just verbally crushed him over the phone. He announced that Mark was going to be released and that the inspector would personally apologize to him. The crowd hailed with joy, although some people called for the policeman's resignation. On Monday, when Mark was going to walk free, the inspector was going to leave his job. After almost 30 years in the system, his professional career ended in just one day. The media went out of their way to show his face to as many people as possible around the world, the face of this cruel tormenter, who had hounded his men on the victim and had beaten him ferociously, hiding under the umbrella of the Law.

Mark woke up in a place that he had never set foot before: in one of the cells at the central police station. The pain in his head was so severe that in the first couple of minutes, he was unable to remember anything about what had happened. Slowly, he got adjusted to the throbbing sensation and looked around the tiny prison cell, where he was clearly the only inhabitant. The hard plank-bed made him stretch like a cat and loosen his stiff muscles. Mark went to the iron bars and looked down the corridor in both directions. He could not see anyone but was able to hear noises from the one-man cells next door to him. He shouted a few times the key word "guard" but no one came. He sat down on the hard bed, trying to comprehend the seriousness of his situation. It did not take him long to come to the conclusion that he was condemned to a long-term imprisonment. He was very well aware of the harsh measures the authorities took against the energy campaigners, who breached the Law. Then, he saw the positive side. In prison, he would have all the time in the world to get into one of his numerous scientific projects that he could never get round to do. Quite calmly, Mark accepted his fate as a prisoner before he had actually become one. When one of the guards appeared around lunchtime and brought food to the detainees, the accountant made an attempt to get some information about his case but to no avail. The man of law seemed indifferent. Later that day, only an hour after the first press conference, the very same policeman was now piercing Mark with his eyes, as if he was ready to kill him. The accountant had never bothered to pay attention to how people looked at him because they usually stared at him funny. He realized that the only time that he had committed a crime was going to affect the rest of his life. Mark did not blame himself for what he did, he felt totally ready to spend as many years in prison as he was given. He knew that his project was feasible and had no regrets. He had to try. The nasty stew he was offered made him almost puke but he forced himself to eat a few spoonfuls. He doubted that he would be getting anything better in the future so he should just try to get used to it. His headache was gradually getting better but not quite going away. A little before he fell asleep, he was wondering how a person like him was going to be treated by all the degenerates in the prison. Bad, actually, too bad was the answer.

The demonstrations in Mark's defense in front of the police station were loud enough but the noise could not reach the cells, which were two floors under the ground level. The media had managed to get hold of his name from the conference guest list and now hundreds of people were shouting from the top of their voice: "Freedom for Mark Eos!" The humble accountant, as boring and disorganized as he was and only interested in his science, never really had any influence over more than one person. And now, he had managed to engage thousands of people with his own persona.

On Monday, at 9.30 am, Mark was released. He could not understand why the chief inspector was looking at him as if he wanted to tear him to pieces and at the same time, apologized for all the suffering he had endured. There were a few cameras, recording the absurdity of events in the foyer. Mark felt he had to accept the inspector's repentance, although the look on his face showed clearly that he had no idea what was all this about. After all, he was the criminal, was he not? The accountant was quietly driven home by a van and no one knew about it. This was supposed to be the fired inspector's revenge, so the crowd in front could not great their hero. The media was also robbed from the opportunity to cover the event of how the victim of police misconduct was leaving the building free. Dozen of reporters failed to get their so longed exclusive interview.

Mark thanked for the free 'taxi' and went up the stairs to his untidy small room. During the last two most turbulent days in his life, he had completely forgotten about Timor and the fact that all his stuff was still in his friend's house. The first thing he needed to do was to call him. However, Mark's sudden and unpredicted fame had affected the executive director in the most unfortunate way. He was the head of the company, which was responsible for the logistics and the advertising campaign for the conference. At first, no one could explain how Mark had managed to get hold of the priceless conference pass. Then, soon after his identity was disclosed to the public on Sunday, it was also revealed that one of the organizers had known him very well. In the employment registers of the neighbouring town, there were clear records of him being the accountant's boss a while back. How the media found out that Timor had arranged the pass was only for the media to know! The speed with, this information was acquired by the reporters should only teach the Police how to do their job. At the end of the day, Mark was a hero, whereas Timor got the sack from his job. The accountant never meant to hurt anyone but just wanted to share his solution of the energy problem. Inadvertently, he had ruined two people's lives and one of them was his good old friend Timor.

The phone was ringing for a seventh time but no one picked it. Waiting to hear Timor's voice or that of his wife Ella, Mark suddenly remembered about his work at the Accountants Office. He felt only slightly worried that he did not turn up for work on the first day of the week. After all, he had an excuse: he got arrested by the Police.

His parents had opted for a peaceful and quiet life, as they did not have a television set and were never interested in the news. They were also going to receive a phone call from him. They had heard of the events from one of the neighbours, the so-called good-wishers, but really, just a nosey parker. Mark was calling Timor first because he was worried about the suitcase he had left there and which was not his. Whenever he had to borrow something, he liked to return it back and on time. He would feel awful when he was late giving the item back even if he was told that it was not a problem.

As there was still not an answer to his call, Mark decided to dial his parents' phone number. His mother, who usually never listened to what he was saying, was very pleased to hear his voice. She did not miss to tell him off, though, for going to 'that dreary conference'. The woman was not worried in the slightest. Lately, one or two insidious memory-related illnesses had made her a real happy-go-lucky, as she could hardly ever remember what she was supposed to worry about. Her very good friend, from the house next door, had told her everything to the smallest detail. However, Mark's mother had forgotten it all, nearly. She did not even remember that her son spent almost two days in a prison cell. His father was in a better physical and mental health but they had not been on very good terms for the last twenty years. This was because Mark did not follow into his footsteps and become a lawyer. His devotion to science was something like eyesore for the attorney, who

33

rightfully regarded his son as a nutcase. The accountancy job was the last nail in the coffin for their relationship. Mark calmed down his not so worried mother and dialled again Timor's number. Yet, there was no answer again. It was getting towards lunchtime, so he decided to go to his local stress and buy something to eat. He loved instant soup that took two minutes to prepare in the microwave.

Mark had no idea how it felt to be famous. And now, he had become a real celebrity in such a short time. He was not familiar with the vulture mentality of reporters, either. They soon found out that the former chief inspector had taken their "big news" back to his hometown. A dozen of television crews rushed to the address of Mark's bed-sit. He had just decided that it was time to get some lunch. The moment he opened the front door, he saw people with microphones, running towards him from all sides, followed behind by the cameramen. The interesting part was that all of them shouted his name. Stunned by this unexpected journalists attack Mark hurried to get back in his room. He ran up the stairs to the third floor and realized that he was streaming in sweat like when he was at the conference. His heart was racing. "And now, how am I going to get out?" He kept asking himself while striding across his tiny room. He looked out of the window to check if they were still waiting for him but it was silly to think that they would just leave. Quite the opposite, when a few photo reporters spotted his face, they immediately turned their large camera lenses towards him. Mark just could not think of a way to get rid of these leeches outside. He decided to call Timor again, who might be able to help him, or even come to his rescue and take him away from here.

"Hello?" Someone said after the second ring-tone.

"Eh-r-r, well, hello, Timor? Hi, it's Mark, here… Look, Timor, I've left my things at your house, well, the Police brought me straight back home and I forgot I left at yours, and now, there are these reporters outside my place and I can't get out… I was wondering if you could help me and…"

"To help you?!?" Timor, totally drunk, shouted in the receiver, so that Mark had to pull his ear back from it. "You, idiot...! Nutter! You, imbecile, you promised me you wouldn't do anything stupid! How could you? Why?" Timor was almost crying. Mark could not understand quite what the matter was. It was a happy end, after all. He was free.

"Well, Timor, but... but what is it? Are you alright?"

"Am I alright? Is this a joke, you dimwit? You're a celebrity now, a hero... Oh, the poor innocent citizen, tortured and everything... And guess who got the blame out of all this and your presence at the conference? Can you guess?" Mark's left ear got almost deafened, so he moved the receiver to his right side, holding it 15cm away from his face.

"Well, no. I can't... but what happened...? Because I just don't..."

"I lost my job! I got fired straight after the first press conference, when everyone was still thinking you were a criminal. But guess what? When you were hailed as a hero, I didn't get my job back. Because I'm good-for-nothing, yes, if I wasn't that, I wouldn't have let an idiot like you get in."

"Well, I'm sorry to hear that, Timor! I had no idea! But you're a good specialist and I'm sure you'll find a much better job. You are always wooed by different companies, aren't you? Or if you want, not that I try to... but, well, I could ask if they give you your job back, when I explain everything..."

"God, no!" Timor screamed again. "I don't want you to do anything! I don't want to see you or hear from you. I don't care about my job, but my wife... How are you going to make her come back? Ella got her stuff and left because of you! Everything is your fault! The hero of the day! So what did you achieve by getting inside? Did you manage to solve the energy problem? Never mind, you're insane! The only thing that has come out of your wacky head is that you've ruined my life!" These were Timor's last words before he slammed the phone down so hard that he broke the receiver. Reclining on the sofa in his empty house, with a bottle in his hand, he started to cry. He had nothing to live for – no personal life and no career. Yes, Ella and he, had problems, but things were not that bad. In a month to one year, they could have patch things up and have a good relationship again. Well, this was not exactly the case. Timor had just got used to Ella, her personality and the arguments. Their relationship was dead. Without realizing it yet, Mark had actually done him a big favour. With regards to losing his job, the accountant was really the one to blame for. However, Timor was not going to stay jobless for long. His professional skills and good qualifications would help him get into a well-paid employment in no time. Competent managers like him were hard to find these days. Right now, though, he was drunk and willing to drink more, as if he wanted to dry up the country's reserves of spirit drinks and so it resorted to imports. He was totally irrational and during the next few days, he behaved like a confused child lost in his parents' big house. A month after the ill-fated events, after some mammoth efforts, he managed to leave the bottle and pick himself together. It was easy to say, but hard to do. He still did not feel like doing anything. Every time he thought about Ella, he felt down again. It would have taken him at least a few months to brush off the habit of her being around him for the last ten years. The same applied for him to feel like working again and go back to everyday normality in his life.

Mark Eos had rarely felt as bad as after his conversation with Timor. It was hard to believe that he could ever affect someone's life in such an adverse way, as he was having hardly any friends, in fact – just one, and was being such a recluse by all means. In this case, he had done totally inadvertently something really bad. Mark was still under the influence of Timor's hard-to-swallow accusations, when he heard a surprising knock on his door. The main entrance of the building was always locked, so no one but the residents could gain access. It was just before 1pm and all of his neighbours were at work. The family from the second floor had gone on holiday since last week and it was unlikely that they got back. So who had let these people here? Mark was certain that there were at least a dozen of reporters outside his front door. There was another, loader knock on the door, speaking for the visitors' impatience. Mark decided that it was better to open the door and just quickly answer their questions. The alternative was to leave them banging but he knew he could not withstand the loud noise for more than ten minutes. The two smartly dressed men, who seemed the same age as the accountant, did not fit the picture he was expecting to see, when he opened the door. Classic black suit, white shirt and mono-coloured tie, red for one of them and orange for the other - their apparel was not typical for the regular journalist.

"How do you do, Mr. Eos?" asked the man of yet non-disclosed occupation, who was stood more to the front. After his greeting, he removed his sunglasses. "May we come in, Mr. Eos? If one of the reporters downstairs manages to open the door, it will be very undesirable to see us here."

"Well, but who are you?" Mark thought they looked like secret agents. Then, it could not be that, because it was only a few hours ago, when the Police had set him free. Why would they want him again?

"Mr. Platt sends us. We have a proposal for you, Mr. Eos, and we hope you accept it. Now, may we come in?"

"Well, of course! Please, come in. I just... I haven't had time to tidy up but you know, I was away for a few days, wasn't I?"

Mark knew the name Platt very well, although he did not know the man in person. He saw him for the first time at the conference. Platt was the chairman of the Global Energy Project and apart of being an outstanding scientist, he had also pursued a great political career on international level. He was very successful at combining science and politics, so he was elected unanimously to lead this project that was so vital to mankind. The other nominees for the chairman's post were simply exceptional scientists but not more.

The two messengers were rather disappointed by the interior design of the Mark's room. They had never seen such an untidy place before. The word 'mess' was simply week to describe it. Well, they had not come to preach, after all. So the gentleman, who had mentioned Platt's name, said:

"We'd like to invite you, on behalf of Mr. Platt, to a private meeting with him at his hotel room. We'll take you there, if you accept, of course."

"Eh-r-r, well, Platt wants to see me? Me? But tell me why? That's impossible! Why?" Mark could not believe that such an influential man would want to meet him in private, him – the ordinary accountant! It did not make any sense and Mark liked to see sense in things.

"I see that you are surprised. But we have no idea why Mr. Platt wants to see you. We simply do as we are told." sincerely replied the gentleman with the red tie, while looking around the strikingly messy room. He spotted the round table next to the window, which was covered with dozens of books, tatty geographical maps, small colourful notes, scattered around, several notebooks, 7-8 pens and a few felt-tips. The three chairs around it were also loaded with all sorts of scientific literature, where the piles of books measured up to the height of a boy in fifth-grade, when sitting down. The visitor's eyes also could not miss to notice all the maps glued to the walls. He was most impressed by an enormous two-coloured map on the ceiling, which represented a detailed relief depiction of the world. Within seconds the man learned by it that plains in the temperate zones covered much more of the terrain than he was aware of.

"We believe the invite has something to do with the conference, where you, Mr. Eos, played a leading part but we don't know any more." Mr. "Orange Tie" interjected. Like his colleague, he also examined the room. He set his eyes onto Mark's bed, where about 15 books covered half of it. The thought that this oddball went to bed with books rather than a woman brought a smile on the man's face and he felt like making fun of Mark. His old-fashioned thick-rimmed glasses also made the visitor laugh.

"Well, right, though, what's the big deal? They just jumped on me when I was handing my research papers on solving the energy shortage to prof. Alex Rice, and then, somebody hit me, and I didn't see who, and after that I was arrested and ended up in custody. I had done nothing, really, and they let me go, though, maybe, I should've been 'fast-track' sentenced. Well, that's all."

"No, Mr. Eos, that is not all!"

"Well, I'm not sure, I can't remember some stuff… my head is still hearting…"

"Mr. Eos, it's obvious that we need to clarify things further, in relation to your case. You're not simply someone, who had been detained by the Police as an intruder, who had disturbed the scientists. You have been the most popular person, worldwide, for the last two days. Haven't you got a television set, so you see what I'm talking about? You're the top news on every channel!"

"Well, I've got one but I don't have much time to watch and I don't find TV interesting, I'd rather read. I think it's broken, anyway, I can't remember well…"

Mark went towards a wooden box, which contained his small television set. He got it out and switched the machine on. He gave it a good slam with his fist as a preventive measure but to no avail. It did not work, indeed. The two men in suits asked themselves why anyone would keep their only television set in a wooden box.

"In short, Mr. Eos, you had incited most of the world leading human rights organizations to step in your defense. The town was brought nearly under martial law after so many activists wanted to siege the police station you were held in. The conference meeting now is associated with your name. It's doubtful that anyone has managed to learn about the topical issues that have been discussed at the forum and the decisions that have been made, whereas everyone knows your name, Mr. Eos."

"Well… really? I thought that it was not such a big deal. Although, I saw that there were lots of protesters… Well, at these meetings, it's been always the case, hasn't't? I did nothing wrong, but to be honest, I

39

deserved what I got. I shouldn't have been there. And what organizations are you talking about? Human rights – how come?"

"Did you get beaten by the Police?"

"Well, might have not beaten me, only that they jumped on me in the Hall where the little party was but I don't remember anything, they might have done it. Well, I couldn't say, I don't know…"

"There, in the Hall, Mr. Eos, you lost consciousness after the heavy measures and physical force, applied by the guards towards you. Then, some reporter had taken a shot of you being carried out in this state and it all started from there. You are free now, the chief policeman is fired and every journalist wants to get an exclusive interview from you as soon as. We are not journalists and we have to take you to Mr. Platt. We managed to get in here through the ground floor of the building next door. There should be plenty of hounds there, too, by now, so we'll just use the front door. Are you coming?"

"Well, now?"

"Now, yes, as at once! The invitation is for today."

"Well, these people outside… They are there and we can't get out, I'm trapped…"

"Don't worry about this. We have some of our people downstairs and they'll bring the car right to the front. We'll form a cordon and you'll jump in. None of the journalists would be able to get near you. We are professionals." The messenger sounded very confident, which implied that this was not his first time to be confronted with a crowd of reporters, hungry for news.

"Well, fine, I'll come but how will I get back in here afterwards? They won't be gone and probably they'll follow us in their cars. How will I get away from them?"

"Do you have anywhere that you can stay for a bit, with someone you know, a safe place? For the time being, that's a good solution!" Mark thought of Timor again. He could not think of anyone else.

"Well, there isn't anyone, I believe…"

40

"Then, Mr. Platt would probably find somewhere secure for you to spend the night, where you won't be disturbed. Don't worry!"

"Well, all right, then. If there's a place I can stay later, otherwise these people outside will just pester me. Well, they might go but I doubt it…"

"Let's go, Mr. Eos."

Mark got all he needed into a small sport bag, which he had owned since his high-school years, and followed the two men. He could not wait to meet Mr. Platt. This was an incredible opportunity that he had never thought it could come to him. The professor would hear him out and in this way, the plan on providing energy for all would have reached the person from whom a lot of things depended on, if not almost everything.

They left the building as planned. No one managed to touch Mark, take photos or ask him a question, as the car was parked only 2m away from the front door and because the two men made him advance into the tinted-window van as quick as possible. It was a good job that Mark dived down at the last moment and missed the top edge of the back door. The other two vehicles, which were full with Platt's people, blocked the road so the reporters could not follow straight away.

It took them almost an hour to reach the five-star hotel because of the horrendous traffic. Despite the fact that cars required something that was very expensive and scarce, this did not stop their owners of driving them. The optimization and further development of public transport did not encourage affluent people, who still lived in the old 'petrol' times, to give up the idea of enjoying their private means of transportation at any time.

The presidential apartment was situated on the eighth and last floor of the hotel, taking up an area of almost 200sq.m. A man of such rank, like Platt, deserved only the best. Before he got out of the vehicle, Mark was asked to put on the hat and sun glasses that he was given. The plan was that this meeting stayed out of the public eye as long as it was possible. It was certain that if noticed, one of the staff or guests of the

41

hotel would boast around about seeing Mark Eos, the hero. From there, the road to blowing the news of his location publicly could not be any shorter. The elevator's display indicator counted from one to eight. The two men escorting Mark led him to the room next the presidential apartment. According to the instructions, the meeting was going to take place in the hotel room, booked for Platt's personal assistant. The reason for this was that the chairman of the Global Energy Project did not want a person from the populace to see his lavish lifestyle. Platt believed everyone should live by their means, and his was virtually unlimited. According to a few leading sociologists and analyzers, Platt's name could be placed up next to those of presidents and prime ministers in the developed world.

After three knocks, a pause, and then three more knocks, the door was opened by Mr. Platt's personal assistant, the errand boy. Platt, himself, was sitting in the middle of the room, calmly smoking a cigar, by the looks of it – Cuban. It was unknown why most people of high status in society smoked cigars. It was an unhealthy habit and a fad that was not going to stop soon. Mark, who had tried this just once in his life, winced at the unpleasant smell of the cigar smoke.

"Please, come in, Mr. Eos. Have a seat!" Platt uttered, pointing at the chair opposite to him. He did not stand up to shake hands with his guest, as if Mark's presence was unwelcome. In reality, this was not the case. The bald, short and overweight host was much of a cunning man, who always managed to get advantage of any situation. Platt had won his good reputation mainly for being reliable when it came down to keeping promises in his dealings with people and companies. He was succinct in words but at the same time, one word from him was enough. The trust he installed in people was more of an innate quality, rather than learned one over the years. The accountant made himself comfortable on his seat and Platt gave his instructions to be left alone with his guest. He did not want to be disturbed in the following 30 minutes or so.

"Well, Mr. Platt, how are you? I just want to say that it's a great honour for me to meet you. I am... I just can't believe it and I've never imagined that I could meet you in person, for me, it's just..."

"Thank you, Mark. It's OK if I call you Mark, isn't it?" Platt asked in attempt to set his visitor at ease in this high-profile environment that was alien to him.

"Well, of course, no problem, Mr. Platt." The accountant gave his permission, not that he had any other alternatives.

"Just "Platt" is fine. Mark, you seem like a nice guy. What happened at the conference was clearly some big misunderstanding and nothing else. Everyone makes mistakes. It happens!"

"Well, I just wanted to meet and speak to one of you, the scientists... I maybe have a solution to the energy problem. I don't oppose to the conference at all. No, not at all, I've closely followed each of them so far and I'm very interested in the subject. Well, when the Global Energy Project was launched, I began to develop my research project that I handed to Alex Rice... but then, he called the guards. I didn't want this to happen but..."

"I fully understand, Mark. That's exactly why I've invited you here today." Platt drew on his cigar and continued. "Mark, what was in the folder that you gave to Alex? When all this happened, I was just a few meters from you two. Prof. Rice said that he had thrown what you gave him away. I'm just curious to know what was inside!"

"Well, it was that, as I said, my research work papers on the energy problem – all my notes, the technological and geographical specifications of my idea, some drawing plans of the basic components, which have no analogue, and I only imagined what they would look like if built. The positioning of the energy capacities, the transport specifications, the safety measures – everything I could think of, had its scientifically substantiated solution."

"Hmm, interesting! And what do you think about the energy situation, Mark? I heard you're an accountant and that you have never specialized in any science." Platt changed the subject in suspicion that

43

the man in front of him was a total nutcase. The professor almost regretted inviting Mark. However, the situation required exploring every possibility, no matter how insignificant it might seem.

"Well, Platt, you know a lot more than me... I've just read the reports, issued by the International Energy Agency and I'm familiar with all that can be explained by different scientific approaches. We suffer now from energy shortages. In some parts of the world, the voltage varies, so it takes people longer to use the same quantity of energy. Low voltage decreases the power of appliances and machines, as far as I know. Energy consumption increases as developing countries are trying to stay afloat, well, the lack of energy resources contributes to them going down, although, those poor countries keep dreaming on... And the fact that the powerful states are in perpetual competition economically makes them blatantly misuse energy resources, especially by not applying strict regulation policies towards the use of energy batteries... This leads, as you know, to the increase of energy needs, which are inconsistent with the manufacturing capacities. Within two years, it's expected that the energy shortage will affect even the richest countries, when less than half of the population would have access to electricity for more than 5 hours per day and if it's used moderately. Small countries will spend time in darkness for longer but it depends on which countries we're talking about... I'm kind of generalizing a bit about things here... There are other adverse results that we could expect in the future. Firstly, the industry won't be at its current poor functioning state but it would worsen. The situation is probably already quite bad but all of it is consciously kept secret. The second effect concerns transport and the decreased level of people's movement, as well as the shrinking sector of transportation of goods, due to the shortage of energy resources. It will simply become impossible to charge the energy batteries and this will result in at least 60% of the transportation machines to stop working forever, unless a source is discovered, a very substantial source within two years, the latest... The third and most significant consequence will be the social impact, caused by the inevitable energy wars between the two main energy centers in the world. In addition, we have a hopeless tendency to praise highly renewable energy resources. They are waste of time as they do not change anything, well, how could they?"

Mark could have gone on for quite some time but Platt was already satisfied that the hero, whose rights were violated at the conference, was not mad and actually had a sound knowledge about the topic.

"All right, Mark, thank you! That's quite enough. I can see that you are very familiar with the problem we've been trying to solve at our meetings. There's just one thing I couldn't get. Where do you have such misleading information from? Energy wars, low voltage… it's not exactly like this!" Platt knew that Mark was right about everything but he was just bewildered by the fact – how an ordinary accountant could learn about the issue in such a detail, when some of the scientists, his colleagues, did not have any idea about the actual energy situation.

"Well, the information, Mr. Platt, which gets released after each conference, has been more often than not inaccurate. It has also been presented in a way that one sees the obvious – you don't have a solution to the problem." Mark explained without thinking whether his words sounded a bit too harsh. After all, Platt was the big boss. The professor's face did not change. He knew that this was the truth and that they were all some light years away from discovering a good and long-lasting energy source as an answer to the crisis. "Well, and the energy wars, they have always been around from historical point of view, since the times there were still natural fuels available, like oil and gas. As you know, oil has been in the center of one of the world wars in the past. I am aware that this happened many years ago but now we've got a similar situation, just the energy source is different."

"You're right, Mark, though, the stuff about the decreased voltage, you're talking about, it's not true. Are you saying that we are trying to deceive the public?" Platt's criticism was not justified and he knew it. He was merely interested to see how Mark would answer that.

"Well, not that I want to accuse anyone… But the electric power that's distributed to the ordinary consumers is somewhat weaker and of lower voltage. And this is not down to the grid's low capacities. On the other hand, what goes to the military plants and other industries that are of greater priority to the State, well, the electricity is of much better characteristics. My point is that people are being ripped off."

"Hmm, that's a very good hit, Mark, for a person like you! But as you know, this can't be proved!"

"Well, I know that I can prove it but if I try to go public, most probably I'll end up in prison again but for a very long time, not just a couple of days. Well, I was there for less, actually. By the way, my project is not about telling people about the present actual energy situation. If realized, there will be a surplus of energy in the future and everyone will be happy."

"Hmm, a surplus… you wish! I doubt that it's possible. Are you certain?"

"Well, I am, absolutely. I've checked everything a thousand times and I know for sure that it is possible. I've discovered a way of how to overcome any political issues that such a huge project could entail. I've thought about where the money could come from, and about the storage and transportation of the energy itself and…" Mark was getting excited as if his plan was not still in its initial theoretical stage but in the full swing of its execution.

"Listen, Mark!" Platt interrupted him, now totally convinced that the person opposite him was not a mere bean counter. "The next conference is taking place across the border, in the neighbouring country's capital. Can you prepare a written copy of your project within a month? I want you to present it at the conference, in front of all members."

"Well… do you really mean I would be speaking in front of all of you?"

"That's right! It's not a problem. I'll arrange everything. After all, I'm the chairman of the Project."

46

"Well, I'll do it. I… eh-r-r, but everything is at home… But how am I going to get back in there? All these journalists are waiting for me and all my stuff is there, my books, the maps…". Panic had set on Mark's stage. Platt, however, had an answer to everything.

"Going back there is definitely not a good idea. I will find you a place to stay until the conference and I'll provide you with everything you need to get prepare yourself. But now, Mark, will you tell me the secret?"

"Well, there is no secret…"

"Common, Mark, just briefly… Where is this vast source of energy coming from? What's the technology behind?"

"Well, the technology has been around for a very long time. I've just altered some aspects, which, otherwise, would make it unfeasible to generate energy in the old ways at this present time."

"Mark, could you be more specific?"

"Well, we're going to build nuclear power plants, a lot of them… that have several thousands of nuclear reactors. That's my idea." Mark spilled the beans. He was not worried about Platt being the first ever person to hear the result of the most important and interesting project that he had ever embarked on.

"Thousands of nuclear reactors? Is this some sort of joke, Mark? You look like a smart boy, also, a very well-read one! You must be aware that these types of power plants have not been built for many years, since the terrorist attacks were directed precisely at them." Platt got slightly annoyed. He decided that Mark was trying to hide the real method he had discovered to solve the energy problem.

"Well, I know that… but I've resolved the issues with the terrorists and everything you could think of! We'll be building nuclear power plants but they will be located in such a place that is on the ground but not exactly… Well, they'll be there but where it's not so popular…"

"All right, Mark, whatever you say. Don't tell me any details if this is what you want. I've made a commitment to arrange for you to get heard out at the next conference, by all the members of the Project. You'll have to convince them, well, and me, as well!"

"Well, I'll try. I will require a bit of time to explain everything as there is a lot of information to cover, and it will take time..."

"Don't worry about this. You will have at least a few hours at your disposal. I believe that it will be long enough." The host put out his cigar to emphasize that the meeting had come to an end, too. "Thank you for coming, Mark, and I hope that you will be at your best next month. My personal assistant will help you with everything you need to prepare yourself." Platt held out his hand cordially to Mark, smiled and wished him a good day. The accountant was left alone in the room for about a minute before the assistant came in, ready to fulfill any of his requirements.

Platt, the influential and affluent professor, missed to mention why he had actually invited one troublemaker to a private meeting, an ordinary accountant, not that an extraordinary one had ever existed. This kind of privilege had been denied, on a number of occasions, to leading politicians, businessmen, scientists, all of them – positioned much higher in rank than Mark. Platt had his motives for meeting him and subsequently, inviting him to present his idea before the scientists from the Global Energy Project. Actually, it was the imminent failure of the Global Energy Project and the despair that had recently gripped the chairman that made him do that. Something had to be done, and very soon, otherwise, the collapse of the world energy system was becoming a certainty. Mark understated the fact that in two years, people in better-off countries would have electricity for just 5 hours a day. The real situation was much worse. The economies of the poor countries would virtually stop working, whereas those of the rich states would continue to regress on every level. Mark talked about wars becoming imminent, and yes, they would simply happen. There was no doubt about all this. As a last resort, Platt believed the story of one man, who had been living almost his entire life as a recluse, in his own universe. Engrossed with science, it was this very subject, which helped

48

Mark discover the right answer to the question that concerned mankind. It was all in the hands of Mark Eos – the humble accountant.

Before the energy restrictions had been implemented, it was never considered that energy was something that could ever be exhausted. People unanimously believed that it would go around forever, no matter how much they used. The energy crisis was regarded as a random and unexpected event. The sustained misbelieves that oil would keep gushing forth for centuries ahead, despite its desultory extraction, had turned out to be untrue, after all. This idea was widely proclaimed by people, who had been naïve enough to believe that natural oil wells would fill up continuously. This theory had never been theoretically proven, however, at several locations, exactly this happened. From completely exhausted oil fields, oil appeared again, as if from nowhere, and no one could find any logical explanation for it. Mark had an answer to this strange occurrence, too, despite his disinterest in the "black gold" as an energy resource. He was aware when and where this phrase came from but still he was not very sure why it was called like this, since it was liquid, not metal. According to him, and anyone with basic logical skills, the fields had never dried up in the first place. When oil gets pumped up, it releases the pressure, which, on the other hand, releases the oil from the pockets, located near the main deposit. It was simply logic.

Another misconception, regarding oil, was that it could be found everywhere, as long as one drilled deep enough. There was an oil sea, apparently, underneath the earth crust, which could be reached from anywhere at the right depth. Well, this theory was eventually refuted, too. Some regions were thought of being huge undeveloped oil fields, which did not let a drop. The reality was being harsh to people, who had been used to the idea of oil being always available. Slowly, the oil fields dried up one after another, extraction and production decreased, and the price went up every day. It was clear that the oil era was coming to an end. Products from oil derivatives kept being recycled and used again, but there were no more raw materials to produce new ones. Not long after, natural gas went scarce, too. Power plants that relied on gas to produce energy had stopped working and became a dear memory of the past. The abandoned power units, the buildings and the imposing chimneys, it was all going to get destroyed.

The military sector, mainly in the rich states, suffered the most. On the great political stage, the fight was over the last few oil deposits left, despite their true insignificance. The heat was getting high and led to yet another energy war, which obliterated one sixth of the world population in just four months and five days. Oil was the cause of so much suffering to so many people that it was never seen before. It was the political race over it, as it was hardly available. The good thing was that the lack of oil prevented the powerful states from relocating their military capacities across the globe. The bad news, however, was the use of weapons, which did not depend on oil. The intercontinental sub-nuclear missiles, powered by small quantity of uranium, were the main weapons used in the last war. The end of it came, when there was one last sobering exchange of this type of missiles, which destroyed a lot more than what the people, who pressed the button, had anticipated.

The question everyone was interested in during the last tense moments, when the oil ceased to flow forever was: "And what would happen after the end?" What followed was a new beginning, when two unknown scientists invented the energy batteries. The rectangular metal container was the discovery of the century, which changed the world. Every car, plane, ship or machine had the battery integrated within its system. People calmed down and felt relaxed again, like in the days, when oil was believed to be inexhaustible. The new device was inapplicable for household appliances but this was not thought of being of vital significance. The energy batteries were not actually that new in their core principle. The mechanism was known to have been developed hundreds of years ago. It was just that some aspects of its functioning had been altered by the two inventors. The batteries worked by being charged with electricity, they had a certain lifespan before they got depleted and need recharging or ended up being thrown away. The improvement was made to the active part of the battery. The more it got depleted, the more the other half of the battery generated energy. These batteries contested any scientific logic, as they could go without charging for 100 000 km in a regular car. The first 1000 km were the hardest because the power was still weak, but then it increased with every 3 000 km, and could get from 2 to 5 h. p., depending on the weight of the vehicle. The only drawback, which actually led to the present tragic state, was that the energy needed for the initial charging of the battery was the equivalent to what was enough to supply the homes of thousands of people with electricity. The mass production of the cars, powered by energy batteries, made a lot of people buy them, despite the fact that they were quite pricy. The grueling charging began and it was not long before everyone realized that energy shortage was at hand. During the first years, radical measures were undertaken in order to increase energy production by all means and the situation seemed to be well in hand. The number of vehicles, however, kept growing; the military incorporated the energy batteries in every military and non-military machine. The industry had been used to operate primarily on natural gas, so when it ran out, the diversion towards the new technology was quite expected.

The important discovery did not alleviate people's life for long and they were soon confronted with the same energy problems from the recent past. This time, it looked like there was no one, who could think of a way to overcome the crisis. Gradually, power restrictions were introduced. The price of cars, powered by energy batteries, was going up constantly, whereas the cost of charging the device equaled the cost of buying a new car. Redirecting most people to use public transport was a good thing. Well, the rich did not want to even hear about giving up their own vehicles. The widely proclaimed measures for increasing energy production proved to be only cosmetic and their sole purpose was to calm down the public. Yes, people did go nuts from time to time due to the tense situation.

The campaigners, who wanted life without nuclear energy, the activists, who organized the global movement against the atom and many other semi-terrorist organizations, were all nothing but 'children of their time'. Most of their actions had insignificant effect but at one point, they did manage to create a huge impact by blowing up three nuclear reactors, located just 10 km from a small town. Those, exposed to radiation, were less than 20 people, but still the international pressure was huge. More terrorist attacks followed in different places around the world and although unsuccessful, they triggered the widespread opinion amongst the population that nuclear power plants should not be built in close proximity of residential areas. Moreover, they should stop being developed altogether for good. The international community decreed a moratorium, which put an end to the hopes of nuclear power engineers to generate energy via atomic fission and thus sate the thirsty batteries. Without oil, natural gas, and new nuclear power capacities, the world was doomed. The energy, produced from the Sun, the wind or water was basically insufficient.

The fact that coalfields had also been depleted and that there was a veto on generating energy from plant sources, comprised another aspect of the crisis. Most coal-fired power plants could not comply with the high ecological standards, so they had to shut down much earlier than it was anticipated. Very little raw material produced less energy. Coal, like the 'black gold', was no longer part of the energy-generating sector. Energy production from plants and vegetation was unthinkable and intolerable, since the world was just about able to feed its population of billions. It was better one to be fed than have electricity. There were people and organizations that opposed this stance. They believed that energy was more important than food and to prove their point, they often went on hunger strikes, refusing to eat or drink for several days. At the end, they, or their stomach, to be precise, would realize that one needed to eat and whether there was a light bulb above one's head or not, this would not prevent them to hit their mouth right.

How?

The way Mark had been driven away in a non-disclosed direction, gave the media reasons for speculations. They were coming up with all kinds of possible or completely crazy scenarios. On the next day all guesswork was drawn to an end, as well-informed anonymous source, called Platt by chance, spread the news that Mark Eos had taken some time off from work and had asked for some help to find a quiet place, where he could regenerate from the stress and recent pressure. In brief, he had been provided with a free holiday on some small isolated place in the middle of nowhere. This was what about 90% of the people, who had read the newspaper article believed. The rest – the 10%, did not miss to accuse the government, well all world governments, in conspiracy against the hero Mark Eos.

People said that if one could not find a solution, this did not mean that it did not exist. They also said that when a problem did not have a solution, then it was not a problem. Mark did not take an interest in any gossip or hearsays but concentrated on getting fully prepared for the next conference, where he was meeting the scientists. Prof. Platt's personal assistant had rented an apartment, which was five times bigger than the attic, the accountant used to occupy before. The secret was kept rigorously and only the driver and the two bodyguards knew the location of the building. Even Platt did not know Mark's whereabouts but this was because he did not care. The accountant was registered under a different name, of course, whereas the hotel staff had been openly threatened if they ever disclosed to anyone about who was in room 505 and since when the person had moved there. Just in case, the warning was issued together with a substantial sum of money.

Platt's "slave" fulfilled every whim of Mark's that was related to the books, maps, papers and whatever else he needed. The assistant had never spent so much time in the library before. For him, this was just another job he had to do, in order to continue being Platt's right-hand man. This position brought him not only a huge salary but also the prestige, which very few other jobs would have rewarded him with. It was often a difficult task to follow the orders of someone, who was egocentric, arrogant and totally insensitive towards other people's feelings. Platt would never raise his voice but he regularly reminded his aide that people were not irreplaceable and that his job was at stake, should he fail to perform his duties according to Platt's expectations. Actually, Platt thought that he was applying the same standards towards himself, although, he did not believe that anyone could depose him from his chairman's position.

The personal assistant's attitude towards Mark was not any different from everyone else's. He did not regard him as a scientist, not that he was one, nor would he consider him as someone, who deserved any special treatment, well, no more than what an ordinary accountant ought to have. At first, he tried to conceal his contempt, but soon he began to openly demonstrate it. Mark, who was working almost 18 hours a day, did not notice anything. He was not a good judge of character, anyway. The accountant had sent his helper twice on a wild goose chase, as he could not remember the titles of the books he needed. The irony was that he knew their content inside out but the exact wording on the book cover had slipped his memory. The lapse made his loyal servant raise his voice in a very inappropriate manner for someone, who was supposed to be an employee. Mark, however, believed that it was his fault and vigorously offered his apologies and thus, making the 'servant' feels superior.

The assistant informed Platt about everything on a daily basis. There was nothing exciting to report. Every day was the same as the one before: "He is writing and reading, he is drawing incredibly badly, he glues maps on the walls and then, squiggles on them. He doesn't want to go out anywhere and he only eats in his room, he doesn't do any sport or exercise." The assistant also emphasized to his boss that Mark had turned the cozy apartment into looking like one in a low-grade side road motel. Despite the daily efforts of the chambermaid, 5 min. later, the special guest would turn the place upside down again. Platt, on the other hand, continued to hope that Mark would manage to present him and his colleagues with a solution of scientific worth. Only once, after their meeting, the professor wondered whether trusting Mark had been a mistake. Platt never asked about any details of Mark's project plan, as one would have expected, because he was a professor in neo-technological physics, a branch, studying the live forms in the physical world, as well as the processes between them. In other words, he was not a narrow specialist in any energy related subjects and mainly his inner feeling made him give Mark a chance, rather than the accountant's display of sound knowledge on the issue. However, his colleagues – the scientists, who had attended every conference, were very much aware of what energy was, or how and where it came from. Some of them were nuclear power engineers; others had been involved in experimental energy research projects for decades. In brief, all of them were comfortably familiar with the subject.

There were some inevitable differences within the team of scientists, which often caused tension amongst them and led regularly to some very heated discussions. The fact that they were united by the same cause did not stop them trying to prove that one was better than the other. Platt, who was diplomatic and patient, so far, had always managed to nip such conflicts in the bud. There was only one man, who could not stand his imperious nature and that was Alex Rice. This furtive man, who had been working on nuclear synthesis for nearly half a century, belonged to the so-called old generation of power engineers. He was one of the few, who would openly barrack Platt and try to undermine his authority. Not that Rice wished to be the head of the

Global Energy Project, however, he was determined that Platt did not feel too cozy on his chairman's seat. Everyone in the team was very much aware of Rice's true spite, so gradually, he was made an outcast from the group of scientist – all friends. Mark had picked exactly Alex Rice to be his uncle and he was the one, who received the black folder. The scientist had ignored it and had just thrown it away, totally unaware that its content was going to be explained to him in detail at the next energy event. Everything was going to unfold and become clear very soon, at the 19th conference.

There was only one day to go, when Mark Eos finally finished his preparation work. The solid scientific project papers reached nearly 400 pages, or just slightly more than the original version that he had brought to the last conference. He also had about a hundred of extra drawings. Mark valued those especially, as they presented his vision of how the elements of his idea, which had never been created before, would look like. His paper work was divided into several sections: type of energy, technology, structure, dislocation, water, defense, politics, resources, funding and the public. Those were divided further into sub-sections but then, Mark decided to omit some of them, so the presentation did not take too long. He assumed that there would be some time restriction, imposed on him, although, Platt had never advised him on that.

Everything that was to do with the organization of the conference had been completed. There was a special department team of the Global Energy Project, which was responsible for doing this to perfection, no matter where in the world it took place. This time, there were more security guards deployed and as for the protesters, they were banned from coming any nearer than 200m away from the building. The Police had decided on some extra security measures. Undercover agents were going to be infiltrated amongst the conference guests, watching vigilantly for any suspicious behaviour on their part. The fear that another Mark could spurt out from nowhere was playing on the police chief's mind. He worried that he could end up in the same unfortunate situation like his colleague in the neighbouring country.

The small private jet landed early in the morning. The wet runway did not hinder the smooth touchdown of the aircraft. It was Mark's first ever time to go to a foreign country. Neither the splendid view from the air, nor the actual flying experience could distract him from his deep thoughts about the day ahead. Mark was an hour drive from the Conference Hall, where he was taken by a limousine. Half way through his journey, he was joined by the chairman of the Global Energy Project. On their way, Platt was constantly on the phone, discussing some last minute arrangements about the conference agenda, so he did not have the opportunity to speak with Mark. They did exchange just a few words, when the professor enquired whether he was all prepared and the accountant, totally anxious before the meeting, managed to mumble: "Eh-r-r, well, I'm ready."

The stylish Mercedes stopped in the near-by underground car park. Above it was a business centre, which accommodated predominantly offices. Platt waited for the driver to open the door, whereas Mark did not take advantage of this silly act of service and just opened his to get out. The building above the car park was connected to the Hall via a tunnel. In this way, no one would have ever realized how the scientists had managed to access the place and later, made their exit. Mark was legging a couple of steps behind Platt, holding tight to his folder, which contained everything that he needed to defend his project. He worried not so much whether they would understand, after all, they were not just anybodies, but rather if they would believe him. He had not thought about this until then. What if they disagreed with his results and conclusions? Maybe, they wouldn't agree with his ideas about the source of energy and methods to combat the shortages! Mark could not think of any reasons of why they might oppose to his project, but it was not an impossible outcome.

Well in their 60-es, apart of one, the scientists, who were all leading authorities, were summoned by their chairman to appear at 9 o'clock in the morning. None of them knew why Platt had required for them to get up that early and it was really quite a precedent. They never really started work until after lunchtime, at about 1pm. Having already had a cup of coffee and a few cigarettes, five people were waiting for Platt's explanation about what was behind this unusual situation. None of them had any doubts that it was something really important.

It was 9:30, when Mark and the chairman entered the huge hall, where the 19th conference was going to take place a little later. In contrast to university halls, where seats were arranged amphitheatrically, this one resembled more an aircraft hall. The floor was flat and the ceiling was exceptionally high. There were four rows of chairs, placed in the middle of this vast space. The enormity of the hall made Mark feel even more insignificant.

"Take your seats!" Platt ordered without greeting them with "Good morning!" There was no time for small talk and he was not one of the most well-mannered people in the world. Mark was not sure about which seat was his, until Platt brought him a chair and placed it in front of the long cambered table, behind which the delegates were already taking their places. He did not wait to be told and nervously sat down. He was feeling quite stiff. He put his folder on his lap and rested his hands on top. Only an accountant could sit like this. Platt walked towards his chair in the middle and on his way he patted a couple of his colleagues on the shoulder. He had ordered not to have any security guards in the hall at this time. What was coming was only for the benefit of the scientists. Mark took off his glasses in attempt to clean them, and then he put them back on again. They did not need to. He had never opted for eye lenses, as he was apprehensive to have anything near such a sensitive part of his body. The accountant felt the intense stare of all these pairs of eyes at his unobtrusive persona and he aimed at looking straight ahead at Mr. Platt only. He was his benefactor and it was him that Mark could rely on in this tense moment.

"Right, my dear colleagues, I see that some of you are not ecstatic about the early hour, at which I wished you all come here. I can assure you that it's worth it! Are you ready, Mark?"

"Well, I am ready..." Despite expecting the moment he would be addressed, Mark reacted as if he was taken by surprise.

"Gentlemen, this is the well-known Mr. Mark Eos, the man, who took the leading role at our last gathering. You all remember what happened then and you know that Mark was released from custody, when it appeared that his human rights have been violated."

"Yea, right!" Alex Rice grunted out. He was sitting one seat over to the left of Platt. The chairman pretended he did not hear the remark.

"It also appeared that Mr. Eos is not one of these crazy activists, who turn up at every conference of ours. Sometimes, I think that most of these people just love traveling around the world and simply take the opportunity to join in the protests." The joke made everyone laugh, although, quite sensibly. "Mark wanted to present us with his realistic way of overcoming the energy problem. We could say that he has also devoted a substantial part of his life to the quest of finding the ever so elusive solution. As Alex has not taken seriously Mr. Eos's attempt to introduce us to his project, today, I am giving him the opportunity. That is why we have gathered here this morning." The man, whose name came up, quickly answered back:

"Platt, how could I know who is this young man?" He pointed condescendingly at the "young man". "You know very well that there are millions of fanatics, all keen to see our heads on a plate!"

"It's true, Alex. I share your opinion. I'm not blaming you for not taking him seriously. If I were you, most probably, I'd do the same. Anyway, I took an interest in what Mark has achieved and I've been assured by him that he's found a way of how we could generate, please, notice, a surplus of energy."

"That's impossible!" The scientists exclaimed at the same time. Their faces showed an utter disbelief and it looked like they could not easily change their expressions. For them, the word "surplus" was

59

incompatible with "energy" and the idea to use both in one sentence seemed irrational.

"I agree with you, therefore, let's give the floor to Mark, who will try his best to convince us that he has a point." The ball was in Mark's court. He was sweating profusely and he looked like as if someone was pouring a tickle of water down his face. Soon he was going to dry out of all liquid.

"Well, thank you, Mr. Platt, eh-r-r, right, where should I start from…" He asked himself and then began to answer. "Well, the energy that we lack and we need to produce could come from one source only. Now that there is no oil, natural gas or coal, and we generate energy just from the Sun, the wind turbines and this …" Mark lost his train of thought for a moment. "And from the hydro-power plants, as well." His brief distraction made his audience, apart of Platt, sneered at him, now, totally convinced that "hero" of the 18th conference was a real nutcase. "Well, we have, as you know, nuclear power plants but there's a ban to build new ones, isn't there? And it's been established that there's no chance for this energy source to be explored further… Well, but this is not exactly the case, in my opinion, anyway. I've read extensively about nuclear power plants and I believe they produce the best and the cheapest energy and…"

"Hmm, the best energy!" Alex Rice repeated in disdain. "Hey, boy, there isn't such term!"

"Alex, please don't interrupt him. Mr. Eos speaks in his own words. We all know that the nuclear energy is really the best. Continue, Mark!"

"Eh-r-r, well, I just meant that it's the most appropriate for covering our shortages and even generate a surplus. Now, I'll explain exactly how this can be done. Let me just see…" Mark opened his folder, looking for the right words, in order to respond to the cynical looks on the scientists' faces. He knew very well what he wanted to say, but the problem was that he struggled to put his words in a consistent and logical order. If he had just regular listeners, he could bend their ears with chaotically presented details, aware that they might not grasp everything. "Well, right, my idea is that we focus on producing nuclear energy and we do this by building… according to my estimates, eh-r-r… between 5 and 6 thousand nuclear reactors, with four in each independent power plant."

Mark was staring at the papers in his hands, without reading the text. His suggestion was met by the scientists' inevitable laughter. They were quite square people but still had a good sense of humour. The silence in the hall, which could accommodate an entire Boeing, was broken by sounds, more suited to a theatre comedy than a serious scientific discussion. Platt stood up from his chair, drawing attention to himself and thus, interrupting what was becoming an incessant guffaw.

"Colleagues, I am asking you again to treat Mr. Eos with all due respect. As most of you know, he is not a scientist but an accountant. He has tried, as a man and a citizen, to find a way and help all of us. Just because you don't make any sense of his account so far, it doesn't mean that his findings don't have a value or aren't worth anything to us. In a little while we are about to open the 19th conference and we have not even come up with a partial solution to the energy crisis. The next person, who laughs, is going to leave this room!" Platt sounded extreme but he had the power to act like this. The scientists seemed as if they had taken a notice and calmly displayed their willingness to listen to the figments of Mark Eos. But Alex Rice had something to say:

"Platt, don't you think it would be best if we asked this young man some specifying questions? That is, of course, if you insist on us taking him seriously. For instance, I didn't quite gather how we are going to build thousands of reactors, especially as they have been banned by the international community! A lot of money will be needed, too!"

"I accept, Alex." Platt quickly agreed mostly to shut him up. "Mark, could you explain to us in more detail how you see us building these reactors?"

"Well, Mr. Platt, until now, the first question has always been "How?" I believe that we are very familiar with the process of nuclear technology. Now, it's more important the question: "Where?" "How" comes second. Especially, because nuclear power plants have been the targets of terrorist attacks and that's why they are all banned and no one builds them anymore. There is one place, where the threat is practically non-existent, there won't be any risk for people and the plants will just keep on working to produce enough energy and more…"

"Where? On the Moon…?" Rice could not bite his tongue anymore, although, he managed to hide his derision.

"Eh-r-r, well, it can't be done on the Moon. Even if it was possible, it would take a long time to harness this energy. But there is a place on Earth that does not touch people's lives in any way, and there we could execute my plan. The area of our working site that I have chosen is approximately 10 million sq. km. We are going to have the 5 or 6 thousand reactors right in the middle. There will be no people living in a diameter of 2000 km. I've thought about the security measures, as well, but I shall talk about them later…"

"Where, then, maybe, you mean in the ocean?" Jeffrey, who was sitting to the right of Platt and was the deputy chairman, asked rhetorically.

"Well, no, it is not possible there, but the vast desert is the best place." The audience was shocked. What Mark had just said was the biggest nonsense they had ever heard. Well, not that the idea was that stupid but it really sounded rather crazy in that moment of time.

"How are we going to build them there?" Platt asked feeling very surprised.

"Well, we will be faced mostly with technical problems. I have developed the entire building project, where I have applied some new engineering solutions, which may prove to be a great challenge for the designers. Well… that's why I've tried to make some drawings and plans, which I have brought, here, with me. You can have a look and see how things would possibly look, when they are built and…"

"More specifically, Mark, be more specific, please! Tell us how!"

"I shall tell you, Platt!" Alex Rice butted in again in his arrogant manner. "It will never... this is impossible!"

"Even if you are right, Alex, it's not helping anyone. What is it? Are you uncomfortable that we rely on some ordinary accountant to solve our problem? You are bothered because Mark is below your level? If you don't like it, piss off!" Platt was at the end of his tether. He had never spoken to any of his well-respected colleagues in this way before. He did it not so much in Mark's defense, but because he had had enough of the old bastard.

"Right, Platt, if this is how you see things, I'd rather stay." He did not try to hide his mocking tone of voice. "This young man has managed to convince the chairman of the Global Energy Project, so he should have a much easier time with me. Alright, Mark?" Rice paused a little before deciding to use "Mark" instead of "young man". "Tell us how we are going to end up with 5000 reactors in the desert?" Alex Rice did not take a step back in retreat. He just felt like staying, so he could witness a few more absurd and farcical moments, which, he believed, were definitely coming. The best thing of all was that Platt was being discredited like never before. It was well worth watching it!

"Well, the method follows the Lego principle. You have children, I imagine?" Mark did not think about the fact that the scientists were about 30 years his senior and their children had probably had their own children by then. "Well, the Lego technology is very simple. It consists of building blocks that fit each other to create a specific design. We are going to build everything somewhere and then take it to the desert. It will all fit together. We will need to find some sort of building site. It could be anywhere, as long as it's flat. We can put the components together and test them, so we can make corrections if needed. Then we'll be in a position to transport the reactors to the desert, four by four and that's it!"

"So this will be the preparatory stage? Is that what you mean?" Jeffrey asked.

"Well, we can call it like that! First, we'll build one complete and independent nuclear power plant with four reactors and then, we just need to repeat everything from about 1250 to 1500 times, so when multiplied by four, it gets to 5000 or 6000." Mark underestimated the mathematical skills of the scientists, although, it was obviously done inadvertently.

"Mr. Eos, you are probably aware that the desert is full of sand and an attempt to build anything on top of it, might prove a challenge. The conditions are highly unfavourable. Have you got a solution to this?" The professor in Energy Processes – Mr. Connor – enquired.

"Well, the sand is no problem because the power plants will be built under domes. I have a drawing of a dome somewhere, let me just find it!" Mark started looking through the papers in his folder until he got hold of his creation. He showed them a badly drawn black semi-circle and carried on speaking. None of the scientists had enough time to see the silly picture, which looked as if it was done by a pre-school kid. "Well, we need some hard ground, so we could position the dome on top. We will have to transfer the reactors through a hatch in the ceiling, as well as everything else that goes inside the dome. With regards to the material that dome will be made from, I have investigated different types of material, and I think that the best one would be an alloy from carbon or titanium. Well, there are specialists out there that know more about this, but titanium is possibly a bit stronger. We shall cast them away from the desert and transport them with helicopters, which will be the only means of transportation we are going to use. And as we can't just place the dome in the sand, we'll have to use missiles to create the foundations." The weapons, mentioned, caused a commotion amongst the scientists. Alex Rice was the first one to raise the obvious question:

"What do we need missiles for in the desert?"

"Eh-r-r, well, the missiles will create the hard even ground for the domes' foundation. As far as I'm aware, the militaries have two types of missiles, which explode a meter above the surface. The blast can flatten an area of about 100 meters in diameter. But what we need is much less. As soon as the missile hits the target, we will have to shift the foundation panels promptly. Otherwise, the sand will pile up and things may fail to stand straight. The panels will be made from re-enforced concrete, where we put the dome on top. We get on with this part first and then, we continue with the rest. The reactors will come a bit later."

"And what next?" Connor asked.

"Well, we just keep building the power plants – one after another, there, in the desert. We launch a missile; lay the foundations, then – the dome. We then, bring the equipment and all the necessary stuff for the personnel and finally, we get the reactors…"

"Despite me trying not to be skeptic, I feel something crucial is missing in the whole idea!" Faulkner, the one of the best nuclear physicist said. "There's no water. There's no water, whatsoever, in the desert. The nuclear reactors can't generate energy without water."

"Well, this won't be a problem. We'll get water from the nearest large water basins. It will flow to us via long underground pipes, which are designed to burrow themselves in."

"This sounds way too complicated to me, if not a total science-fiction, Mr. Eos!"

"Well, not really! It's quite simple, actually! We've got water at about 2 to 3 thousand kilometers, so this is how long we need these caterpillars, as they call them, to be. The technology has been around for a while, though, no one has used very long ones so far. The pipe body has rotating rings, whose cogs dig into the earth and bury the pipe. We just set them at certain depth level and the pipe burrows in by itself, whereas the vibrations, which it produces, automatically fill the hole left behind. We connect the pipe to the sea and voila, we have flowing water as much as we need." While speaking, Mark showed, yet, another of his drawings, which depicted something that looked like a fat worm, covered with axles. No one made a comment.

"I've never heard of such caterpillar. Mark, are you positive that such a device exists?"

"Well, I am, Mr. Platt, and it has done for a long time. It has been developed for the last 40 years now. The initial idea was to use these for the transportation of goods but the technology had turned out to be quite costly. They also cause some seismic activity, so their application proved unfeasible near populated areas. But there are no towns and villages in the desert?"

"That's right, Mark, there are none!"

It had not been that long since the beginning of the meeting, however, the chairman decided that it was time for a break. He and his colleagues could not quite process the information, which sounded more like a fairy tale that had something in common with reality.

"Dear colleagues, we'll stop for twenty minutes. After the break, we shall be back at Mr. Eos's service." Platt announced. He, then, stood up from his chair and walked towards the intriguing quest. "It's all going very well, Mark, you've managed to draw everyone's attention. I hope that you will carry on in the same spirit, after the short break!"

"Well, I didn't quite explain it as I wanted, but I kind of managed mostly…"

"You were good, Mark." Platt said again and then left the hall for the nearest WC. The chairman was totally honest and did not exaggerate in the slightest. He had already started, like the rest of the group, to ponder about the plausible, though, hard to achieve possibility of building nuclear power plants in the desert.

The other scientists also went out to fetch a cup of coffee. Those, who remained rather passive during the discussion, tried to catch up now in the break, debating over the harsh conditions in the desert – their biggest problem, they were going to face. The researchers had not dared to pose their questions inside, due to the rising tension between Platt and Alex Rice.

Left alone, Mark stood up from his very uncomfortable chair and had a good look around. He noticed straight away some strange features in the hall that were unusual for a place of such purpose. He was not the type that paid attention to his environment but that day, the bizarre hall made him think.

Firstly, it was the height of the ceiling. There were not any reasons for this, especially because the floor was flat. It would have made sense if the hall was furnished with balconies like in the opera or movie theatre but this was not the case. Mark was slightly wrong about how high was the suspended ceiling. It was black and looking up, it gave the room a feeling of infinity. Secondly, the dark-brown surface of the floor was way too hard, like concrete, so it was doubtful that the facility was used for any kind of sport's event. There was plenty of space for playing basketball or volleyball, for instance, but who would have wanted to play and risk getting a serious injury? The accountant was right, as a ball had never been inside the hall. Thirdly, the four walls were windowless. Yes, the air-con system functioned perfectly, using solar energy through the panels on the roof, but not having windows…!? This seemed illogical and energy inefficient. Mark was aware that the building was built during times, when energy was aplenty, however, all similar facilities, he had ever seen before, had a significant area that was made from glass, which would let some natural light and warmth through. The tendency in the last two decades, marked by the energy shortages, was towards designs with many windows, which meant – more natural light and less use of such, produced from artificial sources. A popular practice now, was people having their roofs, made entirely from glass. The solar panels had anti-reflex protective layer.

Mark was not sure about the original purpose of the building, as he was not that well up on the history of the neighbouring country. The last century was marked by conflicts and turmoil. During one of the heavy wars in the past, the country had sided with the wrong ally, which resulted in destruction and great number of casualties. The devastation of the war had prompted the government to look in to the future, which did not promise to be any brighter. Therefore, a few of these seemingly pointless buildings were erected. They would have served one purpose only – to accommodate as many people as possible and keep them alive. About 80 000 people could find shelter in there, certain for their safety against the foe's possible bombs. According to International Law, the building would have been classified, as non-military target during wartime and all use of military force upon the civil population would have been prohibited. In reality, the culprit-state was unlikely to get punished in such devastating event, however, all nations abided the rule.

There were other curiously odd things with the hall that came up in Mark's mind, but he preferred to go back to his papers and revise what he was going to talk about, when Platt and company returned. The technical side was roughly covered and explained. The next thing on the agenda was talking about security and defense, mainly against terrorists, but also commenting on protection from nature itself. Then, Mark had to mention politics, as one of the chief factors for the realization of the project and last but not least, funding sources and sponsorship also had to be discussed.

Although, the scientists had started feeling less skeptic about Mark's idea, he still had to "walk" more than half of the long path to the point where he would have fully convinced them. They all sat down in their seats – all eyes pointed at the plain-looking accountant. The researchers waited impatiently to hear the happy ending of the story.

"Let's start, Mark, back to you!" The chairman of the Global Energy Project gave the floor to the guest again.

"Well, thank you, Mr. Platt." Mark kept forgetting that he had been permitted to call the professor simply Platt. "Well, I think, I'll continue with one of the main issues that have been of real concern for the last few decades, when talking about nuclear power plants and that is security, we're talking about, of course, aren't we? Eh-r-r... well, I believe we have the worse situation with security at the Koloss Regions, where incompetence and lack of knowledge on security measures of such specialized facilities, have led to the closure of six reactors. This is a huge lost energy wise! The terrorists managed to break through the outside shell far too easily and you all know what happened there!" In reality, not every one of them was aware of the details about the case.

"Hey, boy, watch what you are saying!" Prof. Merit spoke for the first time and clearly he was very crossed. He had grown up in the area Mark was talking about, and was also one of the consultants, who had advised the government on encapsulating the reactors. So, in effect, Mark had called him indirectly a "good-for-nothing".

"Calm down, Merit!" Platt quickly interfered. "Mark's just expressed an opinion."

"He's welcome to express his opinion as long as he doesn't throw insults at my home region! I, from all people, should know what the situation there used to be, following the attacks, and what it is now! What he's saying is absolute nonsense. We made the best decision, when we sealed the reactors off and right now, we are having a sufficient energy production." Merit's explanation was based on some old information and presented a response that was provoked by emotions rather than coming from a highly respected scientist.

"Well, I didn't know that you were coming from this place. Anyhow, this does not change the situation. I just gave an example, as statistically, there have been the most terrorist attacks and the population has been living in fear the most and…"

"The people there are not cowards!" Quite annoyed, Merit replied again. In different circumstances, he would have jumped at the young man and give him a right-handed blow to his face.

"Calm down, professor! Mark has not mentioned anything like this and I can assure you that he doesn't mean it. Isn't that so, Mark?"

"Well, of course, not. I have not meant to offend you and I'm sorry if this is how you've felt!" Mark apologized sincerely, where the slight shrug of his shoulders, together with his open palms, facing upwards, just emphasized the effect. Of course, his gesticulations were involuntary. Merit accepted the apology with a slight nod, although his sulking expression remained unchanged. "Well, I just wanted to stress on the fact that human psychology is one of the underlining factors in our current situation, marked by energy shortage. People are worried that the near-by nuclear power plant is a potential target for terrorist attacks and this makes them feel on edge at the prospect of being driven away from their homes. Their insecurity is at the heart of their wrath against nuclear energy and the most inveterate antagonists, as we all know, easily become terrorists. Our defense has been upgraded, especially after the series of blows, endured by some of our key facilities, but this has not put people at ease. That is the reason I feel we should build in the desert. There, it won't be any danger because the power plants would be too far away from anyone and anything. Terrorists are very inventive people. I know that. Led by their utter abhorrence for this type of energy, also, having plenty of finances, they could attempt an attack on the desert nuclear power plants, too. And because, the units would be positioned next to each other, it will be far too easy for them not to miss. In other words, wherever they aimed at or threw a bomb, they'd hit!"

"And you have a solution to this problem?" Alex Rice asked, but this time, there was not a trace of provocation in his query. He, too, was impressed by the first half of the meeting, despite the fact that the young man's ideas sounded rather strange.

"Well, the answer is very simple and could be found in the structure of the plants. As I've already mentioned, the reactors are going to be placed under very strong domes and all attempts to break through them with whatever kind of firearms, would come to no avail."

"Fine, but no terrorists had ever gone onto attack a nuclear power plant with just a gun or a pistol. They resort to grenade launchers, throwing grenades, they use T. N. T., and dynamite." Connor was quite familiar on the subject, as he used to be the deputy director of a large nuclear power plant a while back. The facility had been frequently the target of such explosive substances.

"Well, the body will withstand everything you've just listed. But if a bomb is thrown inside, the blast will remain contained and everything in the interior will blow up. To rescue the survivors amongst the staff, we can use special capsules, which will transport the people to safety via the underground water pipes. Every few hundred kilometers, there will be emergency egress hatches, where personnel will be able to emerge unharmed. As you all know, the latest generation of reactors has been designed with having their active zone encapsulated in three layers. And in case of emergency, the entire process is halted immediately, so the reactors cannot explode. In such instances, we just seal the dome off. We'll be one down but people's lives will be saved and there won't be any radiation leaks..."

"You are briefing us on what would happen if a bomb exploded inside. I thought, the point was that we did not allow this to happen in the first place!" Prof. Faulkner made a justified remark in the second part of the meeting.

"Eh-r-r, well, I was describing the worse case scenario, really, but with the security measures, we are going to emplace inside and outside of the stations, then, this will be absolutely impossible, and I also..."

"Hmm, "absolutely", you say!"

"Alex, don't interrupt. Carry on, Mark!"

"Well, the first and utmost security measure will be the control over who would have access to the power plants. These will be only the people, who work there. They will go to work by helicopters, so the most important guys will be the pilots. They will have to be experienced and trusted people, undergone some thorough checks, otherwise, they might do something very stupid and land somewhere they are not supposed to. After the pilots, come the specialists, who will work in each of the power plants. Their selection will also have to be very precise..."

"Mark, when we come to this, we are going to pick the best nuclear energy engineers, as well as the best pilots." Platt uttered, stressing that the personnel related issues are easily resolved.

"Well, so this is sorted and we get some trusted people to work inside. Now we can move on to talking about the resources, which will have to be transported to the sites. There should be a special point, or several of them, where everything will arrive to be checked thoroughly, before being carried on towards the power plants. So if we come across explosive substances or any kind of weapons, they will be stopped in time from going any further. This job will be suitable for the militaries, I imagine, but we'll see. There will be a lot of sand around, dry conditions and temperatures will be very high, but then, they would plunge in the evening, when it gets very cold... In that respect, if someone tries to go near any of our domes in attempt to break its body, they will stumble across the defense system I've developed. I am not very experienced on the subject, but I think that what I've come up with will do the job. We will scatter some small metal particles – smithereens, which will act as defense..."

"Smithereens?" A few of the scientists repeated all at once. Mark was not making much sense to them, here.

"Well, I call them smithereens. When they are well mixed with the sand around the stations, we're going to put weak current electricity through them, as they are good conductor, aren't they, and if there is a man in close proximity he will be temporarily knocked down and stunned by it. In such event, we will be alerted straight away and we'll just send someone to arrest the terrorist or check on some lost Bedouin or whatever it is that has activated the system."

"That's very good idea, but I feel there is a huge drawback." Alex Rice uttered, discovering a weakling in Mark's idea about the "smithereens". "We can't just disperse tons of metal particles over the sand like this. The Ecological organizations would not allow it. The desert is not favoured generally by wild life and plants, but it's a fact that it's a natural habitat for some, which can live in harsh conditions."

"Well, this won't be a problem. We won't bother the several species that live there, like snakes, scorpions and insects. They are far too small to be able to activate the system so they won't be affected in any way. The Eco-organizations could be a pain sometimes. Well, there will be nothing that they could complain about in this case. We won't leave the particles in the sand indefinitely. We can collect them and release them any time we wish."

"How?" Mr. Rice seemed unable to understand. He thought he had an answer but then, his idea to use a sieve sounded rather naïve.

"Well, we'll use electromagnet. The outer skin of the dome will be our electromagnet, which will pull the metal particles towards it. They'll stick to the outer layer and then, we will just collect them by demagnetizing its surface when we turn off the electricity. Then, we could disperse them back again over the sand from a helicopter." This time, the most active enquirer amongst the scientists remained silent. He was obviously satisfied by the answer, so Mark continued.

"Well, there is an important issue in all this, which has caused a lot of damage in the past, to a number of nuclear plants. I believe things have gone wrong in the past, because people ignored the geographical specificities of the regions, where the facilities were built."

"What do you mean, Mark?"

"Well, Mr. Platt, I'm talking about disasters, caused by Nature. On many occasions, power plants have been destroyed or been partially affected. Some had to be closed well before their time. We are talking about the non-human aspect of the security. Desert storms and earthquakes are two of the main causes for worry, I think, but see, I'm not a specialist in this." Yes, a specialist he was not for sure. The low-paid "bean counter" did not have a single document that would have made any of his statements valid and trustworthy.

"Mark, how could we secure the facilities against natural disasters? Earthquakes can be really serious and we should not underestimate them."

"Well, they can be a big problem, especially because some of the cavities and voids, left after the oil and gas had been pumped out, are quite large, so somehow these holes have to be compensated and because of the weight of the land masses, well, the heaviness on top, I mean…" Platt nodded as if to show that he had understood Mark's poor attempt to explain the complex issues. "Well, so far, we've had four major earthquakes, which caused 12 nuclear power plants to be shut down for good. There have been 30 weaker quakes, causing significant damages to nuclear facilities that had to be addressed later..." Mark quoted the statistical data almost without referring to his papers in the black folder. Thankfully, he had forgotten about his drawings, too.

"Mr. Eos, you're talking about earthquakes that happened nearly three decades ago, the big ones, I have in mind, here." Faulkner spoke again, as he obviously had something to share on the earthquake subject. "Even we hardly remember them and since then, the tectonic plates have 'calmed down' and the petrol voids are not such a threat anymore. Basically, there's no danger of such destructive earthquakes happening soon, well, of medium magnitude – yes, but we don't expect any strong ones."

"Well, this is not exactly the case, but you have a point. It is true that there is almost no real threat of earthquakes, bigger than magnitude 7 but the seismically active zones in the Earth crust have never stopped moving. It's only a matter of time when we'll experience some very strong quakes again. I believe that one of the largest cities on earth will be flattened and destroyed within the next ten years..."

"What?" Alex Rice immediately felt outraged at the fatalistic prediction. "Now, you're an expert on earthquakes! So you've come to the conclusion that some metropolis is going to be wiped out by a powerful quake? The irony is that you can't prove anything. Nobody can predict earthquakes."

"Which?" Platt asked in belief that his question is more important than the one of his belligerent colleague. "Which city do you mean, Mark?"

"Eh-r-r, well, I don't want to say, as I don't want to set any panic about and I'm not quite sure if there will be a quake or not, but..." Rice's face broke into a smug grin. He was very pleased with the retreating answer, showing that the accountant is talking at random.

"Common, Mark, if you have solid evidence that this might happen, you should tell us, so people can take measures of precautions." Platt insisted on knowing not so much because he was worried about the population, living obliviously in a doomed place, but from pure curiosity.

"Well, if I say, then it may…"

"Common, spit it out!" Prof. Connor spurred Mark on.

"Well, all right, Metropolis 6 is very likely to be destroyed within ten years."

"What did you say? That's impossible! It's relatively new and built in accordance with all necessary requirements and standards." Alex Rice opposed to the suggestion. By newly built, he envisaged that most of the city's buildings were no more than 50 years old.

This was terrible news for Faulkner, who was sitting next to him. His daughter and her family had moved to Metropolis 6 very recently. She had followed her husband, who had a very high position in a bio-foods production company. Faulkner, shaken by the initial shock, quickly gained his composure. He rested his elbows on the table at a right angle and then he shouted from the top of his voice:

"Prove it, boy, prove it to me!" No one had ever seen the 62-year old scientist so angry before. His eyes sparkled with rage. He was ready to jump over the only barrier in front of him and attack the 35-year old Mark. Also, no one had ever heard him to shout like this. His behaviour was in total contrast with the calm, melancholic temper that people, who knew him, were used to expect from him.

"What is it, Faulkey?"

"My daughter lives there, and the granddaughter… That is why I want to hear a sound explanation; otherwise, I'm out of here! I'm fed up with listening to this accountant's nonsense all morning! Platt, don't get me wrong! The guy has some good ideas but I doubt that he has even the slightest idea about how much all this will cost."

"Well, I do, actually, and I've calculated everything but we haven't come to this, yet. I was just going to tell you about where the money

75

would come from, how much it would cost, what expenses to expect, regarding the…"

"All right, Mark!" Platt interjected. "We'll hear all about it in a bit, but now, I think, you owe Prof. Faulkner and us a rational explanation about your suggestion to do with Metropolis 6."

"Well, I'll explain. The location of the city is in a quite dangerous zone. Well, I came across a map a few years ago, by accident. It displayed the seismic regions on our planet but as they were some centuries ago. The modern maps are very different from this old one, which shows that the metropolis is positioned over an old-forgotten Fault."

"This doesn't prove anything!" Faulkner could not stop himself to speak, although, Mark had not finished.

"Well, it doesn't prove anything, but it's occurred, that, 200 years ago, when this map was used, it predicted all big earthquakes almost 100% correct, despite that the available technology, then, was not sophisticated enough like the one nowadays. You know, the satellite maps, I mean. There hasn't been much deviation from what was determined two centuries ago. Where we have had two tectonic plates touching, sooner or later, they have clashed, creating seismic waves and causing powerful earthquakes. In reality, only few people knew about this map, then, and fewer than that, trusted the predictions. In those days, people made a cult of earthquakes and it was believed that they could not be predicted. Well, this is what I know from history, not that anyone thinks that there could be a prognosis on earthquakes, now…"

"Still, how do you know this will happen to Metropolis 6 within the next ten years?" Faulkner could not find peace.

"Well, it's not that hard to predict, once the speed of moving of each plate is known, its direction, and that's it! One only needs to know how much the plate moves in a certain period of time. I am very good with numbers and I've calculated that very soon there will be a strong earthquake. There is no way that I could be wrong, unless my source

76

data is incorrect, but there is no way it could be, because they've always got it right then. I am very good with numbers..."

"Please, excuse me, everyone!"

"Where are you going Faulkey? I think Mark's answer was good enough." Platt asked. He was confused about why his colleague was fulfilling his threat of leaving, when he got what he wanted to hear.

"I'm going to phone my daughter. I'll be back in a few minutes." Faulkner was very worried and this happened quite rarely in his life. His only child could end up buried under the rubble of some concrete building together with his gorgeous granddaughter...

"All right, dear colleagues, we shall make a break now, while Prof. Faulkner is trying to get in touch with his relatives and then, we'll continue. As I gather, Mark still has to clarify the issue with potential earthquakes in the desert and how to protect the nuclear power plants, if this is possible, of course."

"Well, it's possible! There's no problem whatsoever..." The accountant began answering the question, however, everyone had already stood up from their seats and did not hear him.

In the second coffee break, Mark left again his uncomfortable chair. This time, he followed the scientists out of the room into the large foyer. There, several of them lit a cigarette, some – out of habit, others – possibly affected by Marks ominous words. The cloud of smoke was quickly sucked in through the ventilation system, preventing the few non-smokers from choking with cough. The main topic of their conversation was about the gloomy prediction for the dark future of Metropolis 6. It was a city with relatively constant electricity supply, which mainly came from several hydroelectric power plants in the area. Thanks to them, the population of the metropolis enjoyed having electricity for almost 10 hours. This was quite an achievement, so the city ranked second in that respect amongst all newly built metropolis areas, located in the temperate regions.

The short break finished. The meeting between Mark Eos, the accountant, and the scientists, whom everyone relied on, was about to be resumed. While in the foyer, Mark did not manage to strike a conversation with any of them, and it seemed that the others tried to avoid him. Only Platt and Prof. Connor made an attempt to learn more about him and took an interest in his persona. Platt asked him if he was feeling well and Connor wanted to know about the potential threat of earthquakes on other cities in the near future. After the professor received a negative reply, he returned to his colleagues, who had formed a group.

All topics that Mark had covered so far like the issues about the domes, the missiles, the underground pipes, the helicopters, the electromagnet and the metal particles – everything was feasible in practice. Resolving the issue of how to make a nuclear power plant withstand a powerful earthquake of a magnitude 7-8 and above remained a challenge and could be elaborated on simply in theory. A theory, which only had grounds in Mark's head and which no self-respecting scientist and seismologist would ever take seriously.

Prepared to share his interesting idea, the non-scientist took his seat and continued from where he stopped before the break. This time, Platt just nodded at him to begin, after he made sure that all his colleagues were back on their chairs.

Faulkner also sat down, looking slightly calmer. He had not mentioned to his daughter anything about the potential destructive earthquake, although, his voice was trembling. He simply wanted to hear her voice, so he would try to calm down. After the conference, he was getting on the first plane, determined to convince her, at all cost, to leave Metropolis 6. The reasons now look more than serious.

"Well, I've thought of some unusual way to counteract future earthquakes, no matter how powerful they are." Mark began. He had not said anything that could be considered within the norm so far. "Well, the central part in the Big Desert has not been marked with any strong quakes up this present moment, but they are to be expected in about 50 years time and they won't be that powerful, anyhow! I've got an idea of how to prevent the nuclear power plants from suffering earthquake damages, or at least, how to diminish the risks. Well, so we are going to put several very large metal blocks in the dome's concrete base. Each of them will weigh a few tons. In the same way like with the outer surface, they will be, in effect, electromagnets, again, very powerful electromagnets…"

"What would we need them for?" Alex Rice asked straight away, preventing Mark from explaining exactly that.

"Well, at first, I could not see the logic in having electromagnets underneath the power plant itself. Later, when I thought about it, I realized that they will act as very strong support units, because Earth's core is metal, isn't it? And when we switch on the electromagnets, they will hold the entire structure together and any quakes would be just about felt, if at all…"

"You mean that we will hold onto the Earth's core?" Platt asked very surprised. The idea sounded quite eccentric to him and he could not accept it right away, if ever.

"That's impossible! No magnet on Earth could create an electromagnet field, which is powerful enough to have any effect on the core." Prof. Connor expressed his opinion, based on his solid professional knowledge.

"Well, you are right but we are not after having a direct influence over the core. Actually, the core would have an effect on us and would keep the power plants stable. The more we build, the steadier the whole region would become. It's true that the power of the magnets has any significance for only a few kilometers, deep into the Earth's crust, but I still believe that the core would play a role and help us."

"It's impossible to prove this, isn't it, Mark?" Platt asked again and if he didn't do it, Merit would have asked the same question.

"Well, it is, but one can't prove the opposite theory, either. So I'm right and you're right but I doubt that we'll ever find out who's righter!"

"Mark, do you have any other solutions to how to protect the power plants against potential earthquakes? I have to note, what you've just offered us seems rather unconvincing to me." Platt nearly used the word "absurd", but because he was on Mark's side throughout the whole time, he opted for more of a diplomatic description.

"Well, I don't, but really, the facilities are not going to be under great risk of earthquakes. The daily sand storms are going to be more dangerous. They could hinder the entire operation of the power plants by preventing resources and personnel from being able to reach the units. Well, the good thing is that the storms don't last that long and that the domes are going to be strong enough to withstand them. The longest desert storm that's been ever registered has not gone for more than six hours. This is pretty short time, really!" Mark closed the subject about the natural adversities. He had to move onto the political aspect of things, as well as the actual funding for building the power plants. "Well, now, then, I'm going to continue talking about what must be done with regards to the international political community. Inevitably, we would need a permission to go ahead with building the nuclear facilities and I don't really see us having any particular problems with this…"

"Oh, yes, you think so?" Alex Rice sniggered. "And how will you persuade them so easily? Hey, boy, I'll share a secret with you: politicians can be very stubborn about certain issues and as far as I'm aware, very few of them, around the world, would risk lobbying for the realization of nuclear power projects, unless they are happy to end their political career. This will be like a suicide for them." Rice knew personally many politicians and was certain about what he had just said. He believed that none of them would be willing to part with their power, even if the chances that this would happen were very slim. If anyone gave a "green light" for going back to nuclear energy after such a long period of this being banned, then their power, in a political sense, would simply dwindle as soon as.

"Well, I'm not in a position to influence any politicians, but you can!"

"And how are we going to that, Mark? You know that our Global Energy Project started as a political initiative? We've been hired simply as consultants." Platt did not sound very convincing, considering that he was more powerful than some governments, but he was an exception amongst his colleagues. They were just good scientists before being lured into the project by some leading international politicians.

"Well, that's true. But it's been years, now, since everyone's been trying to find a solution to our energy problem. In the meantime, the problem deepens, so you are in a position that everyone's depending on you rather than relying on the politicians. They are not researchers, who can just find energy from somewhere."

"Hmm, I've never thought about how important we've become dear colleagues!" Platt said jokingly and everyone in the room laughed. "You might be right, Mark. We are in a position to persuade them by scaring them a bit, but it won't be that easy. There are plenty of morons, who I don't even know how they've been allowed to get into politics. It's very hard to negotiate and reason with people like this."

"Platt, don't you think this sounds far too easy? So we just tell them to remove the ban and hurray, they agree immediately to do so? I don't think it will work this way. People will protest. Society won't just take this in."

"Yes, Alex, you've got a point, too! Mark, do you have an answer to this?"

"Well, people believe in things if they can see and touch them…"

"What are you getting at?" Alex Rice quickly interjected.

"Eh-r-r, well, you know, if you tell people that there'll be enough energy for all and that they won't even have to think about the nuclear power plants as the facilities will not interfere with their lives in any way, then, people won't go against the idea. It's important, though, how gently the politicians will present this information. You will just have to reveal the news to the political leaders. You will be the main players in the process, whereas the politicians will just execute your ideas."

"So we're going to change places, then? I've been waiting for this moment for a long time!" Connor joked. He could not stand most of the politicians he knew. They were so much below his level. He remembered how he had to beg them, a while ago, to increase the budget of the organization he was working for – utter humiliation.

"Well, what's important in this case is that the politicians and the regular people, do not have any other choice! None of us have a choice, so we simply need to start building the nuclear power plants as soon as it is humanly possible. We'll do a test one, first of all, somewhere that you decide and later - in the desert..."

"Mark, we are here today to hear you out. This doesn't mean that we are going to automatically approve your project. I admit that you've really given a good thought about the main aspects but this is not a decision that we can take independently before each element of your project is not thoroughly examined and scientifically proved to be feasible, by our team of specialists."

"Platt, he's thought about almost everything. Let's say the ban to build nuclear power facilities is lifted. Where will the money come from?"

"Well, Mr. Rice, that's the final point on my list that I've also taken care of, though, I'm not sure if it'll work… but then, when everyone sees the need, then, they should all accept it…" Mark took a deep breath before continuing to reveal how he would get the money to build at least 5000 nuclear reactors. "Well, the military forces will hand all their money to us for a period of two years. I've estimated that the world military budget of all nations, affected by the energy crisis, will be enough to cover the costs for building 6000 reactors. The funding will be sufficient if we use it for just a year and a half, but as there might be some unexpected expenses along the way, it's best if we borrow the money for two years." It was very unlikely that any of the present people in the room had ever heard so many unrealistic ideas in one day, which, after Mark's sound clarification, sounded so plausible. However, his last proposal about utilizing the world's entire defense budget and build nuclear power plants in the desert was not accepted lightly. As usual, Alex Rice spoke first:

"And you think that the army will hand their money to us, just like this? You've got this wrong, boy! Moreover, the militaries are not politicians. They are hard bastards and it's very doubtful that they'd give you a penny for the desert power plants you were talking about. No way that this is going to happen!" Alex Rice was very explicit on the point and it seemed that his view reflected the opinion of the rest, including Platt.

"Mark, Alex is right. To be honest, we've been listening to you for two hours and despite the fact that we've managed to grasp your idea about the nuclear power plants in the desert to some extent, I have to point out that funding such a huge project is not the same like building a sky-scraper or a bridge, or something of the sort. Mark, I expected that you would have an answer to the financial aspect of your project but obviously I've been mistaken. The army, as Alex said, would never give money for a purpose like this." Platt was starting to feel sorry that right at the end, when everything had started to seem possible, the knowledgeable accountant had begun to talk nonsense.

"Eh-r-r, well, Platt, this is not exactly the case." Mark sensed that he was losing his audience. In order to earn their attention back, he felt that he had to say something worthwhile and in support of his idea about appropriating the military budget of nearly 200 nations for a different purpose.

"I'm sorry, Mark, but all this is too unlikely and you can't really convince us otherwise."

"It's how it is, boy!" Merit joined in. "I have to admit, though, building nuclear power plants in the desert – it would have been a rather interesting endeavour from scientific point of view. Congratulations on your idea. Personally, I like it, some of…"

"Well, hang on. I know how to make them give us the money. It's easy, don't you see?" Mark did not like interrupting people and always waited for them to finish their sentence. This time he failed to abide by his good manners. "Well, the army uses energy, a great deal of it. They own almost 60% of the energy batteries and they simply can't go without energy. So I believe it will be much easier to convince them to embrace our cause than persuade the politicians to change their legislation and remove the ban on building nuclear power plants. Well, every state just spends their money like this, you know, for maintaining mostly the air forces, the troops and the navy, well, some states are land-locked, but this is not important. After the last military conflict, which was over the most important energy resource, I'm talking about the oil, here." Mark clarified what he meant, which was unnecessary because everyone knew that he is referring to the oil. "And, now, the destructive after-effects of the war have led the reduction of weapons in all countries. You see, apart of the fact that there's less energy available and that it's been challenging to charge the batteries, people, really, don't want another war. If there is the fear to live next door to a nuclear power plant, because of the threat of terrorist attacks, then the fear of war in the coming decades should be unimaginably greater."

"We understand your point, Mark. No one really believes that a serious armed conflict is likely to happen. But this doesn't change the fact that every sovereign state would never give their right to maintain an independent army, own weapons, etc., in order to be able to defend its territory."

"Well, Platt, I can't see the problem, here, they could still defend their sovereignty… We need their military budgets for just two years. I didn't mean that we have to deprive them of their troops, weapons or whatever. It will all continue to function and operate as before, so the nations will not feel insecure in any way."

"But the soldiers have families to support. Take their salary away and they couldn't possibly do that. Your suggestion may lead to a very significant shift in the layers of society, when military personnel become redundant or suspended for long periods. The former soldiers will have to re-qualify, find different employment opportunities with no experience. Mark, a soldier is really a soldier for life. They can't change overnight. Although I've served in the army for merely three months, I learned their main values. Their high morale and strong spirit are teamed up to serve the ordinary people. Mark, I just can't see your idea working."

"Eh-r-r, well, the soldiers don't have to leave their jobs and look for a new one…"

"Where would the money come from, then, for wages, for the maintenance of military bases, the military aviation, the navy, and submarines and…"

"Well, their funding will come from other allocations of the national budget, from the national fiscal reserves, as they must have some money for emergencies, crisis or when there's big inflation…"

"I doubt that countries would so easily part with their reserves and spend the money on defense. There will be the risk of collapsed economies, even those of rich states." Alex Rice uttered. Although he was not an economist, he was a keen reader on the subject.

"Mark, don't you think it would be better if we started with smaller number of reactors? Say, we could first build 1000! We are in a position to get the money for that without much effort. All sorts of organizations, governmental institutions and private sponsors would contribute to our cause." Mark had never thought about this option, suggested by Platt, who was very good at finding a compromise in every situation. The accountant imagined that, ideally, they would be able to have 5000-6000 reactors, in order to solve entirely the energy problem as soon as possible. The prospect, his project to start with less, at first, would not supply the world with sufficient energy, but it would, at least, improve the situation temporarily.

"Well, I've estimated how many we'd need altogether, so it's better if we build them in one go… But, well, I suppose, we can do it gradually, too. I just have to calculate to what extent 1000 reactors would do the job for us and to what degree…"

"Mark, don't split hairs now! There's no need to do any further estimations, as they'll be of use to us, anyway! The energy that the reactors are going to generate will help the global economic growth rate and because of it, we'll be able to find the money for the rest of the reactors quicker."

"Platt, don't you think we could start with building more of them?" Prof. Connor asked. "Mark's idea to use the military budgets is not bad at all. I think we can try and ask for half of their financial resources. Of course, we would never get this, but 15-20% is a realistic figure."

"If we press on a bit stronger, they might even give us 25%." Alex Rice suggested, totally in tune with his brash personality.

"It's possible, dear colleagues! It is very possible! We should also never forget that the money won't be coming from just one source. We have a good network of supporters, who would donate a significant sum if initiate a donation campaign on a large scale. The organizations, which are working alongside with us in the quest of resolving the energy crisis, could also raise funds."

"Apart of the military sector, we also have the government funds, which subsidize the current energy projects, related to the hydro-energy power plants, the wind mills and solar panels. The entire resources in these funds could be diverted to this project with simply one phone call, made by Platt."

"That's not exactly correct, Merit! The decision making process in relation to this sort of expenditure is tied to a government approval through a rigid voting procedure. I can make a proposal but I cannot approve it by myself. Otherwise, you are right. Up to this day, I've almost never got a refusal."

The pessimistic air, regarding the financial side of the desert power plants project, had almost 'evaporated'. The notion that money would not prove to be a problem, sounded realistically feasible. The scientists felt convinced and certain.

"Well, now the money's sorted, when can everything, then, start in its essence? I mean, we are running out of time and as you know, my idea is that we need to build one, first of all, so we see how it will work out and…"

"You're asking 'when'?" Platt repeated and continued by outlining the time schedule. "If we all vote unanimously, today, for the proposal to build the desert power plants, after we check and test the main parameters of your project idea, Mark, then, I believe that it won't take us more than a month for this. So we could start with the preparation stage of building the first power plant with four reactors straight after that. The only delaying factor in the whole process could be the politicians! That's it if we don't discover any major errors and missing pieces in your plan that could make it fail. With the political leaders – everything gets going very slowly and by having a lot of negotiations! I do hope to make them move their act, so they remove the ban over building nuclear power plants, also within a month. The funding process of our operation will not delay us, as I consider that the sum, required for the maximum number of reactors that you envisage, as huge as it is, will prove realistic and within the capabilities of the international community. I'm certain of it! I admit that, at first, I could not see a source, which could have provided such a great sum of money. Nevertheless, I think we will find it, if not for all of the reactors, then, we will – for as many as possible. Mark, is there anything else that you haven't told us about and that you think it's important?" Platt asked before he sent the accountant out of the hall, in order to conduct the voting. The scientists might each accept the idea but they all had to approve it with an absolute majority in an open vote.

"Well, I don't think so or I can't think of anything, really. I kind of roughly explained everything, but otherwise, I have compiled a plenty of scientific literature, concerning every component, as well as every stage of the technological process. I'll give all the papers to you, so your experts could examine them, although, I've already checked everything thousand times and I haven't found an error, I think..."

"I am glad that you are so confident, Mark. This means that our checks will take less time if everything is correct in your papers. Mark, is there anything else before I ask you to leave us for a minute, so we can conduct our vote?"

"Eh-r-r, well, I think I missed to mention about how we're going to accumulate the energy and then, distribute it all over the world! Well, I suppose that's quite unambiguous and you all know about it. That's why I haven't gone on to explaining it… but if you like, I could… now?!"

"With energy generators, I imagine?" Alex Rice said not very confidently.

"Yes, Alex." Merit confirmed in belief that this was the right answer.

"Well, not exactly! The generators are far too big and it won't be practical to use them, as well as we would need too many of them. The best way to transport such a great quantity of energy at such great distances is via generators, which operate with conductive liquid and function like ordinary batteries."

"Can't we use the energy batteries for that purpose?" Platt asked, without realizing the nonsense he had just said.

"Well, the energy batteries do not have the same properties as the generators, because the energy they release differs from the initial moment to the stage, when they are depleted completely. It's impossible to control this fluctuation of power levels. The electric grids operate at a constant level of power and certain voltage. Anyway, the liquid generators will do the job!" Mark stressed again on his answer to the question. None of them, however, had heard of this type of devices.

"Hmm, so what is a liquid generator?" Prof. Connor asked simply like a kid. His sound knowledge on the subject could not explain to him what Mark was talking about.

"I've got no idea, either!" Platt added, shrugging his shoulders.

"Well, imagine a container, as big as a car, which is full of liquid that could easily conduct electricity. The hull of the container is made from electricity-proof material, so it does not affect what's going on inside. Well, actually, nothing special is happening on the inside. Just the energy, generated by the reactors, is accumulated in the liquid, which will have the capacity for it, as long as the hull is made from strong enough material to withstand the increased electric voltage."

"And how much could this liquid generator hold?" Faulkner, who had calmed down by now, asked. He, too, like his colleagues, felt the issue was unfamiliar to him. Irrelevant of the source, energy was conveyed to any destination via the standard electrical grids. Generators were only used in far locations, which were not part of the national network.

"Well, I'm not quite sure how many exactly, but probably, we would need about 20 generators altogether for all the continents."

"Wow, Mark, so they do hold a huge volume. Are they really safe? Nothing can dangerously interact with the energy inside? They can't explode, for instance, is that what you are saying?" Platt asked nonchalantly, totally certain that Mark's reply would confirm their safety.

"Well, they can! They are very hazardous, actually, like a huge bomb. If one of the containers exploded, it would destroy about an area of 10 sq. miles, minimum! It hasn't been tested but this is what's been suggested…"

"Hmm, if that's the case, we have to find another way of transporting the energy! We cannot take the risk of using liquid generators if they could so easily explode. Mark, can't we extend the electrical grid right to the power plants in the desert and just connect it to the nearest electrical cable routings?"

"Well, this is not such a good idea because it would prove very costly and also, terrorists would find it a much easier target. We may end up having to constantly repair the damages… Anyway, I think I know how to eliminate the risk, so the liquid generators don't become a threat to nobody! Well, I've thought about it just now, but it could well work… We'll only need some help from the International Space Agency, because I'm not an expert on this sort of stuff, although, I did send them a project of mine for a Moon base, a few years ago. Well, I did not hear from them and then…"

"Mark, how can you make sure the generators are absolutely safe?" Platt interrupted the unnecessary digression of the 'expert in everything' and directed him back to the safety issue.

"Well, I'm not sure that it's possible but I feel this would be the best solution! As I've already said, the liquid generators are not that big and it's not hard to transport them with a truck, ship or airplane. A helicopter is also not out of question. This means of transport can be an easy target for the terrorists, where it won't be too hard for one to launch an attack on them. Still, I think we could shoot the liquid generators beyond the atmosphere and get them back to Earth along a ballistic orbit to the exact spot we need. We will plunk them right in the electric distribution stations, which are guarded very well anyway and so there won't be any danger." No one made any sense of what they just heard. The scientists looked ahead vacantly and the look on their faces was extrinsic to people of their position. Their lack of knowledge about ballistics contributed to their bewilderment.

"Alright, Mark, we'll come to this when we have to. As long as we have enough energy, we will manage to distribute it to all the states in need, somehow. Now, I'm going to ask you to leave us for a few minutes, as I'm beginning to feel worried about all the silly questions coming into my head. We'll be done shortly!"

Platt's fine sense of humour caused everyone to smile again. In a very good mood, the scientists moved on to taking the most important decision in the entire history of the Global Energy Project.

Platt lied. It took them one minute, not several, to vote for and approve the idea of building thousand of reactors in the vast desert.

The 19th Conference was not any different than the ones that took place previously. It came to no fruition. It resulted in a few proposals for taking measures against the energy shortage; however, they were more or less superficial, as usual. Nevertheless, this time, the scientists displayed uncommonly high spirits, which did not stay unnoticed by the accredited journalists in the conference hall, as well as by the millions of viewers of the directly transmitted live Conference coverage on TV.

Mark Eos was not mentioned in any way, nor did his idea become a common knowledge to general public.

Platt prohibited any of his colleagues talking about it. Not that he wanted to hide anything. Just his common sense prompted him to keep everything a secret, as it was in everyone's interest, until the entire project was scrutinized and tested. In addition, it was necessary for the international political community to give a green light to the idea.

Exceptions

No one could touch energy. Mark was no different. Despite this, people all over the world could feel that there was substantially less energy to go about. In reality, this was not exactly the case.

There were 21 small inhabited islands, which had never experienced any energy problems. Thanks to the wind generators, positioned along their windy coastline, as well as the powerful Sun, which was 'working' for nearly 10 months per year, these places could be classed as heaven – energy heaven! This was a heaven that did not require a military defense, due to its 'in the middle of nowhere' location and the ordinary and insignificant existence of the population. The people, who lived there, were calm and happy. They led mundane and simple lives, enjoying what they had. They hardly experienced change and their total isolation did not bother them in the slightest. Quite the opposite, it made them even more content. After the last energy related war conflict, the islanders realized that they did not have anything in common with the rest of the world. The senseless warfare together with the vast number of innocent victims became the basis for the new union of the 21 islands, which broke off any diplomatic relations with other nations. The fact that there were less than 2000 people living on each island did not matter whatsoever. The response to this by the rest of the world was expected and easily predictable. The insignificant Island Union was shunned and labeled spitefully with the medical term: "The 21 Tumors".

Tourists never came to visit any of the 'tumors' and at the same time, the locals were not allowed to leave the island, unless they were going to one of the member-islands of the Union. During the first few years of isolation, it was not uncommon for some nutcases amongst the natives to dream about leaving the archipelagos. However, their attempt was unachievable goal because the nearest dry land was too far away to be sailed across. There was no other means of doing it but via a sailing boat. Some found death when trying on. Those, who were less confident, simply resigned to turning their boats and headed back to their prison-island.

The islands' population did not have to worry about food, either. The Ocean was generous enough and even when there was a stormy weather, the islanders had plenty of reserves to rely on. United by their common destiny, the islands exchanged know-how and learned from each other's experiences and thus, they constantly managed to improve their residents' living conditions. They also benefited from mining iron-ore from a dozen of uninhabited rocky islands, located near-by. It was used to manufacture different metal parts for the ships, numerous hooks, harpoons and all the tools needed by the locals in their everyday life. Wood was also aplenty because of the responsible methods applied in the timber industry. If a tree needed to be cut down, the Council had to vote in order for anyone to go ahead. All issues and problems were resolved effortlessly, due to the islands' small size and tiny number of residents.

There was nothing notable in the way the islanders moved from one place to another. There were not any energy batteries on the 21 islands, because when the devices went into mass production, the archipelagos had been already shunned by the rest of the world. Cars, run by petrol, had also never touched any of the 'Tumors'. The mountainous relief was simply not very suitable for this means of transport to operate efficiently on any of the islands – it did not allow for building regular roads. Hence, the inhabitants generally walked on foot or sailed if they needed to visit a neighbouring island. All home appliances and tools were powered by hands, so there was no need for any extra energy.

Kids and teenagers passed their free time by playing games. The lack of television and any kind of information about the outside world was actually doing the youngsters a favour. Some of them had heard of 'over there and beyond' but that was about it – they would never learn anything more than that. Their curiosity was dulled in the most simple and efficient way. The parents followed meticulously the restrictive order, issued by the Island's Council. They taught their children that if one could not see anything afar from the highest peak on any of the islands, then, this meant that there was nothing further away, but water. Brought up with the idea that it was impossible for them to leave the islands, the youngsters had accepted the world as it was described to them. Any evidence that proved the opposite of the imposed illusionary belief had been destroyed. This isolationist strategy, which modeled human behaviour and views, was implemented in the very first week of the new Island's Union. In contrast to other similar social experiments, where people were simply pawns, in this case, the undertaken measures were for the benefit to all. The purpose of concealing the truth was peace and a better life for everyone. Children had to learn the minimum of knowledge at school, mainly the basics of biology, anatomy, mathematics, etc., but no geography. There was a map in each "classroom", which depicted the archipelagos in the centre of a blue background. This was the whole world.

Very soon, probably 99% of the population was going to believe in this 'reality'. The only enlightened were the high rank governors of the Island's Union, who were traditionally succeeded by their enlightened children. A certain number of elders, who had passed the tricky age of 70, also remembered the past, albeit, they did not feel like talking about it. At first, there was the odd good-wisher who tried to keep the memory of the previous world outside the archipelagos living in the minds of the youngsters. However, the strict regulations, implemented by the governors, soon put an end to it. The control over the population was much easier, when people naively believed that this was it and there was no other alternative.

From time to time, goods from outside had to reach the group of islands. For instance, the solar panels were manufactured by a continental state, which government did not mind having an easy-going trade relationship with the members of the Island Union, although, on theory, it had also signed the isolation pact against the 21 Tumors. Silicon plates were exchanged for see food goods.

Sometimes, other products were needed, too. The barter type of trade was explained in the most simplistic and believable way to those, who did not know the truth and were totally satisfied by this account, i.e.: The big ships crossing the ocean, often explore the far away uninhabited islands, where there was old silicon. So the sailors who had been living on the ship since they were born, collected the precious material and made the solar panels, which they exchanged for fish, as they were not very good fishermen and preferred to get it from someone else. In order to keep the illusion on, the 21 islands did not own and had no intention of building big ships on purpose, and thus, they limited their capacity for long-haul travel.

The half-primitive way of living for the islanders meant that the energy was insignificant factor in their lives. Unintentionally, they had stopped in the right spot in history, energy wise. They used the commodity only for having light in their homes at night. The mining industry consumed the most of the energy, but out of it small but enough quantity of iron was being produced. The electric network worked in a very simple way and it had hardly ever any problems or failures. And if there were any, it usually came to just replacing a few meters of cable.

Even in the past, before the new made-up theory about the outside world had been imposed on the islanders, they had always lived a simple life as fishermen, who had never had any greater ambition than just filling their fishing nets and having a stable family. They did not like newcomers and foreigners and they also disliked traveling far. The rest of the world may have thought that this way of life is not normal, but then, no one could argue now, amidst the grave energy crisis situation that those very people led better and happier lives than everyone else. Well, that was a fact!

There were three other states, apart of the islands, which had never experienced any energy shortages. They were slightly more developed economically and had large populations than that of the archipelagos. The residents of the three countries shared the same origin and ethnic background. This was the reason why the states had elected a supranational government. The people in these states were lucky to have enough natural resources, mainly coal and vast and endless areas, covered in woods that provided them with valuable timber. In the past, there had been attempts to conquer these rich territories but to no avail, due to the extreme average temperatures of minus 40'C and harsh environment.

The cold was a huge problem so there was hardly any interest shown towards the North. Trading with 'the cold nation' was not great. They were selling coal and timber at a very high price. The Northern people did not worry about their food supplies. They grew different crops in underground green houses. Their diet consisted mainly of potatoes, which they could make numerous types of dishes from, even desserts. They designed their homes, so at least one of the floors was built underground for heating purposes. These lands were rich in deer, which were used not only for their meat, high in protein, but also, as a means of transport, too. It was proven and tested that the energy batteries could not operate in temperatures, lower than minus 20, so that was the main reason why the 'evil' had missed them.

Life in the far North was far from perfect but bearable, especially, for those, who had been born and bred there. Very few people ever ventured down South and left their country. Most of the Earth's population lived in the temperate zone and some could not bear the cold temperatures during the cold winters there, which lasted about a month and a half. Many, during this harsh period, would go down south like some migrating birds. Not that there was more energy in the warmer regions, but at least one would not be freezing. Another kind of migration exacerbated the energy crisis.

The migration was somewhat an expected process, in a very similar way to the Great migration of peoples, quite a few centuries ago. There was nothing unusual about people seeking a better life for themselves and their families. Unfortunately, these innocent intentions caused the old metropolitan districts to expand beyond the 100 million citizens. The bad management of these giants of a city, together with the overloaded electrical network, led to the occurrence of the first energy related problems. City after city had become the victim of people's irrational behaviour, which resembled that of a herd of animals, which would simply follow their instincts. There was an attempt to update the electricity grid, but to no avail. Generating energy became insufficient. In addition, a lot of resources were spent on repairs, which was a total waste of time.

There were some real enthusiasts, who decided that they could live like in the old times, relying mostly on fire as a source. This led to the situation getting worse – devastating fires broke from forgotten candles. Lighting a fire was banned, as if the world had become inhabited by kids. These 'kids' decided that something had to be done and not just keep whining about it. People realized they had to act together, if they wanted to overcome their problems. Naturally, the Northern regions and the energy-fortunate lush 21 islands did not need to become a part of this pact. The energy wars had made man to come to his senses. Equal on paper, the most affected countries by all this began to look for a solution to the incipient energy crisis. The beginning was challenging, mainly because of the political nature of the initiative, which was tailored to do the small and poor states down. The deepening problem prompted every state to join the energy union. Democracy reigned within the international alliance - views on solving the crisis were welcomed from every country, which had to resort to their brightest minds in the face of leading scientists. This approach, however, led to no valuable results, as it was obvious from the very beginning that the world was full of a huge number of crazy scientists. Well, there were some very good ideas out there, too, but usually not viable, due to their cost. Proposals, featuring trivial energy sources like water, wind and the Sun, very well hinted at the helplessness of the global scientific community.

The experts really struggled to come up with answers, not realizing that the problem was not down to the energy, overused by conglomerations of people, which was also hard to produce and transfer along the obsolete grid system. The lack of development was the key issue. The energy batteries, the discovery of which made any type of means of transport function, were the main reason for the energy shortage. Of course, it was understandable that a 100 million city would be hard for one to supply efficiently with electricity at 100%. But when this city had 1 million energy batteries implemented in different machines, each one charged at the cost of thousands of households' worth of energy, then the estimate went pear-shape. From the very beginning it was clear that the miracle device that inundated the global market was going to cost everyone rather a lot. The inventors of the technology made sure it became open knowledge worldwide, so the batteries were easily accessible. That was the reason why their production rate was steady, however, energy was available to the ordinary citizen for less and less periods of time, as it was all used up by the very same energy batteries. A vicious circle was in place. All this led to a new type of dependency, where the previous master-source that was retrieved from the depths of the Earth had been replaced by a new one, simply called: energy battery. Was it possible that a few thousands of reactors in the vast desert could lead to a new dependency?

Stage 1

Mark Eos did everything in his life, by being led by some strange kind of science related idealism. Thanks to this, he had managed to develop his detailed and somehow reliable project plan, designed to solve the energy shortage. As soon as the 19th Conference had finished, the meticulous process of testing every detail of Mark's plan began. At the same time, Platt and his colleagues went on to visit different parts of the world. The reason for that was not their love of traveling or curiosity for exotic foods and places but rather they were trying to convince the world political leaders to lift the ban on building nuclear facilities. Instead of charging across the globe, they could have decided to wait and meet all the key players at the Temperate Regions Economic Alliance Summit, as they were all going to be present there. However, the meeting was not until 8 months later and they did not have that time to waste.

Platt played the key role in these important meetings, as expected. His personal connections with a lot of state and political leaders had turned him into someone, who was rather difficult to refuse, if he asked for a meeting. The other five scientists from the Global Energy Project were left to handle those statesmen, who Platt did not know personally very well. The members of the Project did not have to worry that much if their negotiating skills were not at their best, simply because they only had to make sure and convince the politicians in the only possibility and chance that it was left before mankind. Platt had really made a decision to always bring up what Mark had told them at their meeting -

everybody was doomed if people did not realize the lack of any other alternative.

The world was a colourful and interesting place to be, but it could, sometimes, become too interesting. There were so many different countries, which meant that they all had their own agenda and interests to defend, often, at the expense of others. The scientists had to deal with some really stubborn lead politicians quite a few times.

The initial few meetings, organized by Platt, went really well. As soon as it was mentioned that there would be energy for all and at any time, the politicians just bit into the whole idea straight away. Their hidden plan was so obvious: if the energy problem was sorted while they were in power, it meant that they would remain in power for longer. Platt put their lust for power to his advantage. He used his words cleverly, describing the future position and greatness, awaiting anyone, who backed the idea of lifting the ban. All fears of the possible danger to people were dispersed, as soon as the location of the future nuclear power plants was made clear.

Understandably, the issue about the cost of this venture came up at every meeting. Platt was very surprised to see that it actually turned out not to be such an issue after all. On the contrary, the world leaders were prepared to fund the building of 6000 reactors, as Mark initially aimed for. Some of them offered even a greater sum of money than it was asked from them to begin with. It probably made them look more important or it helped them shun some of their inner deep insecurities. The total cost was estimated in a very simple way: the cost of one nuclear power plant that had four reactors was multiplied by 1500. 10% was added to account for all those expected logistical expenses, and there was another 10% on top of that for all the quirky inventions of Mark that no other similar facility had, like: the domes and self-burying pipes, etc. So every country that had placed their signature under the Global Energy Project, excluding the 21 Tumors and the three Northern states, were about to invest as much as they could afford, according to their GDP rates for the past year. It was fair that rich economies were going to contribute more to the project, because their use of energy was higher. Platt was aware that, eventually, the developed states were going to try and push the smaller countries out of their way, but this was how things were in life, where justice and fairness hardly ever reigned. The fact that a substantial sum of money had to be redirected from the state' military budgets proved to be hardly an issue. In effect, this was praised as being a very smart move. Platt was a very perceptive man and he could see through the transparency of his clever and experienced politician friends' strategies. Yes, it was a difficult decision to part with money, designated for defense, however, the leaders knew that once the reactors started to gush out the energy, the first thing they would do was to increase their arsenal and the production of military machinery. It was a known fact that the army needed the largest quantity of energy batteries and it used energy more than any other industry. One step backwards meant three moves forward.

Not everyone was that easy to convince. The president of one of the key states, which played a major role in establishing the energy project, was firmly against the new proposals. He hardly knew anything about nuclear power, but he was an avid follower of the conferences and he still believed that Platt and his colleagues could come up with alternative ways to solve the problem, which would never become a target of terrorists. The statesman did not want to even hear the theory that a possible success in targeting the facilities in the desert was not an issue. He also believed that the energy situation was actually not that bad and that it was even improving in his own country.

Platt was going to remember this meeting for life. He had never had to contradict so vigorously his own believes and ideas that he consistently had been presenting in a succession of recent conferences. The chairman of the Global Energy Project quickly explained that so far, everything said had been a big lie and that the world was going down. There was no way out, unless we all did not embrace the ideas of an anonymous accountant, who took science as his hobby. Realizing that he had been very much misled, the political leader of the country in question refused to look at the suggestion to agree on lifting the populist ban. The two men had known each other for quite a few years, and for the first time, one of them felt betrayed. At the end, the only thing Platt managed to get as a promise from his, now, former friend was a call for a national referendum after hours of begging. Platt did not like begging and he did not resort to it lightly. The last time he asked someone for a favour, was when he and his older sister went to get an ice cream and the short chubby boy asked for another one. And this was really a long time ago.

The shuttle diplomacies carried on for a little bit more than three months. Platt did not fail even once, especially, when it became clear after the polls that the ordinary people were also on his side. The citizens happily went to the ballot box to give their favourable votes, knowing the geographical peculiarities of the project, i.e. the reactors would be located thousands of kilometers away from them. The unpleasant outcome from all this was that Platt's presence in that country was going to be unwelcome for years to come.

His colleagues also accounted for the odd negative result from their international meetings. Alex Rice had managed intentionally to enrage one of the leaders of a country in the Far East. The president was quite fine with signing but his visitor's excruciatingly bad attitude made him say "No", just out of spite. Prof. Rice had gone to the meeting, determined to get that negative answer. He detested the short happy-go-lucky subjects of this artificially happy and untroubled country. The reason for this was going back in time. More than three decades ago, the young Mr. Rice had to visit the Science Institute in this country. It was an honour for any young and prospective scientist to develop further their academic qualifications in this establishment of knowledge. The duration of the postgraduate PhD course was two years, which turned out to be the darkest four years of Alex's life. He was kind and tactful, when he was young, well cultured and behaved. This sort of attitude was a rare gem then, let along now. His family did everything possible to ensure that their only son received the best of education and have a good life. His insulated kind of upbringing and the fact that he got everything he asked for had made the young scientist slightly blinkered to what was going on in the real life. Alone abroad, in a far away country, with no family and friends, was a situation that many students regularly fell into across the world. Not a lot of them, however, had to go through what Alex had to.

The student residential quarters were located on the edge of town, where the university was. The remoteness of the campus was not accidental. Over the years, it had been proven that students excelled in their studies only if the option to frequent the nearest town for recreational purposes was brought down to a monthly visit. Any more deviations than that led inevitably to lower grades for the students. There was really no need for anyone to leave the campus, but of course, the forbidden fruit was always sweeter, even when it was not. The gates of the university campus closed at 10pm and did not open until 6am. Those, who happened to be late had to find a place in town to stay over or simply stand outside the gates and just wait.

Alex Rice had devoted himself to his studies and was easily in support with the idea that there was no need to leave the student quarters more than once a month. At the end of his second year, just before his final and most challenging exams, the pressure had accumulated quite a lot. Alex realized that he had to somehow release that pressure. He agreed to go out with a few of his fellow students, who always had rather average results on their exams and who often went out and about in town. They all decided to go to one of the posh bars in the center.

The city, which was completely flat, had two sides to it. One was represented by a modern science institute, a business park, a few decent residential districts and a beautiful historical center that attracted plenty of tourists. On the other hand, there was a part, which was sleazy and shady, notorious for dozens of casinos and bars, where alcoholics and druggies went about, undisturbed, their everyday business. Frequent visitors of this side of town were some students, who were not exactly friends of Alex, but at least they knew how to have fun.

Slightly drunk, Alex Rice left the bar at 3 in the morning, leaving his pseudo pals behind to continue drinking until dawn. The alcohol had hardly affected him and his mind was engaged in thinking about his forthcoming exam, which was turning out to be rather easy, in terms of the subject matter, but at the same time – quite hard, with regards to whom the examiner was going to be – a real nasty piece of work. He had no means of transport, public that was, to his room in this early our, and a cab would have cost him as much as his monthly rent. The taxi drivers were always keen to prey on some drunken student, who they were happy to hit with a double fare on arrival at the student campus. The distance of 5 km was not to be underestimated, but in a steady pace, Alex would have reached the gates just in time for when they opened. He anticipated some sleep until 10am and then, some mental exertion for the rest of the day. The temperatures would fall to 10'C during the night, which prompted any forethoughtful person to bring a warm piece of clothing with them, when going out. The Eastern parts of the temperate regions were known for the pleasant climate and nice weather throughout the year, where the temperatures during the day were about 23-24'C. The tall young man was striding in a slow and even pace, placing one foot in front of the other. He walked in this strange manner, because he was in deep thought about some of the questions from the examination synopsis. Therefore, Alex did not realize that, from aside, he looked as if he was drunk and high on drugs at the same time. His black leather jacket made him almost invisible, especially because there were no streetlights along the road. In those days, there was plenty of energy to satisfy the 24-hour needs of the population, however, the local tradition called for the idea that there was no point to waste electricity after midnight.

He did not feel anything. The blow was so hard and out of the blue that by the time he fell on the ground, his brain had switched off like a technical device, when it stops to prevent further damage. Alex had no time even to experience pain. When he woke up, he was very well aware that he was in a hospital and this fact made him relieved and slightly pleased. Lying flat on his back, with no pillow under his head, he did not have a good view of his surroundings in the hospital room. From what he could see in his range of vision, he realized that he was not in a standard in-patient's room. The ceiling was painted dark-blue and was rather depressing. He looked to the left, then, to the right, but he could not see any medical equipment around. There were no monitors, nor there drips, attached him, nothing. The room could fit four more beds, but it was just he, lying in there. His thoughts could only come up with: "If I'm here, it means I must have been pretty ill. And if I'm not in pain now and there are no doctors around me, it must mean I'm fine now. Hmm, but why can't I move my arms and legs…?" was the last question that popped into his head before a doctor entered the strangely painted room.

The bad news remained bad news no matter how it was presented. The doctor tried to lay it out gently, the seriousness of his condition to the young student, but he did not quite manage to do it well. Alex listened, with his eyes wide open and tried to accept the terrible diagnosis like a man. A few minutes later, he was alone again in the room and began to cry like never before in his life. Alex Rice was brought in a very bad state, as he had lost a lot of blood. After the initial life-saving interventions were completed, the doctors had established that the young man was paralyzed from the neck and that both his legs were broken. Luckily, they would heal alright, without the need of surgical procedures. The plaster would help his broken bones heal for the next four months, at the minimum. To this very day, Alex sometimes felt a slight discomfort in his left leg but tried suppress it with the occasional painkiller. His immobility was described in medical terms as something temporary that was supposed to get better with time.

The wording "with time" bothered him the entire first night. On the following day, Alex, whose eyes were very red, got his first breakfast, brought to him by a petit and jolly nurse. They talked a little and the conversation was all about the reasons he got beaten. The nurse, though, was careful about it, because she was aware that it was not beneficial for the patient to bring back the nightmare of events that he had been through. She did mention to him that according to the Police, what happened to Alex was standard mugging, which was not something that rare these days. The inspectors had another theory, too, about possible personal motives for the attack, the evidence for which could be sought in the severe brutality of the assault. To be fair, the city was famous for its low level of crime. The penal system was pretty harsh, so the locals, the visitors and the students from overseas tried to avoid any conflicts. Alcohol consumption and drug use were not classed as crime, but these activities were regulated. The spot, where Alex had been attacked, was also interesting. There was no case like this, recorded in the last twenty years: a student, beaten in such a severe way, on a road, leading back to the student campus. Whenever people clashed occasionally, it resulted simply in the odd broken tooth or a bruised eye, and usually arguments occurred in busier parts of the town.

The days that followed looked alike due to the common characteristic they shared – Alex could not do a single act independently, but speak. His parents arrived within a few days. They could not come earlier, due to the far distance of the country. They did not quite manage to encourage their son or give him hope. He needed a long time before he could begin to accept his condition and recover from his psychological distress. The invisible trauma was far more serious. The exams, thanks to which he would have fulfilled his dream to gain a PhD, passed without him. Twice a month, the doctor carried out some special tests on him and every time he would confirm that things were getting better. It seemed, however, that only the doctor and no one else could see the light at the end of the tunnel. After one year, Alex could feel his arms and legs, but he could only move them by a few centimeters. His muscles had vanished completely. Although, there were not any neurological reasons for him not to begin to move, it was not for another year until he made a full recovery. What helped him the most in the final few months was his determination to graduate. After all, that was why he had come to this Far Eastern country.

Only a week after he had regained 98% of his health, as the doctor described it, Alex got his PhD. He passed successfully his final exams. His fellow students and tutors, the entire university, everyone was shocked at what had happened to him. So their sympathy probably helped him to get the highest grade at the end, even if he did not quite deserve it. The local media also covered extensively the incident. They were the first to give reliable information about the case to the authorities and help with the investigation. It occurred that there was an organized gang of some aggressive youngsters, who went out on a mugging rampage, targeting inebriated customers of the city bars. They would wait for their victim to leave the pub and then follow them. Applying some physical force, they would deprive their prey of all valuable belongings. Alex had lost his wallet and his black leather jacket, which the attackers had obviously considered expensive. The place of attack had also been thought to be rather convenient for them. The detained individuals self-confessed to several robberies and muggings but denied any involvement in the attack on Alex Rice. Nevertheless, it was fastened on them and they were put behind bars for 7 years.

Alex did not care about whose responsibility was and in any way, he never saw the perpetrators. What was important to him was to graduate and leave this terrible place that was full of terrible people. He detested everyone and was blaming each of them for his mishap. The inhabitants of this country were generally short, about 5ft4". They had wavy hair that seemed they never combed and chubby sly-looking faces. There was no scientific explanation to why the locals always looked happy and jolly, no matter what mood they were really in. Their faces seemed extraordinarily the same and never changing. These features, unpleasant to most foreigners, put aside, the people of this country actually had one of the highest IQ, which placed them amongst the smartest nations in the world. It was not uncommon for one to turn quite racist after experiencing physical or psychological abuse from persons, who came from a different racial background or religion. Alex even went beyond that. When Platt told him that he had to pay a visit to his old chubby "friends", his face broke into hideous grimace. All these years, in which he had promised himself never to go back, he had managed to accumulate even stronger hatred for them. It would keep burning him until the day he died.

The happy host, who was no taller than 5ft, had been the president of the country of "Lilliputians" for the last 6 years. According to the local legislation, the president had to change every ten years. There were many pros and cons about this practice, but at the end of the day, the current leader had been seen in a positive light. He and Alex shared a common background. They had both graduated the same university, although the president had specialized in Humanities. The meeting between them did not last for more than 20min. The guest presented, in brief, the good ideas of the unknown Mark Eos. Then, suddenly, he set off a completely unprovoked verbal attack against the innocent population of the host country. Alex went on to pointing out how they deserved nothing and how the chairman of the Global Energy Project was determined not to include them in the business with the desert nuclear power plants. He dropped Platt's name on purpose to emphasize the importance of the entire venture. The host, who would have accepted wholeheartedly the idea if he had been treated appropriately, actually firmly refused to become associated in any way with the bunch of 'energy idiots'. He left demonstratively his own sleek and luxurious office. The evil grin reappeared on Alex's old face. It was another triumph of his everlasting hatred. Thanks to him, the Far Eastern country and its population of millions of riffraff were going to be left out of the distribution of energy, generated by the reactors in the desert. The current energy situation showed that the shortage was in a far gone stage and people had only about 6 hours of electricity a day. The diminished power of the Sun, the light wind and the lack of large rivers, basically everything that had been valued in the past, was now becoming a big problem. The vast number of energy batteries was using up all the energy, as little as it was. The batteries were not going to disappear; it was unthinkable! This would lead to a total crash of the transportation system, which would respectively result in a collapse of the economy, then a downfall in people's life, in everything.

Prof. Rice did not feel any hatred, nor love during the rest of his meetings. There, he managed to achieve his aims without any problem. This was down to Platt, really, rather than him. The news about the chairman's achievements was spreading fast, which meant that his colleagues' foreign visits became simply perfunctory. They just went to their appointed meetings, where they did not need to even try to negotiate or convince their opponents. The latter were already convinced and it was actually impossible for anyone to discourage them.

Merit failed just once. He was on a visit to a country, which was known for some unorthodox views. The population there believed that God would provide them with enough energy, as long as they all collectively keep making their prayers. Hence, the idea of building nuclear power plants in the desert sand was not approved by the spiritual leaders of this nation, which really consisted of naïve believers. Prof. Merit was not that disappointed by the decline of his offer, because he was very much aware that sooner or later the country would join the project, due to the large quantity of energy batteries they owned.

His colleague Connor felt quite uncertain about the success of his last trip. He had received a firm "No", from a state that hardly resorted to using batteries. This country had imposed some strict rationing laws. There were restrictions over all unnecessary use of energy. The problem, there, was the not great level of effectiveness, rather than insufficient energy production. The population was against nuclear power energy generation. They were getting used quite easily to the restrictions. Also, the insignificant increase in production had caused a slight optimism amongst the people. Connor realized that at that moment of time, he could not make the leader of the country accept his proposal. It was an open secret that the head of state had been trying to impose his separatist policy and break his country away from the rest of the world, very much like the 21 Tumors had done in the past. The fact that the most active terrorist in recent years, came from this country, made the entire idea of the visit pointless. Connor, like his colleague Merit, hoped that when they see the completed power plants ready to go, then the state would decide to join the alliance. Well, this was probably unlikely. The six scientists were very well aware that not everyone would join and that the realization of the project did not really require every single state to participate, although, it was required for each country to be asked to join.

Jeffrey and Faulkner, they, too, came across a dead end, at some point, but no one thought of it as being a that much of a deal. So at the end, without any major problems, the first stage was concluded successfully. The ban was lifted, the allocation of sufficient financial resources was arranged and the global community "swallowed" the idea of building nuclear power plants again without too many significant protests. The condition that the new rules would apply for initiating the nuclear energy development only in the Big Desert, additionally contributed towards the smooth start of the venture.

Mark could not celebrate, yet, hearing the great news, because it looked like they were not going to start building soon. In the last three months, a large group of scientists and him had been trying to prove that his ugly drawings and his logical theories on paper could actually be put into practice. They could not quite do this, but they were close. They still needed a major revision of the theoretical plans.

The accountant had totally accepted Mr. Platt's model of work. In accordance with it, they had to thoroughly scrutinize each step of the project idea, where Mark was going to be interrogated in detail by 80 expert-scientists. The team included engineers, who directly took part in the development of some of the last nuclear power plants before the ban was imposed. In addition, there were also a few nuclear physicists, geologists, meteorologists, machine technicians, a dozen of security specialists and some experts in subjects that the regular citizen had never heard about before. So many clever heads in one place made the achievement of some sort of coordination rather difficult, but the task was getting even harder, when all those scientific answers were sought from a man, who was not a scientists, a man, whose drawings were simply appalling and whose elocution skills were rather strange, to say the least. Communication in so many foreign languages was also making things tricky. There was a bunch of eight interpreters, who followed Mark relentlessly. His home country had provided a decent administrative five-storey building to be the scientists' working ground for the purposes of the project. A week after the start, things were not going that well. The first conflicts arose from the fact that some foreign experts had become a bit too keen to spend as much time with Mark, so they could impose their views. Their respectable status as scientists did not stop them to start behaving like some squabbling housewives, getting vexed over the last box of washing powder, left in the shop. The lack of appointed coordinator made Platt's assistant go and report to his boss about the inefficient working environment everyone was experiencing. The chairman of the project managed to calm things down, by issuing the order: "Do as Mark tells you!" Well, Mark really had no idea how to give orders to the venerable scientists so he simply delegated this to his and Platt's assistant to relay what was required from them.

Every time the scientists looked at the undecipherable information and drawings in the black folder, questions arose straight away, reflecting the scientific field, in which each of them was an expert. Their critical approach inevitably led to a widespread skepticism amongst the specialists. Some of them even thought that the entire idea is a waste of time, but took into consideration that Platt and the rest of his team had given their support. Well, then, it must be worth something.

The location was the most unique feature of the nuclear plants project. Never before in the world history had such an energy development been designed in such a hostile environment. The statistics showed that all working nuclear power plants had been situated in areas with favourable climate, unlike the deserts, where the temperature amplitude was rather significant. Mark did his best to convince the biased engineers that outside elements would not have any adverse influence over the sealed structure of the plants. He half-managed to persuade the experts. Similar doubts arose when discussing the water supply methods. The idea about the self-burying pipes was already known technology, however, their length seemed to create a problem and also there was the question of how would they be lowered to a certain depth. The geologists believed that some areas in the desert, where the pipes were supposed to go, were simply difficult to drill through. Day after day, Mark was trying to clarify every next component of his project plan and his opponents swiftly refuted his ideas. They were beginning to think of him as a pathological fantasist. No one denied Mark's originality and his exuberant imagination in relation to energy solutions, but the scrutiny of their scientific checks pointed at the unfeasible outcome. Not in this format, anyhow. When the ban was officially lifted and the permission to build in the desert was granted and signed, the 80 scientists and their strange host were firmly convinced that the initial idea was not viable for millions of reason and therefore, the plan would require some significant rectifications. Mark Eos was about to discuss precisely those with the chairman of the Global Energy Project. The brief meeting between them was going to take place in the office that Mark had occupied for the last few months.

"Come in, Mark, have a seat!" The guest said, feeling much more as the host rather than a guest.

"Well, hello, Mr. Platt, I was just discussing with some of the scientists a few details about the new dimensions of the domes and the possible traction needed for their transportation... and then, my assistant, well not that he's mine, but your assistant, and he came, didn't he, and told me that you were here... though, when we spoke on the phone last, you didn't mention you were coming, but only talked about the ban being lifted, and if I knew that you'd be coming..." Platt took the chance to light his cigar during this never-ending and typical for the accountant sentence. The explicit non-smoking policy in this building was not going to disturb his intentions whatsoever.

"Right, Mark, I've surprised you, then?" He could have abstained from interrupting him, but sometimes this was the move, when there was someone like Mark Eos opposite you.

"Eh-r-r, well, you have, quite a lot actually..."

"You mentioned that some alterations are needed, what sort?"

"Well, Platt, as you know, I was telling you, wasn't I? Some of my ideas are unattainable, well they are out of question and my colleagues..." Mark could not remember everyone's name, so he just referred to the scientists as his colleagues. "They also think that this is the case. Moreover, they pointed out to me some errors of mine. Well, I'm not an engineer, aren't I? Well, I did say I was not one. I'm an accountant." He paused as he had exhausted the air, left in his lungs. He topped it up, so he could continue. "Well, we've determined a few points and we've been working on them for the last few weeks, and it's been much easier, now, that so many of us are thinking together about how to solve the problems and..."

"Mark, tell me what changes need to be done, but please, be brief." Platt did not feel like talking, nor did he feel like listening, either. He was more than exhausted from the long flight and had no time to get some rest, as he came over straight from the airport.

"Well, the things that don't add up are as follows: the question about how much resources we need and their location; the size and transportation of the domes; the water provision and supply; the reactors and finally, one of the most important things, I believe – how to provide enough uranium for fuel. In addition, the idea about the Lego principle of construction is only viable for assembling the large parts. Well, we now know how to deal with this. We're going to transfer the inner parts of the reactors into the dome and then, we'll put them together and assemble them. We really can't take them inside already pieced together…"

"Mark, I have a feeling that you'll need a few hours to really fill me in on these matters. I don't have that time. Tell me is there any point for us to go ahead with the whole thing at all?" Platt had talked beforehand with some of the scientists, working with Mark. They believed that it was really possible to produce enough energy in the desert nuclear power plants and overcome the global energy shortage, as long as some significant alterations of the project were made. The professor was only asking to see how Mark would react to his provocative question.

"Well…" Hesitantly Mark began, taken by surprise with the blunt question. "There is a point and we just have to go ahead, though, it would take longer than I imagined, eh-r-r, well, it's alright to build now, so… and also, you've said that the money's available, therefore, I think it will all work out at the end. I thought that it would take a year if the whole world joined forces in the project. But maybe, this was too optimistic and we'd need that sort of time to just complete all the important modification of the plan before the start of the actual building work. Six thousand reactors are a lot to do… Not that I thought they weren't a lot, well, I recommended this number, didn't I?"

"Right, then! Keep working at full capacity! I want results as soon as possible. A year is far too long, Mark! Make sure you're ready before this time. Together with my colleagues, we will do the rounds again around the world and tell our partners that things would be paced down a bit. We'll schedule a new energy conference soon to calm them down." His cigar was not quite out, yet, but this did not stop Platt to throw it in the bin and leave the room. He did shake Mark's hand before that without changing his frozen face expression.

The chairman of the Global Energy Project was actually in rather delicate situation. It appeared that Mark had turned out to be more of a dreamer rather than a scientist, which was causing some stirs between the other 80 "colleagues" of his. There were even indirect suggestions that Platt should be replaced from his chairman's position. He, of course, did not really feel threatened by this and just kept his trust in the accountant intact. He truly considered Mark as the only person who could change the grave energy situation. Well, like before his belief was more of a sixth sense, really. It was something that could not be rationally explained. The five members of the project were not that bothered about the delays, whereas Alex Rice openly did not care about it or who was going to be his boss, now that he had managed to throw out the object of his hatred from the entire project, even if it all did fail at the end.

One of the biggest drawbacks in the list of problems was the lack of sufficient quantity of materials, and one type of which that was located too far away from the vast desert. The uneven level of concentration of natural resources across the globe aggravated even further the inequality amongst the states, which were taking part. For instance, the largest depot of titanium, needed for building the domes, was in a country, which was supposed to invest in the project a relatively small amount of its budget. However, if it was the only state that contributed the necessary titanium, then it would appear that this nation donated the most, leading to the higher expectations with regards to receiving more energy, which the country actually did not need. This, on the other hand, would have to result in the other countries paying the 'titanium' state, because the value of the material was much higher than the supposed monetary contribution the country was expected to invest, with respect to its GDP. At the end, it was decided that the surplus given would be covered by the rest of the participants. There was another problem, too. The titanium was going to be enough to build just 1000 domes, instead of 1500. The experts opted for the only solution possible – to make an alloy with titanium, copper and nickel. The dozens of professors became stuck with resolving yet another issue within the project. It was less of a problem in contrast with the titanium, but still. They realized that the concrete sites under the domes would require the same quantity of material, used by the entire world for a whole year. This would mean that the states, nearest to the desert, had to cover it. The problem was that even if they applied their full capacity, they would produce about half of what was required. The solution was resorting to extensive import and building the rest of the concrete panels in these countries, in newly built factories. The additional cost for this was going to increase the project budget by about 5%.

Things became quite a mess, when it occurred that to cast just one dome, first it had to be done several thousands of kilometers away from where the material was extracted, which was located quite far from the desert, anyway. Therefore, the scientists decided that the only solution was to build a new foundry next to the titanium mine. The problem with the domes wasn't completely solved. Mark wanted them to be very big, so they could accommodate everything necessary for the proper operation of four reactors and the reactors themselves. He had not taken into an account, though, that if the dome is one whole, then it would be rather heavy. So it might be impossible to be transported to the desired location even by the biggest helicopter that was out there. This issue was resolved by modifying the initial plan. The domes would be smaller, with a slightly altered shape, and they would be designed to cover two reactors, not four. This would make the titanium 'cap' almost half as light than the originally thought. So the nuclear power plants were going to be 3000, with two reactors each. These changes increased the cost further by one fifth, but there were not any other clever alternatives on offer.

The concrete platform and stable dome, now sorted, it was then the turn to the actual nuclear power capacity equipment to be placed in the enclosed space. At least, this stage was straightforward. The latest generation of nuclear reactors, the experts were going to use, were relatively compact and no bigger than a truck. They were easy to transport from one place to another and most importantly – they were safe. Thanks to several secure 'coats', embracing the active part, there was a zero possibility for any radioactive leakages, so radioactive exposure outside the accepted levels was out of question. The most developed states were going to manufacture the reactors and thus, decrease the sum they would be required to invest in the project. Some smaller countries also had the know-how and the technology to build them but it would have taken them the same time to make one, what it would take the richer partner states to make ten. In the name of justice and equal distribution of tasks, the less powerful states were going to produce the equipment, responsible for the nuclear fission process that took place in the heart of the reactor, in order to generate energy. In contrast to the first years of the nuclear era, when the equipment was bulky and heavy, taking up an area of several hundred square meters, the new technologies, now, allowed the control system facility to be no bigger than an average wardrobe.

One could not generate nuclear energy without water. The scientists decided to stand against the idea the precious liquid to be transported via pipes, which were thousands of kilometers long and two and a half meters in a diameter wide. The problem was not so much the long distance, although, pipes so long and wide had never been used before. The issue seemed to be the fact that they were planned to go under the surface. The accountant's idea was to connect many short pipes into a long one. The problem was that he had not thought through the self-burying concept, which was limited to ten meters and depended on the density of the top layer of soil. It would have been ideal if the surface was nice and evenly soft everywhere, but the diversity of Mother Nature never offered conditions, too perfect. The vote went on different directions. After some lengthy debates over the matter, the scientists, who were concerned about security, agreed that the pipes should partially go above the ground at some places. The visibility of the facilities was going to attract terrorists like a magnet, so army guards had to be deployed in certain areas. No one wished that the water-main got damaged in any way, but if should something happen to it, then, a second stand-by pipe would have to substitute the first one. It would also have some of its sections above the surface. Security would be required at the coastal base, too, where the pipes met the ocean. Hopefully, the guards would do their job properly.

The assembly-point, where all equipment and materials were going to be thoroughly checked and tested, before dispatched to any of the nuclear facilities, also required the highest level of security. Mark had thought in detail about all this, but even he was surprised to find out how many human resources needed to be employed, so the safety of the non-nuclear parts of the facilities was guaranteed. The nuclear power plants themselves did not require live protection. The scientists really liked Mark's idea to secure them by dispersing tons of smithereens around in the sand. This was one of the few elements of the entire project, which was approved unanimously because of its ingenuity and effectiveness.

The nuclear reactors would generate daily quantities of energy, which would be distributed proportionally to every country involved. The methods of transportation and its distribution caused some differences in opinion. The most ineffective and expensive way was to develop a few main electric routings to the nearest states, which would then, transport the energy via their national electric grids to their neighbouring countries and so forth along the created chain. This was far from the best option and the experts knew it. Nevertheless, they did spend some considerable amount of time to discuss the idea. Another not very cost effective alternative was to collect and store the energy in regular generators, which would be transported to the desired destination. The motives against this suggestion concluded in the fact that hundreds of thousands of these generators had to be transported daily across the globe.

Mark had proposed a different option, involving generators again, but of a different type. The technology proved to be unpopular amongst the scientists initially, but after some extensive deliberation, everyone agreed that it would be the most cost effective, though, the most dangerous option, too. A few intense weeks followed, during which the experts overcame the risk elements after some strenuous mental work and long hours of discussions. Several months ago, when the accountant presented his project before Platt and his colleagues for the first time, he had shared his idea that concerned the safety of the transportation. He had suggested that the liquid energy generator could be sent into the sub-space ballistic orbit and then, they would safely reach the energy distribution centers around the world. The military specialist had already confirmed that this was possibly by deploying the ionospheric airplanes, used mostly for exploration and research. In order to diminish every undesirable eventuality during take-off, the flight itself or landing, when such a "short-tempered" substance was on board, a remote control center was going to be employed on stand-by, just in case. The generator, charged with energy, could turn into a metal box, full of liquid by just a click of a button, and thus, converting its valuable load into a safe substance. This was easily done by simulation of grounding within the container. This sort of deactivation had a price. To press the button just once would have used up energy, generated by four thousand reactors in two days. When there was no cause for emergency, the liquid generators were going to be lowered in the heart of distribution station, from where they would keep feed every part of the country and its neighbours, via the local system of 'blood vessels'. The surplus energy was going to be stored. It was a top priority for the energy-storages to be protected against terrorist attacks. The evidence of the authorities' serious intentions against anyone, who would dare jeopardize the safety of the energy, generated in the desert facilities, could be seen in the large military presence, protective barriers and heavily armed soldiers. The army personnel had to get used to with their new role of becoming ordinary security guards, since there were no military conflicts and wars anymore.

The theoretical preparation was entering its final stage, when the most important element of the whole project needed to be looked at, as without it, nuclear energy production was going to be impossible.

Uranium could be found in different parts of the world, but for obvious reasons, there was no clear information on the quantity available, or on the exact location. One nuclear reactor required very little uranium, in order to operate. However, the problem was elsewhere. The long period of banning the development of new nuclear facilities had prompted people to believe that the use of this type of energy source was coming to an end. It was also thought that after the current nuclear plants exhausted their working life and reached their limit, then, they would turn into enormous monuments – a reminder of the dangerous past. Of course, this belief was accentuated by the idea that very soon, another source would be discovered - a source that was safe, cheap and aplenty. So the available uranium was only enough for the current facilities until their lifespan ran its course. Most of the mines were actually deserted and neglected. Some countries even went to the extreme of burying their uranium deposits under tons of concrete, and thus, showed the world that they had called it a day about relying on nuclear energy, in the name of the peace and safety of their people. After some scrutinized checks of the uranium mines with an easy access, the scientist had determined that they could not sufficiently supply the six thousand reactors for more than two years. The sealed off mines had to be reopened again and new ones also had to be discovered. It was not going to be an easy task, due to the stupidity of those upright politicians in the past. At least there was plenty of time for this, which had to be a good ground for success.

Plutonium was a chemical that shared a lot of its characteristics with uranium, so it could be used as an alternative. A slight drawback was that one had to drill deeper to get hold of it and also, there were fewer sites across the globe. Still, whatever quantity Mark and the scientists could get hold of – it would be of use. In contrast with uranium, a chemical that became useless radioactive matter after fission, 40% of the end product, when using, plutonium could be recycled to generate energy again. Mark was aware that there were other chemicals that could be employed in the energy production process, but they were far from efficient, due to the insignificant quantity of energy they would generate during the nuclear fission process.

In Mark's imagination, everything was perfect and the thousands of reactors operated like clockwork in a safe and isolated place, with the help of tons of uranium and plutonium, and where millions of liters of water had been harnessed for the smooth function of the facilities, only to generate energy for all mankind. The accountant's fantasy, no matter how realistic it could be, had not catered for one very important issue, which came up at one of the next daily scientific discussions. Usually at these, the blind optimism always ended up shattered by sound logic and real facts. The question was how the energy would get to the people. Yes, it was agreed that the liquid generators would facilitate the process, however, the issue laid elsewhere. Problems were likely to occur after the energy left the distribution center points.

When millions of people migrated towards the big cities, the network grid could hardly cope. Trouble-shootings, failures and power-cuts increased until it became rather difficult for the system to withstand the great energy demand. Not long after, the energy batteries took over the consumption, 'sucking' away what was before designated for the ordinary citizens. Power restrictions were emplaced, initially – in some locations, but then, it became a widespread policy and practice. So now, when the new project envisaged the incessant flow of energy towards every household around the world, an obvious issue came to light. It would be a real challenge for the grid to endure such non-stop power pressure. The scientists realized that the initial estimate of the costs would ultimately increase. Further investments in new power system facilities in the big metropolises were a must. The smaller towns did not encounter so much this problem, but even there, measures were going to be taken if necessary. It was going to be labour-intensive and rather costly to adapt and expand the power supply infrastructure across the globe.

Mark had an interesting, although, not very efficient idea up his sleeve, which could facilitate the entire process and maybe, reduce the necessity to resort to patching things up. "Why don't we entice people to return to their hometowns – usually, smaller places, where drastic power network alterations would not need to take place?" The state could opt for introducing the policy of economic decentralization by offering preferential conditions to investors, ready to part with their funds in places with population under a million, in contrast with the practice from the past – investing in the suburbs of the multi-million people metropolises. If the proposal was to succeed, a number of administrative units and services had to be relocated in place. In that respect Mark would note that "I'm not familiar with this sort of thing, but in this way, it seems, things might work, I think…" The scientists could not quite grasp the accountant's suggestion completely, but Platt felt the idea was feasible. He committed to meeting all the political leaders of countries that had gigantic cities and talked them into convincing the people to move back to where they came from, along with updating their national grids. It was clear that mass exodus was not on the cards, as very few people would agree to go backwards. However, it was calculated that even if a small percentage of them did, this would have a positive effect. At the same time, certainly no one could stop newcomers to move to the big cities; therefore, it was unlikely that a metropolis of more than hundred million people would ever become one with a population of under that figure.

The physicists and chemists amongst the scientists, who were experts in energy conductivity subjects, seemed to have a better idea. They proposed something innovative and never done before that would guarantee the stability of the power grid, no matter how many millions of energy units would be passing through. A modern cable had a copper wire in the middle, because of the good quality characteristics of the metal. Before the energy crisis, there had been a research development program, trying to find an alternative to copper that had the ultimate conductivity. Unsurprisingly, the program stopped shortly after that. The material was expensive then, and it was now, although, the global community could foot the bill. There were no two ways about it. According to the idea, the entire energy "spine", starting its route from the distribution centers, along with every component on its way, it all had to be replaced with the new material. The secondary and less pressure loaded energy routes drew from the main spine and thus, covered and reached the peripheral parts of the cities. The new power system grids were going to be designed to fit each metropolis, according to its strict individuality and structure, but following the same principle. Although the technology was experimental, the scientists believed that it would work, as it had been very well researched and tested.

Platt got absolutely excited about the new conductor-material and the moment he was confident that it was going to work, he issued an order for its production and implementation. This process began before even building the first nuclear power plant. The additional spending was enormous, but the more money Platt demanded, the more he was offered. Moreover, the world was prepared to give as much as it was required. There was hidden logic behind all this.

Finally, Mark and his 80 collaborators had managed to prove the realization of every controversial point of the plan and were, now, convinced that they could be put into practice. The long waited moment had arrived – it was action time!

It was difficult to choose and appoint a coordinator of the complex logistics of the entire project. Platt thought that one of the more ambitious scientists could take on this important role, but then, he quickly changed his mind when he saw their profound lack of leadership and organizational skills. Mark's proposal for someone, who Platt did not know in person, seemed fair, so he decided to look into it. He had agreed to meet the candidate for the post first, so he could see for himself whether the person fitted the job requirements. Mark wanted so much to make it up to his only friend that he was prepared to tell Platt off for doubting his judgment of Timor's unquestionable skills.

Back in the game

The accountant, who was world famous for his rebellious actions, had a small cozy office located on the fourth floor. The room suited Mark's needs and taste perfectly. It was his 'cell' in the voluntary prison, where all the scientists had committed themselves to work. The complete isolation of everyone, working in the building, was guaranteed by dozens of armed guards who were providing a secure perimeter. Media also had no access to anyone to bother for an interview. Reporters had to satisfy their hunger for news by resorting to the official information, released weekly by the press-office of the Global Energy Project.

Platt had an acute self-preservation instinct and he tried to impose the same on the people, he cared for – all the scientists and one man that was not. All of them were convoyed to work on a daily basis, and then, returned to one of the army barracks-complex, which accommodated the lodgings of reverent intellectual. Most of them were not happy with these settings, especially those pretentious professors, who were used to be a center of attention in their respective countries and who always sought after comfort and luxury conditions. They had no choice, but accept the situation. A hotel accommodation would have jeopardized their safety, so it was out of question. Mark had his own room, which he had managed to turn again into a pigsty. He got used to it very quickly and hardly ever thought about his den of a bed-sit. Actually, he had not visited the place since the 'Red' and the 'Orange Tie' took him away from there. He did not miss his old job, where he successfully played the role of a walking calculator. He did not miss his work colleagues, either, as there was no one like Timor.

The first checkpoint was situated ten meters away from the building. The visitor, surrounded by three armed men, was made to present his ID and display all his belongings out of his pockets. Body checks were slightly crossing the limit of what was legal and what was not, but Timor did not intent to rebel even if this limit was overstepped. The absence of a gun, knife or another dangerous metal item shortened the procedure to last no more than a minute. This exercise repeated immediately after he entered through the spinning doors of the foyer on the ground floor. Mark's former boss was very well aware of his whereabouts, although, he had not got the slightest idea about the reasons of his summoning. Anyhow, he let the security personnel to perform another body check on him. The staff was professional in doing what they do. Two civilian guards took over and convoyed the guest to the lift. It was just a few meters away, but they could not possibly allow him to get to it by himself. Timor pressed the only button that he spotted. The short noiseless trip ended on the appropriate floor. When the slide doors opened, he saw two polite guards, stood before him and ready to show him into the right direction. For a moment, Timor felt like a celebrity, and as if he had a dozen of private bodyguards. He smiled. He nearly laughed out loud, but who knows? It would have been probably seen as a bit of an aggression and they could have simply jumped on him.

There were many offices behind the doors, situated on both sides of the long narrow corridor. No people could be seen around, apart of Timor and his escort. They reached to the third room on the right, where the visitor had to wait for a couple of minutes, after being asked in a polite, but peremptory way. He sat down in the comfortable chair, placed in front of the desk, and crossed his legs. He was not nervous, although he didn't know who he was about to meet. His curiosity preyed on his mind only for a little while, because the person came in shortly.

The conversation lasted a little bit more than half an hour. It resulted in the domineering host being convinced that Mark was right. The chairman had no doubts that the combination between impressive physique, broad intelligence and commanding tone of voice were exactly the qualities he sought in a person, who would be fit to head the largest energy project in history. Platt had scanned through Timor's CV, just before the meeting took place and he felt contented with what he had seen. After talking to him face to face, he only reconfirmed his opinion about the recommended man and about him being the right candidate for the position. The chairman had asked Timor a few provocative questions, to which the latter answered in a just about acceptable, totally correct way. Very pleased, Platt left to find Mark and tell him the good news, while Timor stayed behind in the office. The accountant, who was waiting next door, felt sincerely happy. A second later, however, he felt scared that Timor might be still crossed with him: "what if he hits me, what if he refuses the job because of me?" He was standing outside the door and all these questions kept coming in his head one after another and every each of them raised his body temperature, which resulted in him profusely sweating. Finally, he decided to go in.

"Well, hello, Timor!" He said hesitantly, still stood near the open door and ready to run off if he needed to. Timor recognized straight away who was behind him, not only by the characteristic voice, but also because Mark was the only person that started his sentences, 9 out of 10, with "Well..." He got up slowly from his comfortable chair and came very close to his former employee, without changing his icy face expression.

"Hey, you bastard, did you just arrange this job for me?" Timor shouted and then, his frozen mask changed into a broad smile. A bear's hug followed. This dispersed completely Mark's fear that his friend was still mad at him for the things that went on during the conference. The accountant opened his eyes, which he had preventively closed, expecting a powerful right-sided blow. Even his glasses could not protect him against it. "I knew it was you! My God, I still can't believe it! Can you imagine, I just had a meeting with Platt and he told me that I'm going to be the chief coordinator of this whole thing with the reactors in the desert?" When Platt mentioned that an old friend had recommended him, Timor thought of several people that could have said a good word about him here and there. But when it became clear that this was the crazy scientific project, then, it was just one possible person that could fit the picture. Well, after all, the media had already announced officially that Mark Eos was behind the whole idea. Despite all this, Timor did not expect to see him here. He believed they had been hiding him somewhere out of the country, according to the rumours.

"You, bastard!" Timor repeated jokingly and gave Mark another hug. The accountant calmed down from his initial panic, though, he was still a bit shocked. "Mark, I know that I've said a lot of nonsense to you in the past. I thought that I was right at the time. Got fired because of your antics, remember? Anyway, I want to apologize now. I'm sorry, my friend!" The third hug was one too much but it was good one to let it all out, rather than keep it in. When the big hands let go of Mark, he was relieved to find that his vocal abilities were still intact.

"Well, you know, Timor, it was my fault, then, and I didn't want you to lose your job because of me, and things got out of hand. Then, Mr. Platt helped me and now that the project is ready, I've though that you're suitable for the job... I'm sorry about your wife that you two had to split up, Timor!" Mark remembered all the shouting on the phone, word by word, and how he was accused of causing Timor's break-up with Ella.

"Are you kidding me? You've done me a big favour. After Ella left me, I felt rotten for a few months, I admit. The divorce was over very quickly, but the bitch took my house!" Timor's hatred for his ex-wife was very obvious. He released the tension in his jaws and continued. "But then, I met Jess and I've never been happier in my life, since we got together. She is so cool and I feel ace with her. We are renting a place near the center, so why don't you pop and see us one day soon?"

"Well, I'm glad I could help! This is what friends are for!"

"Mark, thanks to you I have a beautiful woman, and now, I have this unique job that millions could only dream of. I will remember this!" Timor raised his right index finger symbolically. "So, whenever you need something, I am the person to ask. I will do anything for you and even, then, I'll be still indebted to you."

"Well, Timor, I don't need anything, just your friendship, like in the old days... As you know, I don't have many friends and..."

"Ha-ha-ha! You are easy to please! You want a friend – you got a friend! You can count on me!"

"Well, I know, Timor. You can keep your promises and you're trustworthy man! That's why you've been a director, as you can take responsibilities and you are good at managing staff..."

"That's right, Mark! That's me – a big shot!"

After the laughter, coming from the newly employed chief coordinator, and after a final exchange of questions, clarifying who was angry with who in the past, and whose fault it was, the host nodded at his dear guest to sit down. Mark closed the door, blocking the route for the escape that never happened and then he sat in Platt's chair. Timor settled in the one, opposite him.

"Mark, we haven't seen each other for a long time and there is no one else, who can open my eyes for all this. I've heard all sorts of nonsense in the media, but are you sure that the whole thing is not doomed? A lot of people laugh at the idea that the global community is going to resolve the energy crisis with a few thousands of nuclear reactors in the Big Desert. I'm not going to blemish my career as a manager and great image for one big nothing at the end, am I?"

"Well, Timor, you know, at first, it was not going to work in the way I thought it all out. But now, together with my colleagues, we've changed a few details for the last several months, and it's going to work. In theory, it's all fine and it's been proved. But I wish we see all this working successfully in practice."

"You don't sound very convinced, Mark."

"Well, how do you mean? I'm certain, I'm convinced now, and it's not just my opinion, here. Everyone in the project, believe in the idea and think that there will be enough energy and the reactors will work fine, without a problem."

"I hope that's the case. In my neighbourhood, they've cut the power with another half an hour per day. So, I'm thinking that we're really going down. Mark, we are very close to the bottom!"

"Well, Timor, I don't want to make you angry, or anything, but when our country starts producing the elements that it needs to contribute to the project... You are aware that there is an agreement amongst countries about what parts each of them is going to manufacture! So when all this starts, there will be further power cuts for the ordinary consumer and..."

"What?" The guest shouted, making Mark jump in his chair. "So, it will be us, the regular citizens, again, that we'll have it the hardest... and carry on going to the bathroom with a torch in the middle of the night. I have four or five in every pocket of mine. That's not normal!"

"Well, there's no other way, Timor! At first the energy needs to be redirected towards the factories, but, then in around three months, when the first reactors begin to generate energy, the people will feel they have some for longer periods. Platt has told me this, and also, the idea is that there'll be energy for all at the end and people..."

"Yes, yes, yes, I get it, Mark. I understand you completely. I just don't feel like waiting that long."

"Well, the project implementation could have started much earlier, if I didn't make those mistakes. The domes were too heavy, and generally, I misjudged some things..."

"Don't beat yourself about it, Mark! What's important is to work at the end. I'm sure you've done everything how it should be." Timor noticed the guilt on the accountant's face and quickly decided to show some tact and change the subject of their conversation. "So, do you know what my position will involve? Platt's told me that I'm going to find out at a later stage, because there isn't much to coordinate right now. He also said something about the basic components being manufactured now!"

"Well, that's how it is for now. Platt ordered a few days ago, to cast the concrete elements that would make the base, as well as the domes should be created as soon as possible. The idea, really, is to try to do everything cost-effectively so we don't transport them to the desert one by one. We need to build most of the components first, even the reactors have been started, too, and other things. As far as I know, the actual assembling work will begin in about a month, where your expertise will be most needed. You'll be the chief coordinator of this process."

"I can't wait, Mark. My current job can't be even compared with this. It's unreal! And what is your position in all this? The right hand man for Platt, or the seventh member of the Global Energy Project, what would it be?" Timor joked around with a few more suggestions, but in reality, Mark had no idea what his role would be, after the theoretical part of the project was concluded and his mental efforts would be no longer needed that much.

"Well, I don't really know, I think I've done my job and now, as it all starts in the desert, I've never been there and there is no point of me going there..."

"Mark, you don't need to fill your shoes up with sand! They'd probably give you some millions now, so you can just live you life, spending, with no worries about the future."

"Well, Timor, I don't think I really need money right now. I have some savings in the bank, don't I? Since I got on the project, I've been provided with everything I need, so I haven't been spending anything, really!"

"I don't need money!" Timor repeated, imitating the squealing voice of the accountant. "That's unheard of, nowadays! If I was in your shoes, I would have asked them for ten million, at least!"

"Well, I wouldn't want that much? I wouldn't know where to start and how to spend it all…"

"You can always call me and I'll help you with it!" The offer sounded serious and like a joke at the same time.

"Well, I don't know, Timor. I'm not going to ask them for money and I just don't know I…"

"Hmm, Mark, this humbleness of yours makes you simply look like a complete idiot, but I do understand where you're coming from. You put science first, before money. Anyway, I won't hassle you about it anymore."

"Eh-r-r, well, then, but, hey, you don't hassle me. I should ask for some payment but, as I don't need it, there you go, I don't…"

"You know what, Mark? Why don't you ask the big boss whether it would be all right if we worked together, like in the good old times? Platt is very clever so I doubt he'll say "No". And they'll offer you some sort of salary."

"Well, I haven't actually thought about this, but it's not a bad idea, if Platt agrees. But what am I going to do exactly?"

"Nothing. You'll just keep me company. It would be best if he makes you the deputy chief coordinator. After all, you are behind this whole idea. You won't be doing anything, but if things start to go wrong, then you could help with some advice and generally stay close. Don't forget to ask him later, when you see him!"

"Well, I'll ask…" Mark was brief because Timor's phone rang, otherwise his reply would have definitely been one long ranting sentence, as usual.

"Yes, honey, I'm coming!" Timor was beaming, talking to his new girlfriend. "I'm sorry, Mark, but when Jess is calling, even these guys outside would not be able to stop me from picking up the phone. I

131

have to go now. I've made a promise to take her out for dinner tonight."

"Well, Timor, I have some work, too. I'm glad you've accepted the job and that you are not angry with me anymore…"

"Enough with this story, now! Friday, I want you at ours for dinner. I'm not taking "No" for an answer and don't dare come alone!" Timor winced in the same frozen expression as when he did at the beginning of their meeting. He realized that it has an effect on Mark's tendency of being scared of him.

"Well, we have security and I'm not allowed to go anywhere. Whatever I need, they just bring it to me… and I'll have to ask Platt whether he'd let me come to yours. He has not done so for the last months, not that I've asked him… And I don't really have anyone to bring along and if I turn up alone, then you…"

"Mark, you're going to finish me off with your gibberish. Come by yourself. It's not a problem. You could let me know, then, about what Platt has thought of our idea. I have to go now. We'll be expecting you on Friday, for sure!" Already at the doorstep the newly employed chief coordinator raised his long arm to wave 'good bye', and put an end to the pleasant meeting with the man, he could definitely call again his best friend.

"Well, bye, Timor, I want to come, but…" said Mark too late, as usual.

After the meeting the accountant started walking up and down in the building, in search for Platt. None of the security guards could tell him for sure where he had gone. Then, Mark met their mutual assistant, who informed him that the boss had left the building straight after his interview with Timor and had headed for the airport. Platt traveled a lot anyway, but since the start of the actual implementation of the project, he had to visit different parts of the world even more often, in attempt to please all the political leaders and find a mutual balance in achieving a compromise. The perfect balance probably did not exist, but this did not stop Platt from trying to convince everyone in its existence.

Everything was in Platt's hands. His colleagues had less of an authority in these matters.

Mark hated talking on the phone, so he avoided it at all costs. He always worried that people would not understand him and would keep asking him to repeat himself. So far, it had always been the case. Even Platt realized that Mark was not the guy to speak to over the phone, when he needed some updates on the project. Therefore, the professor made sure to call the rest of the scientists, who were familiar with some of the details, he was after.

The brief conversation resulted in achieving a partial success: Mark was not permitted to visit his friend for dinner on Friday, but he was promised that his request to work with Timor would be considered in the future. Platt was aware that Mark was no longer needed that much for the project, but he did not intent to reduce the level of security around him in the slightest. The terrorists were very well informed about whose the idea about the nuclear power plants was, so the risk could not be still ignored. Mark could be seriously in danger. With regards to the new tasks in store, the accountant and the 80 scientists were going to be briefed at the start of the week.

The 6 000 reactors would not require too much manpower, as the entire process would be computerized. Powerful computers would be designed to sense the slightest problem in their function and then, would be able to fix it. However, without human resources, the smart machines would not be able to operate. Platt had assured Mark that staffing would not prove to be a problem. He firmly believed that there were plenty of skilled and qualified scientists around the world, who were able to go and work under the desert domes. He was right and someone had to select the best specialists from the global nuclear engineers' guild to work at the power facilities. There were about 30 days left, during which Mark and his colleagues had to look at the CVs of all the candidates, who wished to get a lucrative position on one of the desert power plants. A lot of HR specialists and psychologists were going to assist the selection process, in order to guarantee its objectivity and the professional criteria implementation.

The project envisaged that there would be three people, working under every dome. One would supervise the fuel supply to the reactors; the second one was going to control the whole process of energy production with the help of the specialized equipment, whereas the third person was going to manage the smooth transfer of the energy from the reactors to the liquid generators. The selection process was going to involve scanning through the candidates' CVs, without actually meeting them in person. Basically, the administrative building did not have the capacity for conducting interviews with so many people from around the world. The psychologists were very much aware that many insecure individuals would embellish their skills and experience. However, as they could not get an impression from a direct contact with the applicants, one had to trust what was on paper. Mark had never taken part in such a selection process. He had only been on the other side. Therefore, he approved all the candidates that he had checked out, as their CVs surpassed the job requirements. The rest of the scientists were slightly more selective. Whether the best and most suitable people got the job was rather difficult to say. If some of them failed their duties with time, there were plenty more that could replace them.

The pilots were selected under a strict military set of conditions. Platt did not have a mechanism to distinguish the best of them in the process so he relied heavily on the judgment of military officers. The main requirement was 10 000 flying hours, irrelevant to what country the pilot came from. Platt got this advice from a friend of his, who worked in the Military Air Force, and he trusted his opinion. They did not look for young and promising pilots, who had insufficient experience in the sky. Of course, everyone could make a mistake, even the experienced ones, but there was no way one could have guarantees about anything.

The issue with the actual helicopters had to be looked at carefully before the start. A former military base was provided, where all the helicopters could be accommodated in huge hangars. It was not going to be hard to find machines in good condition. Presently, they were the most used in the army, whereas fighter planes were less popular. The reason was, of course, in the helicopter's energy battery, which provided much longer period in the air than that of a supersonic plane.

The energy batteries were going to be the main problem in the following months. The countries, located nearest to the Big Desert, had to go out of their way to produce the elements for the base, and thus, the energy that was left available for the population needs did not amount to more than three hours per day. Moreover, extra energy was required for charging the helicopters. The machines could not be provided with energy in countries that were further distance away, because it would counteract the whole purpose of saving energy, by the time they reach the desert and making in this way the venture pointless. The solution was, to stop the entire energy supply for the people from the neighbouring countries, until the helicopters were fully charged. The process took a few days and then the standard 3-hour per day restriction was resumed for two weeks, until the machines needed another re-charge. The energy 'genocide' for these people was going to last around three months. Then, some of the nuclear power plants were supposed to be completed and it was expected from them to take over. In order this to be achieved, a new chapter was added to Mark's project, which envisaged several underground power-lines, made from the new conductive material. They were going to connect hundred of the power plants with the central base. The base itself was going to operate, relying on solar energy as it was surrounded by silicon panel fields. The star in our solar system ensured life on our planet but in terms of being a source of energy – it was rather unreliable. Actually, before the invention of the energy batteries, the Sun was regarded as an alternative, but progress "stabbed it in its fiery back", too.

The will and ambition could do wonders sometimes. The whole world experienced a real and unseen sense of unity – all states put in the effort to do their part of the project, avoiding any delays at all costs. The miners in the biggest titanium mine were proud to work 12-hour shifts under ground, very well aware that the bright future of their children and grandchildren depended on this. The workers in the new foundry, where the huge domes were made, had no time to complain in the unbearable heat, either. Some people moaned a bit as the energy flow to their households was reduced and redirected towards the factories. Well, it was accepted easily enough. Everyone was aware of the high purpose the world had and looked forward to the beginning of the new light era, which would never end.

A month later, enough domes and concrete components were made. There were about a few hundreds reactors ready and the two long water pipes were nearly completed, too. It was time for all the parts to be transported to the distribution base, which was situated right next to the desert. A second base was being considered in the near future but for now, they were going to use just one.

Under Timor's strict supervision, the workers followed the order, planned by Mark: a missile, a base, then the dome, the reactors and the rest of the equipment that was going to be on the inside. The militaries would first make the surface even and after a few minutes, when the sand particles settled back, about 30 helicopters would come, carrying the concrete blocks. Their form facilitated the process of putting them in the correct position, so the pilots had to apply the minimum of skills and effort, aided also by the people on the ground. About twenty workers, well equipped against the heat, had to make sure that accuracy was observed in this process. While the "puzzle" was being set, another special helicopter was bringing the dome. The design of the machine was altered purposefully. It had its center of gravity moved towards the back, in order to counteract the inevitable swaying and wobbling because of the heavy load. The computer simulations had demonstrated that a standard helicopter was not up for the task – the lightest breeze

136

could bring down everything in the most unfavourable way. Mark had designed things in such a way that the dome could be placed in without the help of the workers. Some slits were cut in the base beforehand, where the titanium 'hats' just fitted perfectly. The same thing was repeated 44 times during the first week. This number could have been 50 if it was not for the huge sand storm that lasted a few hours on the second day. The weather conditions, generally, were not that severe as thought before. However, the teams above ground had realized that speed was the key to overcome any climate adversities.

The Big Desert was uninhabited and no one ever went there as a tourist. People felt apprehensive about the sharp temperature differences, forgetting that not so long ago, several tribes used to call the place a home. The odd Bedouin was still roaming after their herd of camels, but usually at the periphery of the sandy plain.

The entire staff, employed to put Mark Eos's desert project into practice, were accommodated in the distribution base in especially build underground residential compounds. Above, there were huge hangars for the helicopters and an enormous open area, where the domes were placed next to large stacks of concrete blocks. The modern coordination center was the heart of the Base. It was located at the top of the radar tower, from where all the deliveries were closely watched. There was the working place of the chief coordinator. Timor had less work than he expected before his arrival and he did not appreciate this in the slightest. He had twelve assistant directors, who did most of the job together with their personnel. So Timor had not managed to feel that he was in charge that much, due to the perfect working organization and the infallible equipment. This motivated him to go and supervise in person the laying of the first few foundations and then, the domes being placed on top. Soon, very soon, he realized that he was out of place. He simply stood boiling in the horrendous heat. Therefore, he decided to go back to the air-conned command room and just issue the odd order now and again, perfectly aware that things would get done without him saying so.

Mark was not around. And this was Platt's fault. After the selection process for finding the right staff was over, where Mark took a humble part, he was left with nothing to do. The chairman of the Global Energy Project was not in any rush to send him to the Base right away. He was going to fulfill his promise and get the two friends working together, but not before he received the security report. There were some indications that amongst the employees, one was a supporter of a certain terrorist group. It was believed that the person was simply waiting for the project to get into more advanced stage, so he could do more serious damage. In contrast with the helicopter pilots and the scientists, who had undergone some very thorough checks, many of the regular personnel in the administration consisted of anonymous people. They only passed a scan, whether they had ever been convicted. Who was the baddy if there was one and how would he do the harm? Platt really hoped the security services were going to point at the potential villain, so he could be eliminated immediately.

Within the first month, it was clear that everything ran efficiently by almost 100 %. All the equipment was being carried through the special hatch at the top of the already positioned domes. The reactors were about to arrive any day, too. It was going to take about 30 hours to fit them and then the power plant was going to be connected to the pipe, which had to supply the facility with the valuable water. The connective element was another pipe that 'liked' to hide itself underground, but it was much shorter. Only patience was needed until it was ready and fully functional, which was expected by the middle of the second month. The schedule envisaged that from the moment the first missile was launched to flatten the ground, it would take no more than 90 days for the reactors to start charging the first liquid generator.

It occurred that there was no terrorist on the horizon, nor there was anyone from the staff that deserved the sack. A special multinational military team provided perfectly the security for the Base. The completed power facilities were not yet working, but they were under full protection. They were patrolled from the air, whereas the surrounding area was scanned 24 hours a day for any suspicious changes and events. As soon as the reactors were fully operational and started working, their own protection system was going to be activated and the additional measure of watching over them from the air was going to be no longer necessary. The smithereens were waiting in storage, all ready to contaminate the sand in the name of security and prepared to shake any adversary, who had dared to set foot near the power plants. Finally, Mark, who was no threat to anyone, either, joined the fully secured base. His arrival coincided with that of Jess, who had not seen her beau for ten weeks, two days and 6 hours. That was how long their imposed time apart had lasted. The woman, madly in love, had truly counted every minute. Mark and the girlfriend of his best friend were traveling on the same flight and even looked at each other a few times. They had never met before and it was going to remain in that way until the chief coordinator did not introduce them to each other.

The accountant had never been down south before and had never experienced extreme high temperatures. The only time he left his home country was when he went to the neighbouring state on his fateful visit, to present his crazy project to Platt and the others. Mark was so excited and fidgety that he felt the urge to get off and go for a stroll but there was nowhere to do this. This strange feeling was rather common on helicopters. The crammed space, together with the deafening noise, coming from the vanes, affected badly the passengers' central nerve system. The rule was: no one was allowed to vomit until the machine had landed, so people could step outside and proceed with it if they had to. Mark was trying his best to keep his breakfast down, but it seemed the meal had a mind of its own, dying to come out for a breath of fresh air. The ugly scene reoccurred with everyone on board, who had not had the experience flying on helicopters. The soldiers waited, smiling, for the out of control food incident to stop, so they could check the passengers' IDs. That included Timor's girlfriend. Mark was told he would be joining the scientist's team responsible for testing the thousand times already tested theoretical side of the project. The most capable colleagues of his had already settled and they would all "collaborate" again. Platt had missed to inform Mark about his responsibilities unintentionally. He had too much on his mind and his memory failed him occasionally.

The residential compound had been divided into three underground sectors, where the entire staff was accommodated. Mark was led there, despite his pleas to be taken to see Timor. The accountant had been feeling guilty from the moment Platt prohibited his dinner visit over to Timor's that unfortunate Friday. Although it was not his fault, Mark felt somehow of being in the wrong.

Jess was dying to fall into Timor's arms to the extent that she would punch any of the strong guards should they try to stop her. The fragile lady was deservedly escorted to the coordination center, where her potentially future husband was doing his best to supervise the working processes in the desert. Thanks to his efforts, the nuclear power plants sprouted like mushrooms. With time, Timor had realized that his task was not to be underestimated and although his physical presence on site was not mandatory, the supervision of placing correctly the concrete elements was a crucially important job. At the end of the first month, he had prevented two teams from being sent to the same place, at the same time. Two missiles had made one of the foundations rather uneven, so it had to be redone a few hundred meters away, in a different spot. At least, the desert presented enough space for things to go wrong. It just did not matter, really. As chief coordinator, Timor immediately fired the persons, responsible for the mistake. He had enforced strict discipline and uncompromising manner of management, and his reputation amongst the staff got higher. No one thought of him as an expendable figure anymore.

Unauthorized individuals were not allowed to visit any of the personnel. Friends and family could be contacted only via telephone; so many of the employees developed a strange numbness in their hands, due to the prolonged clutching of the receiver. Jess was the only exception and she had been permitted to stay over for a week. During this short period, Timor, Jess and Mark were inseparable. The trio turned into a couple only at night. The three of them were back together at breakfast. Then, they go up to the coordination center, where the chief coordinator had work to do. The center was actually a spacious round hall, located as high as what equaled the 10th floor of a building. When in there, one felt as if they were in a flying saucer. The room was crammed with aviation controlling equipment, which gave constant information on the whereabouts of every single helicopter in a radius of several thousand kilometers.

Jess hardly listened to the boring rant of Mark about the history of radars and so on. She was more interested in enjoying the surreal view that the window screens revealed in front of her eyes. One could see the vast site, the size of which equaled about 100 football fields. There were rigid lines of numerous black titanium domes, in contrast with the chaotically piled concrete blocks in front of them. It was a waste of time to put them in some sort of order, as they were too many. At the background, one could notice a line of the grey tin hangars in the distance, which had rounded roofs like the domes. Further aback on the horizon was the barrier-fence that prevented the desert from invading the base itself. However, as high as the wall was, it could not stop the occasional desert storms from carrying in the inevitable dry sand. Also, it did not have a control over the scorching heat in the day or the plummeting temperatures at night that could have endangered the entire project if they did not rise again, once the Sun was up.

Jess went out only once during her 7-day visit. She actually liked the powerful hot wave that 'slapped' her in the face. It was a different sensation that she could never experience in the temperate regions, where she had to return and wait for Timor until he completed the 3 000 nuclear power plants. It was another nine months of separation, which would make their feelings for each other even stronger. The decision was made. When Timor returned to her, he was going to propose. His failed marriage to Ella had made him precautious. He had

141

even sworn to never get married again. Well, this time Jess appeared to be different, did they not all?

Mark Eos had no experience with women and one could see this from afar. When Timor was busy in his 'flying saucer' and he could not delegate his tasks to someone else, the accountant had to keep Jess a company. He failed to notice that his long and monotonous tirades about every stage of the project did not provoke the slightest scientific interest of Jess. Timor had warned her that Mark was a bit strange but her expectations were surpassed in terms of the level of his oddity. Despite this, the woman, who was rather superficial and worked as a simple secretary, realized that it was better to just nod occasionally and leave the man talk. She did not want to offend him. Mark was also her guide in the complex network of underground tunnels. In reality, thanks to this labyrinth, people had not got the need to go out to the surface, so they could enjoy the pleasant temperatures below. The well-organized set of connections included horizontal 'elevators', which made their venture rather pleasant. Jess could not wait to tell her girlfriends all about it.

Left without the female presence, Mark and Timor carried on working as before. The chief coordinator made sure errors did not occur, whereas Mark kept testing and proving the validity of all aspects of the project, together with his scientist-colleagues, despite the fact that everything had been already tried and tested numerous times before. Whenever the accountant got fed up, he would go up to his friend at the center and just spent time looking at the never-changing view. Everything repeated every day until it was eight months into the project.

Mark was still not very social. Although he had to communicate daily with dozens of people, there was no one he could call a close friend, except Timor, of course. The situation with the ladies was even worse. He felt nervous to look a pretty woman in the eye. He would avoid looking the plain ones all the same. In his former life as an accountant, he had a couple of female work colleagues, but he did not fancy any of them. One morning, while he had breakfast with Timor in the staff's dining room, she appeared and passed by their table. Whether it was the beautiful love he witnessed not long ago or there was another reason for this, but Mark felt the urge to speak to her. He had never seen such eyes before.

Jennifer

The interior regulations applied to everyone, who worked in the Base. The list of all possible punishments, starting with a warning and finishing with instant dismissal, was long, indeed. The section with the fines resembled a pocket-size book. It was shockingly stupid in places, where instead of preventing staff from erring, it actually gave ideas to the employees to how better they could spend their free time.

One of the amusing possible offences was to urinate out in the open, which would immediately result in parting with a substantial chunk of one's monthly salary. A few followers of the empirical science had a go in testing this rule. They were pleased to discover that at 55'C the liquid matter evaporated at once, leaving no evidence of their breach of regulations.

The fine, related to the working dress code, was less amusing. It was definitely not that funny to part with half of one's wages just because they wore socks that did not match. The rest of the apparel included the obligatory trousers and long-sleeve shirt. This did not prove to be a problem, as long as everyone washed their uniform and ironed it daily. Staff wore different uniforms, according to their job and position. The pilots, who were really the biggest show-offs, had khaki uniforms, as they spent time in the desert, although more often than not, they were in the comfort of their helicopters. The personnel in blue were engaged in the everyday service tasks. The scientists, including Mark, were not dissimilar to doctors, wearing white. Staff, employed in the administration, had to wear grey. Everyone permanently employed in the coordination center was dressed in black uniforms. Timor and his 'brothers in color' did not like at all their grim deathly attire, which made them look like funeral agents. No one could change or oppose to the color code, despite how much it might not correspond to their inner fashion sense. Off work, the employees were free to wear whatever they wanted and express their individuality or class. Eventually the color code was adopted across the globe, at many airports or military bases.

Mark Eos was not picky, when it came to food, so whatever was on the menu, he did not mind. His bachelor way of living, deeply engrossed in his science, had turned him into someone, who did not pay much attention to what they put in their mouth, as long as it did not make him sick.

The queue resembled a colourful snake, formed by the lined up workers, was getting shorter quickly, thanks to adept movements of the cooks and their assistants. The khaki and camouflage green were not present. The pilots and the military personnel had their food intake after the rest of the busy-bees had finished and left. The diner-room simply had not had the capacity to accommodate everyone at same time. However, the pilots really felt very special by this unintentional instance of segregation.

The accountant had breakfast, lunch and dinner always with Timor. If his best friend did not feel like eating, he happily gave it a miss, too, in the name of solidarity. Often, some of the department managers joined them at the table for four, in attempt to sweet-talk the coordinator, who was now becoming more and more respectable amongst his employees.

Mark could swear he had never seen her before. The grey uniform looked too good on her and suited perfectly her lean figure. When she passed their table, he looked her directly in the eye for slightly longer than it felt appropriate. She also met his eyes, behind his glasses. He smiled. This was one of these brief moments that could affect tremendously one's mental state and physical being. Mark's heart was racing, and although sitting, he felt the wobble in his legs. He blushed. There was, of course, a scientific explanation of the state he was in – the excess production of hormones, was due to the emotional reaction caused by direct visual contact with a suitable sexual object. Well, he could not care less about science in this moment. He stopped fiddling with his fork and turned around to see where she would sit. Naturally, she settled at a table with three of her colleagues from the administration – all dressed in grey. A few minutes later, after the initial shock had passed and Timor had asked him three times about why he was not eating, Mark got his sense back. Back to reality, he realized that he would have no chance with her. Beautiful women attracted men's attention and this was no secret to no one. But how men would catch a woman's eye was a question that he did not like the answer to, at all. The pilots or the military guys would suit best any free lady within the Base. They were fit and strong, had a dream job and were not massively stupid or anything. But above all, there were lots of them. Mark was the complete opposite to those men. He had an average body, no prominent muscles; he was modest, despite the whole project being his idea; he was smart, but in his own way; in short – nothing would come out of all this.

Mark put aside any logic and for the first time in decades he began to think of a way about how to introduce himself to her. The approach was crucial, but he had not got any ideas of what strategy to adopt. He could always ask Timor, who was a king when it came to what women wanted, but he was too embarrassed to go to him for advice. They were close, but Mark found the coordinator's constant jokes about women unpleasant and he did not want to be ridiculed further. He felt his brain did not work and experienced a mental blockage. No ideas of any worth came to his mind. Timor had just finished his breakfast and was talking to the guy next to him about the daily tasks ahead of them. Every morning the table conversations were pretty much the same so there was always something to talk about. Mark stopped eating, leaving most of his food and started looking across his left shoulder every ten seconds, without realizing he was doing it. His strange behaviour made Timor stop talking to his colleague. The chief coordinator decided to enquire after his friend's well being. Yes, he was aware that Mark was a bit odd, but this... now...

"Hey, Mark, Mark, what's up with you today? Is it something with the eggs?"

"Well, they are tasty, but I'm not hungry and, you know, I don't have much of an appetite sometimes..." He had stopped turning his head for a few seconds, but this brief moment of not being able to see her agitated him even more. Usually calm and composed, the accountant was feeling exceptionally anxious.

"Are you alright?"

"Eh-r-r, well, I'm fine..."

"Mark!" Timor raised his voice, like when he was telling one of his workers off. "What's the matter? If you don't feel good, just go to get checked out. It could be something with the food."

"Well, I'm alright. There's nothing wrong with me..."

"Mark, you know you could tell me, whatever bothers you... Don't make me feel like a policeman, interrogating you... Tell me, what the matter is!"

"Well, I can't, Timor. I'm fine. Please, don't ask me questions right now... It's probably because I couldn't sleep much last night. I had a few things that I needed to check and was reading till late, as well, and I feel a bit... But I'm not ill. Still if you insist, I will go to the doctors." The pressure rose. There had been already a whole long minute, lost in small talk, preventing him from looking over his left shoulder.

"Later, come by and let me know what happened."

"Well, I'll come and tell you if there's something wrong, but I doubt it..."

"You doubt it, but if it's some nasty virus, then, I'll have to start bringing you warm soup three times a day, and you know, I have more important things to do." Timor laughed. The third person at the table smiled at the joke, as well. Mark also smiled, pleased that he would be left alone, at last.

Such a long time had passed. Would she be still there? He turned around at the minute she and the rest of her colleagues were just leaving their table. He was going to miss the opportunity but what could he do? Usually not very impulsive in his actions, this time Mark stood up abruptly and went after her. He heard Timor's voice behind, who asked him where he was going. With eyes still fixed on his target, he answered: "to see the doctor…"

Her figure from behind was perfect, too, standing out against the rest. The long and straight black hair came down nearly to her waist. It was interesting that when he looked her in the eyes, the emotions took over and he did not actually see her face properly. So the lack of a facial image of her in his mind urged him to speed up his pace and shorten the distance between her and him. What he would do, when he caught up with her, he had not decided, yet. Maybe, touch her on the shoulder, or he should try to stop her by standing in her way, or simply start speaking to her, while she was walking? What was the right thing to say, Mark did not know.

The long corridor leading to the administrative department presented sufficient number of horizontal elevators. Four people could fit in each of them, by simply lining up inside like fish in a tin. They would rest their backs on the wall, awaiting the acceleration to begin. In contrast with their vertical predecessors, these ones were as wide as a standard human body size could fit in. The device was designed in such a way that there was no free space between the front and the back wall, so when it accelerated or it was about to stop, it did not cause a chaotic movement of bodies on the inside. Mark got in the next elevator. Three scientists were with him aboard and although, they politely greeted him, he remained silent. He did not return their greeting until the doors opened and he managed to turn around, while getting off. The scientists knew him reasonably well, but even they felt bewildered by the strange behaviour of Mark Eos.

Jennifer intended to go to work earlier today, so she could have a look at the documentation, left for her to check the previous day. Then, she would deal with the new information. The administrative job involved putting in order all official documentation, related to the work activity in the Base. Food deliveries, all other stock and supplies, including every piece and element that was necessary for building the desert power plants, they all came daily with the appropriate papers, attached to them, which certified their availability and that everything had arrived at the right place. Jennifer was about to turn and walk down the short corridor, leading to her office, when she heard Mark's direct invitation:

"Hi, I'm, you know… If we could meet? My name is Mark Eos." This was on the border of unthinkable introduction, which started without the 'well' that he was known for. She turned around, giving the nervous accountant even more of a shock with her beautiful white face and her huge dark eyes. She had pretty plump lips.

"I know who you are! Everyone knows. My name is Jennifer." Her voice, which Mark heard for the first time, affected him in the same powerful way like when he met her eyes back then, in the dining room. The symptoms reoccurred – wobbly knees, a racing pulse and of course, he had a face, red as a tomato.

"Eh-r-r, Jennifer…" Mark repeated after her as if he was under the influence of some drugs.

"It's very nice to meet you, Mr. Eos." Her arm, offered to him for a handshake, was a standard gesture – a sign for her readiness to begin some closer relationship. But this 'Mister', he felt, was inappropriate.

"Well, no, I'm not a Mister, just 'Mark' is fine. It's nice to meet you, too."

"Are you after something from the administrative department? I'll be glad if I could help you. I'm just about to start work in a minute." Jennifer kindly offered her services in belief that this was the reason she was stopped right outside the administrative department.

"Eh-r-r, well, no, I'm not. I'm looking for you, you know, to introduce myself, and maybe, some time, if you have the time…" Mark was so insecure that he felt ashamed. He looked down at the tip of his shoes and paused. He had not gained his composure back but still, he needed to carry on. "Well, if you like, we could go for a walk by the wall, after work!" Her confused look on her face and the strange frown on her forehead was a sure sign of her forthcoming negative reply. Three seconds later a promising smile appeared:

"Alright, maybe after work? Are you going to wait for me at one of the exits or we'll go there together?"

"Well, it would be probably better if… well, I'm not really sure whether it's better if…" Mark realized that the last thing he should do in front of her was to speak to her incoherently. So he quickly stopped and uttered briefly:

"Well, I'll come to pick you up at 5."

"See you at 5, then. I have to go now. Until later, Mark!" When she turned round, her long black hair nearly touched his face and he smelt the nice scent. He had no words to describe the feeling.

Mark was standing in the middle of the corridor, in the way of rushing personnel, heading towards the administrative department. He simply could not move. His physical state had gone back to normal, but somehow he did not feel he wanted to go in any direction. When he regained his mobility at last, the accountant headed towards his room. He was not going to work that day. His colleagues did not need him. Anyway, they got together every day to discuss everything else but what they were being paid for. His visit to the doctor was completely forgotten. Mark had no wish to go up and see Timor, either. He was going to wait between the four walls of his small room until it was time to meet her.

Mark was thinking over the how emotionally he had shot out his invitation to Jennifer for a bizarre walk by the wall. Although there was this tradition for the staff to go out for a stroll by the wall after work, this usually did not happen before 8 o'clock. Around this time, it was the most bearable temperature for going out. Then, at about 9 o'clock, it would plummet rapidly to nearly 0'C, whereas at 5 pm, it could be as hot as 50'C. This was how quickly the sand, heated all day, would cool down. Everyone was aware of this information. There was no way that Jennifer could have not known this, too. Why did she accept, then? Mark had become a bit of a celebrity since his antics at the 18th energy conference and everybody in the Base knew that the odd accountant was behind the entire project. However, it was very doubtful that she had agreed to go for a walk in the horrendous heat just because he was Mark Eos.

The excited 'bean counter' did not own a watch and usually resorted to the services of the big clock in the corridor, opposite his room. He would open his door every few minutes to check the motion of the clock hands. Time was going slow, despite the scientifically proven consistency of its speed. He had never experienced before the torture of waiting before a date. At first, it was a real drag, but later in the afternoon, the time went a bit quicker and less painful. Half an hour before 5 o'clock, Mark was on his way to his new female friend. He had made a couple of promises to himself. The most important thing was to try not to rant on, but give her the chance to speak, too. Also he decided they should not stay out for more than ten minutes, otherwise it was going to be a truly sweaty ordeal. Lastly, he was determined to tell her how much he liked her. Mark was quite inexperienced, but he knew that no one did this in such a direct way. He was lovesick and the only cure was to confess how he felt, without worrying about the consequences, which were most probably, going to be unfavourable.

He arrived at the right place and at the right time and waited. He could not have known that the object of his affections was going to be late by twenty minutes, due to the unexpected amount of administrative work there was to be done. Mark had his eyes fixed on the door, as if eager to find out what was going on behind it, and what she was doing. It did not work. The image remained blurred, despite his efforts. Different thoughts were racing through his head. He really thought that

Jennifer had done a runner on him and had left work earlier. His low self-esteem plummeted by the minute. He actually started to convince himself that this was the normal development of the situation, because he was obviously not good enough to be with a woman like her, even if it was just for a short stroll in the heat. With a back, resting on the wall and his head down, Mark had given up. The battle was lost before it had started and he had succumbed to a true despair. He had the type of personality that by the end of the week, he would forget about her in the same way he had forgotten about a lot of his scientific projects, which turned to be a total rubbish. He was already starting to picture how he would see her on the following day at breakfast time and he could feel the shame and the embarrassment about her not turning up at their date, because of not fault of his.

"Hello, Mark, I'm sorry I'm late. I had to stay for a bit as we had some work to do. Have you been waiting for me long?" Her gentle voice got him back to reality, which turned out to be not so grim as he had imagined.

"Eh-r-r, well. Hi! Ah, I'm waiting. Have been for a while… but it's not a problem, and as you've had work to do, I was wondering if you'd come, and I've been waiting here… Well, you're here now. And in the administrative department, you all probably have a lot of work to do, well, not that I know for sure…" Feeling sorry for himself a minute ago prevented him from noticing when Jennifer appeared. He was surprised to see her and her beauty just stunned him to the extent that he forgot his first golden rule – to try and avoid ranting on his long gibberish.

"Mark, you talk in an interesting way." She smiled playfully. Clearly, she did not mind his strange way of expressing himself. "Shall we go?"

"Well, let's go, if you're ready, but where to, first…? I mean, if you want to change or straight to exit 7, which is not far from here! I've checked on the map. It's been most used by the staff, according to the statistics."

"I'm ready."

"Well, let's go to exit 7, then!" Mark was about to fall into another daze, overwhelmed by her presence. She was the most beautiful woman he had ever seen, the most perfect, in his eyes, even if others did not think like him. To the rest, Jennifer was probably a regular good-looking woman, who was slender and a bit too slim, with nice dark hair and really big dark eyes. If there was a poll, more than half of the male employees in the Base would confirm they liked the way she looked, and the rest would probably say that she is just ordinary. Mark had never cared about what other people thought, and he was convinced that she was the most wonderful thing around. He could not see any faults in her.

"Mark, what is your job exactly here? I'm aware that it's been your idea, this project, but what are your responsibilities now?" Jennifer asked, trying to interrupt the uncomfortable silence, while they were in the crammed horizontal elevator for several minutes.

"Well, my colleagues, the scientists, and I, we are checking different stages of the building work, we test the project plan and if there are some problems, we make sure they are solved promptly. Eh-r-r, well, not that there are any problems… everything seems fine after we've made the first alterations to my initial plan." Mark uttered without taking a breath or looking at her. She was so near him that their elbows touched slightly. He wanted to hold her hand, even before they got into the elevator, but he felt it would be too intimate to do this.

"Aha." She said briefly, waiting for the sliding doors to open.

There were two military guards at exit 7, who made sure the number of people leaving the premises equaled the number of those coming back in by 10pm, when the gates were locked. If anyone was left outside after this time, they had to wait in the minus temperatures until the morning or venture the 15km trek to the hangars that could be seen in the distance. They looked as if they were nearby, because of their size but the distance could not be underestimated even by the fittest members of staff. Mark and Jennifer got their IDs logged on the way out and they started climbing the stairs up to the exit, looking forward to the "fresh" air in the sands. The view was incredible and it managed to interrupt their slow conversation. It was the sheer scale of things that struck them, as there was nothing really to look at, apart of the high wall, swerving, on their right and the back of the hangars – in the far distance, to their left. The heat, of course, really hit them, when they opened the exit hatch, but this was expected. There was not a cloud in the sky that could stop the sunrays from heating the sand up to 10 cm deep. In contrast to the delivery depot, where all the elements were being unloaded, and special machines constantly cleaned the area, making sure that small dunes did not pile up, here, at the bottom of the seven-meter high grey wall – nothing of the kind was done, as long as the sand did not pile up higher than 20 cm.

Mark and his 'girl' stood still for a minute, giving a chance to their lungs to get accustomed to the heavily heated air. Then they followed the path in the sand, formed by other enthusiasts, who had felt they needed to experience the extreme temperatures and harsh conditions of the desert.

"Well, Jennifer, do you like it here? I thought that maybe, it's not the best time to come out, but you agreed, didn't you?" Mark said nervously and wiped his forehead of the first drop of sweat. It was a good job that at least his white uniform was protecting him from the unforgiving sun.

"I like it!"

"Eh-r-r, well, I like it here, too, but I haven't been out that many times, just a few, and... this heat, well, it's fine, but only for a short time... We're not going to stay out for too long, are we? Unless, you'd like to..."

"Mark, don't worry. We'll stay as long as you want to!"

"Well, alright, then. We'll do that. Other than that, eh-r-r, how do you like your job in the administrative department, I wanted to ask..." She sincerely smiled at the jumbled order of words he used to form his question.

"I'm just used to it and I like the job. I know, most people think it's boring but it's fine for me."

"Well, and what did you do before this, I mean, job wise? Probably something in administration, again, well, it's logical... But I can't know that for sure, because we just met and I had no information about you..." Mark simply did not know what to ask her. He actually wanted to tell her how he felt about her and until he was confident to do this, he was going to ask her general questions.

"Yes, back in my country, I worked in administration, too, and then I got a better offer. Here, at least we've got enough energy. I came just before the start of the project."

"Well, when all the power plants are completed and there is energy for all the states across the globe and the restrictions get lifted, then, are you going to return to your homeland or you feel like staying here?" Mark asked this question in attempt to find out how long his unsuspecting sweetheart was going to hang around, close to him. The thought that she might leave one day was beginning to torture him. It did not matter, whether this was going to happen in a week, after a year, or she would be here for another decade.

"I will go back. I miss my family." Jennifer got slightly upset at the thought that she was not going to see her mom, dad and younger sister until at least, the end of the working year. This was in her contract. "When the energy problems are solved, the economy would be expected to pick up, again. So I think, I won't find it hard to get another good job. Also, the references from here will help me tremendously!"

"Well, when there's enough energy, this is how it's going to be!" Mark was not really listening to her but was mesmerized by part of her naked neck. Then he looked at her perfect profile, with this dainty tip-tilted nose.

"And you, Mark, what are you going to do after?"

"Well, I don't know what I'm going to do, I have a few scientific projects I'd like to look into, really, and that I don't have the time for, right now. But when we're done here, and there's no problems with the energy no more, then, I'll do something and I'll go back to work."

"What did you do before?"

"Well, I was an accountant, I'm good with numbers and I like it. Eh-r-r, my job is also a bit boring, like yours, but I'm used to it and I find it easy to just get on with it."

"Mark, don't you think that it won't suit you to go back and work as an accountant after all this?" Jennifer asked with irony in her voice. She truly thought in disbelief that the man, who had found an answer to the global energy problem, could not possibly go back to his old low-paid job. It sounded naïve.

"Well, why not? I like it. Also, I really don't know what else I should do. My scientific endeavours, you know, I get into these in my spare time, after work... And what do you mean by this?"

"What I mean is that you can find something better. It won't be hard to become the head of some company, for instance, which is involved in scientific research!"

"Well, I'm not like Timor. I couldn't possibly become a head of anything. He is born to be a director and I find this hard. I simply don't like telling people what to do."

"Hmm, don't we all secretly dream of being in charge, Mark? What's the matter with you?" She joked playfully. His answer, however, was very serious:

"Eh-r-r, well, not that anyone had ever offered something like this to me. They might, in the future, but I doubt, it will be something, related to science... I'm not a scientist, anyhow, and as I can't deal very well with people, well, then, the work won't be efficient, but ..."

"Ha-ha-ha, I'm joking, Mark!" Jennifer burst into laughter at yet, another of his brilliantly entertaining sentences.

"Well, that's fine. I just didn't get it." He felt embarrassed again, thinking how he made a fool of himself and really doubting that she would respond to his feelings and powerful attraction towards her, which some people simply called love at first sight.

"Mark, shall we go back?"

The heat was unbearable. They both had managed to become profusely sweaty after just 50m of walking, and both had swallowed enough sand particles that the hot wind had swirled their way. Their shoes protected their feet, although, the rubber soles were on the brink of melting. The couple really had to get to a cooler place within the next few minutes.

"Well, alright. It's getting rather hot, not that it wasn't, when we got out... Now that it's getting late, it will become cooler, but let's get inside, I'd like that, too."

They turned round and headed back next to each other, like two good friends that had gone for a stroll after work. If one was watching them, they could thing that they were colleagues, though, their differently coloured attire, refuted this suggestion straight away. Then, maybe, they were brother and sister, who were lucky enough to get employment at the same time and at the same place, and now just leisurely discussed how their day at work went. Jennifer and Mark looked like everything but not a future couple, let along – like people, who had been together for a while. They had the same height, and the fact that Mark constantly looked down, made the woman next to him look taller. Not once he tried to look her directly in the eyes, and when she asked him something and looked for his behind his glasses, he would always turn his head and look at the hangars in the distance. An onlooker could read into this slightly offensive attitude, a bit of boredom on Mark's part. However, no one could really be further from the truth, as no one could see through what was really going on with Mark, namely – his doomed struggle for happiness. At last, only a few meters away from the hatch, leading to the well-controlled temperatures of the indoors, Jennifer gave him the opportunity to get his all locked feelings off his chest:

"Mark, why did you invite me here?" Her eyes were looking hard to meet his eyes.

"Well…" His side vision sensed what was about to happen, so he quickly turned his head into the safety of the opposite direction. "Well, I just thought that… and because people come for a walk here, don't they? I just didn't think about the heat at this time of the day, well, I realized later, but…"

"Mark, I asked you something different. Why me? I've only seen you with Timor so far."

"Well, Jennifer, how can I put it? When I saw you and these eyes of yours, I got all nervous a bit, actually, I felt very nervous, and I decided that I have to meet you…" The sweat was running down his face. Drenched, his face was very red, not just because of embarrassment, but also, it was the Sun, which had made some significant changes to the first layer of his skin. He kept avoiding her eyes. He just could not look at her and tell her about his feelings. At this moment, more than everything, he preferred to stare at the sand under his shoes.

"I think it's not just that." Jennifer confidently grabbed Mark's hand and stood in front of him, blocking his way to the entrance. She could clearly see that her strange new friend was badly trying to conceal the fact that he had some sort of affinity towards her. It was all written on his forehead. Everyone in the Base knew that Mark Eos did not have a girlfriend. She liked him, too.

"Well, Jennifer, I… I've liked you at the first moment I saw you, you know, when our eyes met, and I just don't know what actually happened, I've never experienced this before, but I can only say that it's incredible and I like the way I feel… But now, telling you all this and knowing that you'd never… with me, there's no way, I mean, there's no logic. Well, at least, I've had a good time, and I'll remember it for a long time, I won't bother you again…" Mark could keep going even longer. The words were just going to come out of control and he was going to look where he should not. Jennifer intercepted the chaotic long sentence, which was somehow meaningful.

"Thank you, Mark. I like being with you, too." She was still holding his hand. Her delicate fingers and smooth skin provoked his senses yet again.

"Eh-r-r, well, but... really?"

"Yes, Mark, I like you, too."

"Well, no, you don't have to say this. There is no logic!" The accountant in love was prepared to argue against the idea that they could ever become an item, which in effect, was rather silly.

"Don't worry, Mark, not everything has a logical explanation! You seem kind and the way you talk is really funny." Jennifer laughed as if to emphasize her statement. What next? Maybe, he should try to kiss her – something he definitely thought of doing, but then, this heat... and she was still laughing!

"Well, shall we go in?" It was the only thing he could say, this time, confidently looking at her beautiful face. His nervousness had disappeared as if with a magic wand. He realized that the impossible had suddenly become something very realistic. He took and gently squeezed her hand, their fingers locked together. Jennifer rewarded his initiative with a peck on his left cheek. She felt the salt of his sweat, but this did not matter to her. The gesture was important. Mark smiled like a child, who had made his dream come through. The dream, however, involved something much more valuable than getting a toy-truck or a ball for Christmas. The couple climbed down the stairs, where their ID numbers got checked out by the two military guards.

Timor had plenty of power and he had to use only a tiny portion of it, in order to find Mark's whereabouts. He discovered that the accountant had not been to the doctors, had not seen his colleagues that day, nor had he visited him at the tower. Timor concluded that he had been lied to - something he had never experienced before with Mark. His friend never lied. He was too honest about everything and even if he tried, he would have failed. White lies or innocent fibs would eat the accountant's conscience. The chief coordinator remembered too well the instance, when Mark could not keep a secret about the surprise birthday party everyone at work had prepared for their boss.

The computer was never wrong. He had left the Base through exit 7 at 17:48. Timor was staring at the screen, in attempt to find a reason behind his friend's strange behaviour, but to no avail. Then, he headed directly to Mark's room, where he should have gone, according to the electronic admission system of the residential quarters.

"Mark, open the door, Mark. It's Timor." The chief coordinator could not wait to go in and just kept banging on the door. For some unknown reason he did not make use of the doorbell.

"Eh-r-r, well, Timor, Hi! I was going to come up and see you… but, I wanted the day off today, I'm fine, really, and I haven't been to the doctors, you know, I don't like going there… and the smell is nasty, isn't it? They also use these big needles and I'm a bit scared, you know…" Mark sounded sleepy, despite not feeling tired. The adrenaline he had received in the last few hours was unlikely to leave him alone in the next couple of days.

"Look, stop this nonsense." Timor raised his voice and forced his way in.

"Well, Timor, I…"

"Don't bother with this 'Timor, I…' Tell me what's happening and don't dare lie to me! You know I'll catch you out if you do."

Mark realized that there was no point of hiding things from Timor. Sooner or later his best friend would simply find out the truth. So he decided to tell him everything. He had not stopped thinking about her since he came back into the room. That was until his visitor barged in and interrupted his happy thoughts. He pictured Jennifer again, now, his Jennifer, and smiled.

"What are you smiling at? Do you think I'm joking?"

"Well, no, Timor, I'll tell you. Just calm down! You are right that I've been hiding something from you, but I'm going to tell you now. I was going to tell you a bit later, but after our stroll, we got straight back, so I thought, tomorrow, at breakfast… And, maybe, she'll be with us, if you don't mind, well, I was going to ask you in advance about that…"

"She!?! A woman? You're telling me that you've found a woman?" Timor shouted in some sort of elation at the news. For him, it was like the hunter's young son had just shot his first doe. Well, Mark was not that young, but that was irrelevant. "Who is she? Tell me, who is she? If she's ugly or if she is not for you, I'd tell you straight away. I know you may not like this, but true friends would never leave you fight the enemy alone!"

"Well, but, Timor, what fight are you talking about? I like her and she's told me that she likes me, too, and…"

"You listen to what she says now just to blur your mind, but then, it all becomes very different. You can't recognize her after a while…"

"Well, when we were out, it was me, who did the talking and I…"

"Listen, Mark, I meant something else. All day I wonder what's wrong with you and it appears everything is alright."

"Well, I'm sorry, Timor, I should have called you at least, so you stop worrying about me…"

"Yes, you should have. Don't forget to do this next time! Right, so she'll come at breakfast time, then? What department is she from?"

"Well, the administrative, she works in administration. I haven't asked her exactly, yet. We only saw each other for a little while, as she's back to work tomorrow, isn't she? And she needed a rest, and after our walk, together, we got home straight away and…"

"The administrative department?" Timor frowned not because he had anything against the idea of anyone working there, but because he did not know anyone personally from their staff. He knew the department manager by face, but not by name.

"Well, she works there, Timor. Her job's alright, I think, but I'm not really sure…"

"Mark, isn't this the girl you were staring at like some fool, this morning?" Timor had noticed that his friend kept turning his head in the same direction, that day, where a female worker was sitting.

However, he had quickly got rid of the thought in his head that Mark could have been looking at a woman. It was not in his character, well, until today.

"Eh-r-r, well, so you've noticed, then? Well, I wouldn't have wanted for you to notice, really, then, as I didn't know her at the time, and it all evolved so fast, and I was a little nervous, well, quite a bit, actually… I don't want to lie to you, but you know me, I'm quite shy…"

"Everyone noticed and by the way, there was just you there, who fidgeted like crazy in your chair."

"Well, so the others saw me, too, then… that I was looking at her, but, maybe, they didn't know that I'm looking at her, but then, when they see us together tomorrow, then…" Mark felt rather embarrassed that apart of Timor, others amongst several hundreds of people had seen his odd behaviour.

"Hey, calm down a bit. It doesn't matter who saw what. You got hitched with a woman, so it's all clear. Tomorrow, after I tell you what I think – the hard part will be over and done with. Now, though, I need to ask you a few things that your colleagues could not clarify for me." Timor consciously changed the subject. He knew that if he carried on digging, he might offend the sensitive love-boy. There were other reasons, too.

"Eh-r-r, well, what about? The scientists know everything, some things – even better than me. It was them, who suggested that certain aspects need changing, am I right? I wouldn't have the slightest idea if it wasn't for them…"

"They know everything, but their estimates, related to the energy generators are all wrong. I don't know how you all did your calculations but we need two more. I want you to personally call Platt and tell him to arrange this."

"Well, what do you mean, Timor? Everything should be correct. There are so many reactors that will produce so much energy, and this will require a certain number of generators. This number is unchangeable, at least for now."

"You are partially right, Mark. What about if we are forced to deactivate one of them, or God forbid, if one of them explodes, what then? We don't have a substitute. You haven't thought about this, I see."

"Well, Timor, you know, as the power plants are not yet ready, and we've got all the generators here now, so we've got a replacement if something happens, and later on, when all the facilities are completed, then, you are right and you have a point, but that's not until much later, so we've got time, haven't we?"

"As a chief coordinator, I need to be sure that whatever happens in the future, even if it's just one liquid generator, we're talking about, people won't suffer with getting their energy supplies cut." The human aspect in this affected Mark, who allowed friendship to intercept his better judgment.

"Well, alright, Timor, we could order another two, it won't be a problem, but why do you want me to call Platt? You know me; I hate talking on the phone. I suppose, you could give him a ring, if it's not a problem for you…"

"Of course, I could." Timor replied haughtily. "But you see, these colleagues of yours, they will call him, too, and I doubt very much that he'd take my side in this. I'm not a scientist, after all. That is why, Mark, you should call him, because he'll believe you."

"Eh-r-r, well, you're probably right, but does it have to be over the phone? He's coming on his first official visit to the Base in a month or two, isn't he? I'm not sure exactly when, but I can mention it to him, then, can't I?"

"No, Mark, it's better to do it now, because when he comes, together with the rest of the Global Energy Project, I doubt he'd want to be bothered with some petty administrative details. Come on! A simple phone call won't kill you!"

"Well, I'll phone him, I don't like it, but it's just two more generators, you mean, isn't it? I'll ask my colleagues, as well, to see what they think, as they are all familiar with the…"

"No, no, no, Mark. I've already talked with them about it. There's no point to bother them. They are so stubborn and pig-headed, being scientists; they think they know it all. You are calling him tomorrow!" Timor ordered, although, Mark was not under his command.

"Eh-r-r, well, Timor, if you say so." The accountant gave in. He was feeling uncomfortable that he had not been able to think about Her for the last few minutes. Timor noticed the drifting look on his friend's face, and now that he was done with what he had come for, he decided it was time to go back to his work.

"Bye, Mark, and I hope the bird's fit, otherwise I'm not giving you away. And if she's not fit, I'll find you a better looking one!"

Jennifer was also moved by the hot stroll, even if her emotions were more controlled than those of Mark's. What had just happened affected her tremendously, but she experienced things in much more mature way. Jennifer had been regularly chased by admirers, who had, unfortunately, always been total idiots. Her misfortune with men followed her again, when she got her job at the Base. She ran into the same type of superficial men, who always regarded her as yet another easy-to-get girl. Two pilots had tried to entice her into going out for a dinner-date. She agreed to see one of them. He was good-looking and seemed kind. It appeared, however, that all this was just one of these silly games, pilots get into, where pretty Jennifer, as a person, was the last thing they cared about. Disappointed yet again, she decided, while here, that it would be best if she just got on with her job and stopped going out on pointless dates with men. A colleague of hers, who was very well aware that she did not have much of a personal life, also asked her out. She refused, because she was not impressed with his personality, nor was he that great looking. Mark was not that much of a catch, either, but he had some rare qualities that Jennifer found intriguing. He never pretended to be something that he was not, he was not arrogant - he was simply Mark. Being shy around women was actually funny and she was really taken by his strange way of talking.

At last, the morning, when everyone was going to notice the newly formed romantically involved unity of two people – Mark on one side and Jennifer – on the other, arrived. Mark was waiting in front of her room, well before breakfast time, despite their agreement that they were meeting straight in the dining room. His red puffy eyes gave away that he had not slept all night. He had strained them additionally by reading something he, now, could not remember. He thought that this would distract him from having her image constantly appearing in his mind, but it proved impossible. While waiting for her to come out, so they could head together towards their morning meal, he wondered about what he should do: take her by the hand? Yes, he would definitely do this, and by the way, this type of move was warranted to him the day before. Or should he kiss her? This did not sound bad but where? On the cheek, or he should head for her pretty soft lips? Mark acted impulsively and completely out of character. He gently took her by the left hand and gave her a clumsy peck on the cheek. His teenage-like behaviour made Jennifer smile. She went over the limit by tenderly biting his upper lip. After a short exchange of saliva, the taste of which, both found rather pleasant, it was time to get in front of the 'testimonial committee', consisted of the only member and chairman – Timor.

Every day, the chief coordinator sat at the same table. No one dared break the tacit rule that it was reserved for him, and even when Timor and Mark were not present, none of the staff ever sat there. This was down to fear, rather than respect for the boss. Although, he had no power over dismissing anyone, but his staff in the tower, he still, could have easily applied pressure on the managers in the HR department, who could then fire anyone from the other departments, irrelevant to how well they were doing their job. This had happened a few times, so far, where the dismissed ardently believed that they had been released for no good reason, but under the obvious pressure on Timor's part.

165

Well, the truth was that these people really did not perform as expected, so they had to be replaced with more efficient workers, who had a better motivation.

Jennifer passed her 'check' within a few minutes. Timor did not sit to have breakfast but just asked several trivial questions about the beautiful young woman's job. The 'interview' concluded with the apology that he had no time for eating and had to go back to his work. Mark believed he knew Timor well. He expected from him to start with his usual sexist and demeaning jokes and questions, but this was not the case this time. It seemed something was different about him this morning. Jennifer answered briefly each question the chief coordinator had asked her and she did not feel nervous by his presence at any point. The couple in love found the plain breakfast, which most people detested, delicious, so they quickly emptied their plates. The looks around, the accountant had feared so much, happened to be not that intrusive or a nuisance. On the contrary, it seemed no one cared that those two were an item. They fed each other with a spoon, a demonstrative sign of closeness, which yet again, remained unnoticed. This calmed down Mark and put him at ease.

Timor also did not get much sleep the night before. He had no problems at work. Everything was running smoothly, according to schedule and it was only a matter of time when the last dome was going to be fit in place. His personal life was good, too. He spoke to Jess every day on the phone and was still very much keen to make her his second wife. Physically and mentally sound, the chief coordinator had problems elsewhere. Something was playing on his conscience. Very good at manipulating people; Timor had involved his best friend in something that no one should ever know about.

It was greed that made him do it. Well, Timor was not greedy or at least, not excessively greedy. He had not realized that he had been trying to maintain a very high standard of living. Of course, he could afford it alright, but there was nothing wrong if he could have some extra money for rainy days! Now, the situation was different. Yes, his monthly salary was huge, in comparison with his last position, however, the responsibilities now were much greater, so it felt as if he was almost working for free. He had thought about that when Ella got the house, after the divorce, he had no property in his name and if he was about to get married again, he had to provide a home for his new wife. What about if they had children together? It did not look good if the chief coordinator of the most significant global energy project lived in a rented property. His annual salary, for the first year, would have been enough to buy a detached house in the suburbs of one of the big cities in his home country. But then, if he invested all his savings, he and his wife would be left with no disposable cash. Her pitiful wage would not be sufficient to cover even the property tax and maintenance of the house. Probably, all these progressively increasing future costs were only in Timor's head. But this was enough to make him do something, the consequences of which were going to have a negative effect on everyone. Mark was going to lose his best friend. Good job that Jennifer would stand by him!

Are you ready for this?

A year after the beginning of implementation of the slightly crazy idea of solving the energy shortage, an idea of an ordinary, low-paid accountant, the result was: almost every household in the world enjoyed having electricity 24/7. The population was ecstatic and there was hysteria, never unseen before. A lot of people just turned crazy in a very short time.

At the beginning, most people were skeptical and this was understandably justified. They started to believe a lot more in the whole project at the earliest news and media coverage about moving the first domes in place. Before the eyes of the citizens, major energy routes were replaced and updated, by applying new sophisticated conductive material of enormous capacity. Dozens of working teams were digging all day long to create a 'comfortable bed' for the thick energy-supplying sheaf. The military presence around the factories, where all components for the desert nuclear power plants were being developed, was also very much noticed. Heavy defense equipment kept being piled up outside the distribution stations – a sign of the seriousness of all the stuff that was going on. People realized that this time, their problem was going to be resolved for real and there would be no more pulling the wool over their eyes, like it had been, so far, at all those past energy conferences.

Very few asked themselves about what they were going to do, when the moment of constant electricity supply arrived; when everyone could afford a car, run by energy battery, which could be charged without any adverse effect on others; when the world economies would pick up and every country would begin to compete, again, trying to show that they were richest and most powerful. The human nature would be always full of surprises.

To live for so long, abiding the Law of Darkness, only to realize one day that it was no longer valid, was a truly scary affair. At first, the Law was created and imposed by the think-tank heads, in order to teach people to be responsible and more economical, so they did not waste energy in vain. Slowly, the rule became a necessity, simply because energy was scarce and not for any educational reasons. For the first few years the electricity supply had been intermitted for several hours in the night. The big cities, then, would turn into dead dark concrete compounds, until light returned in the early morning. This was the reason why, not just Timor, but everyone had to resort to a torch on their mid-night visits to the bathroom. The power restriction regime expanded further power cuts even in the day, following the increased shortages and the dried-up energy resources becoming a fact. People accepted the inevitable reality. At least, their daily activities were not that much affected. Further restrictions followed year after year. There was also the propaganda campaign for people to do more sport and apply themselves at fitness activities, when electricity was off, and many people did so, as there was not much else to do. The Law of Darkness was rather mean for everybody, who had his private solar panels, but was prohibited from switching on anything electrical after 11pm. The purpose for this was to avoid any aggravations between residents, who had and those, who did not have. The reality was that even the entire roof of a building was covered with solar panels the energy from them would have been enough to power only the elevators and anti-fire automatic system in the building. In houses, where lifts were not necessary, the energy was sufficient enough to keep the security alarm alive and the house telephone, which was not much, indeed.

And suddenly, there was energy at large. The older generation took the new changes in their stride. After all, they still remembered the times, when resources were available to them and energy supply was not a problem. However, their sons and daughters just went totally crazy. Throughout most of their lives, they lived with the thought that they had to be frugal and careful, as there was hardly any energy left. They were aware, from their parents' stories, that in the past, there was time, when things were different. Usually these stories were more or less regarded as bedtime fairy tales. But now everything was for real and the youngsters became extremely keen to catch up with everything they had missed on.

Stress was the main culprit for so many to be affected at the very beginning of the era of Light. The sudden change logically had an effect on people's sleep. The restrictive regulations' legacy was that there were not any nightclubs or bars anywhere in the world. Restaurants in the most affluent parts, energy wise, could be open only for 5 hours and had to close by 11pm. Of course, it cost them a bob for this privilege. Now, non-stop pubs, clubs, bars and restaurants sprouted like mushrooms everywhere. There were even kindergartens, which proudly announced that they enjoyed electricity 24 hours a day. Many young people suffered from the newly offered entertainment services at night. They often found themselves unable to perform their duties at work on the following day. Well, this applied for those, who actually bothered to turn up for work. Most did not make it at all, waking up at lunchtime, when it was a bit too late to do anything.

Lack of sleep led to increased level of road accidents, turning motorways into dangerous death traps. People, who were late for work, drove like maniacs in fear of being fired. Good job that there were not that many private energy battery powered cars like in the past, however, the prediction was that this would change soon. Fatalities on the road were on the increase. The calm drivers had suddenly turned into crazy race drivers within few weeks.

Crime doubled in just less than two months. The simple truth was that when people roamed the streets from pub to pub at night, it was the perfect time for the burglars to pay a visit to their homes. Conscientious citizens, who had been dismissed from work for their systematic absences, turned into petty thieves overnight. They were wandering about aimlessly, anyway, so why not help some drunk and lost gentleman accidentally lose his personal belongings and wallet! If chance was not enough, they would apply some gentle physical force to their victim.

Was everything going to get back to normal soon, after the novelty wore out? The scientists, who had observed closely the changes, were very clear: No! Not a chance! It was a new opportunity, which people could not easily miss and ignore. It caused their adrenalin levels to increase, and this was addictive like a drug. The lack of sleep and generally going out at night became a habit that had spread out widely amongst people that it would have been very hard for them to give it up. History spoke for itself. In the past, when petrol prices were at their highest, making it the most sought after commodity in its time, people behaved in the same irresponsible way, ignoring their own health or that of others around them. The evidence for similarities between then and now could be found in the medical and police reports from those days. The situation with drug use was also repeating itself. The same boom of drug addicts was becoming a fact, as it was before the last energy war. Then, people abused illegal substances out of fashion and after the sobering experience they had, during the military conflict put them off - sanity seemed to have overthrown the fad. In effect, what happened was that the vast cocaine fields got eradicated for good, whereas the synthetic drugs required too much electricity, in order high quality to be achieved, making them unaffordable. The marihuana remained a 'good old friend' - simply, there for you. At least, it was not that bad for one's health, as so many paid 'experts' were trying to prove in the past.

Now the cocaine was still hard to get, but the market, was rapidly flooded with a variety of pills, coming in different form, shape and color, and which successfully messed the brain of their brainless user. This stuff required a lot of energy, in order to be manufactured, energy that Mark Eos so kindly have provided for. Joint, good old joint, was still ubiquitously used, as if it was full of healthy vitamins.

Bad health and the desire to catch up with everything that people had missed out on were not the only issues people experienced. New types of mania suddenly became apparent – the psychological effects of the incessant flow of energy. Statistically 38% of people began to leave some electrical appliance switched on, even after they had gone to bed. Falling asleep with the light on or in front of the working TV, something impossible in the past, was now easy. Clearly, people got hyped up about that the power restriction days might return, so their sick brains were obviously bothered at the thought. They would open their eyes every few minutes to check, just in case, although the human eyelid could not fully block the light. Another strange obsession had spread out amongst car owners. Most of them got it into their heads that they needed a new energy battery after the old one had run out of power. They believed that it was no good anymore, because it had partially run on the old type of energy, whereas the new one would be charged with energy, coming from the sophisticated nuclear power plants in the desert. This was, of course, totally stupid, but people simply freaked out at the slightest hint that they could recharge their fully operating old battery.

Sleepwalking was another thing. Many citizens would get up, wandering in their sleep and trying to console their sleeping bodies that energy was freely availably, by switching on every appliance on their way. This usually provoked unbelievable arguments between them and their mentally sound neighbours, and often ended fatally for one part. The constant disputes raised the level of noise in the cities to unseen before heights and additionally stressed out the already edgy situation. Interpersonal conflicts and fights boomed to unprecedented and strikingly bloody levels.

At first, the authorities found it hard to cope with the enraged mob, which clearly suffered from sleep deprivation. Everyone wanted to hurt their opponent, to subconsciously revenge for their loss of sleep. Harsh measures were taken by the governments. The results from them were going to be noticed after several months, but still, they had a positive and literally a soporific effect on the population. Police applied unparalleled repressive measures against everyone who had breached the Law even in the slightest unnoticeable way. The brutal and sometimes totally unnecessary force was strangely approved by the older generation, which had had their fun in the past. The authorities successfully applied the regulations and control, checking nightclubs and bars. Shockingly high fines were issued on the spot even for minor administrative violation or offence. Discipline and order ruled and even some of the more liberal counties did not compromise with them. For now.

Unequal equality

Timor was the ideal candidate. Mark Eos was also checked out very carefully, but he had an odd personality, so he was dismissed as a potential player. His best friend, however, possessed certain suitable qualities. He did not adhere to any principles and this could be cleverly used against him. The thorough checks pointed at this weakness of the chief coordinator.

It was eight months into the implementation of the project, and two days before Timor had learned that Mark had got a girlfriend, when he received an interesting phone call in the middle of the night. A voice, insisting that it was that of Prof. Connor from the Global Energy Project, told him that it was very likely for him to lose his job after the end of his first year. Platt was apparently going to decide on discharging him, when the six scientists come to visit the Base. However, if Timor wished to continue working as a chief coordinator and even better – earn some extra cash, he had to demand further two energy liquid generators, which later on would be sent to the listed seven countries. Connor described the way this could happen without anyone ever knowing. Timor considered how wrong the proposal was, determined to say "No" to the professor. The offer was so unrealistic. Connor offered him a million for each generator, he would provide for him. The professor also promised his help in making sure he did not lose his job after the nuclear facilities were completed. Whether the reason was the late hour, he got the phone call or the chief coordinator simply did not think the proposal through, but he said, "Yes", or was it his greed that did so! Connor, if it was him, of course, was in a different time zone, when he called at 8 o'clock, his time.

To carry such burden for four months was definitely an unpleasant experience. Timor felt bad. He looked distracted at work. The chief coordinator often thought about Jess. He tried to get her support, but managed to keep his deal a secret. At the end, he convinced himself that no one would ever know, he would earn a lot of cash and no one would get hurt. Well, actually, quite a few countries were going to get affected, but if people were not aware of it, then no loss would be caused to them. And after all, these states would keep getting their regular quota of energy, right? His attempt to clear his conscience worked for a short while, until the moment he personally dragged Mark into all this. Timor did not want for anyone to know. The scientists were all against his idea, so he really felt he was at a dead end. Money, again, came first. Good job that Mark was not so shrewd, when making personal favours for his friends. He never questioned the real motives of people, who openly misused his trust and benevolence.

The project was completed exactly within the 365-day period, set at the start. This meant that the global community was determined to solve the energy problem and "bury" the two decades of restrictions and shortage forever in the past. There were a lot of popular and not so well known high-ranks at the grand ceremony, celebrating the success of the venture, together with the six scientists from the Global Energy Project. Timor had not managed to speak to Connor in private. After the helicopter landed, he met the professor's eyes and discretely raised his thump up to say that everything was how it should be. Connor read the sign simply as a friendly greeting. The chief coordinator managed to exchange a couple of words with Platt, while showing him around in the coordination center. He briefed him about every building procedure and explained to him the importance of this "intelligent" hall, in relation to the system control of every action and process. Timor also hinted at the fact that he regretted that Platt had not visited earlier. He simply tried to ingratiate himself with the chairman, despite detesting such attitude. Platt listened to everything very carefully, commending and shaking hands with anyone from the staff, who tried to approach him. He did not mention anything about replacing Timor then or later, at the actual ceremony, which meant that his contract was automatically extended for another year. The chief coordinator felt over the moon with happiness. He could not stop thinking about the piles of cash he was about to earn without anyone knowing about it. He left the Base immediately after the party, when all the guests left, too. His aim was to see someone, a female, who he had been missing tremendously.

Timor returned in after 52 hours stay at home. He did not feel that sad, parting with Jess, as she was coming to visit very soon for more than just a week. She was going to meet Jennifer, too! They might become friends! Well, Timor hoped that this would be the case, but if not, he did not think of it as a big deal.

All was going too well to be true. The additional two liquid energy generators arrived on time. The opponents of this, Mark's colleagues – the scientists, were foresightedly kept in the dark about this delivery. The military personnel, responsible for the ballistic arrival of the generators, did not doubt Timor's clear orders. So as a result of this, seven states continued to receive illegitimately more concentrated energy than they should. It was interesting how it was generated. The chief coordinator increased the capacity of all six thousand nuclear reactors. He was very well aware that this was only possible by changing the settings in the control center, and thus, squeezing a bit more energy from the reactors. If someone from his employees, dressed in black, questioned the alteration, Timor readily replied that it was ordered by the guys in white. If he had the same query from those in white, the answer was obvious: someone had made an error at the command center, which he was going to correct at once. Of course, after the amendment, Timor would quickly reinstate the old incorrect settings. Unexpectedly, after a month of this wicked practice running, and with a couple of millions in his bank account, Timor's best friend was about to catch him and put him on the spot.

176

In the evenings, Mark and Jennifer loved going for a long stroll by the wall. They preferred to use exit 7 most of the time, but sometimes, they would opt for a different one. Straight after dinner, they headed towards the unpleasant sandy desert reality outside, which gave them a speck of hospitality only at about 8 o'clock, when the temperatures went down to the perfect 25'C. On these outings, Mark was the one, who had plenty to talk about and was less inclined to take the role of the listener. Jennifer, on the other hand, preferred to speak less. She openly demonstrated how interested she was in yet another of his odd and funny stories. Usually there was really nothing exciting to share about her work in the administrative department but today that was not the case. Jennifer had something very important to talk about. She intended to share it with Mark much earlier in the day at meal times, but the person that she needed to speak about was always present. One could clearly see her concern on her pretty face. Her eyes were struggling to conceal her worry.

"Mark, do you remember the time, when we met, and later, you told me about how Timor had come to your room, asking you about your day?" She began in a roundabout way. She was usually quite straightforward, but tried to be tactful with sensitive people like Mark. He was her loved one after all.

"Well, I do. Of course, I remember! Timor almost broke through my door, then. He believed I was lying to him, well, I was in a way, and then... I told him about you... eh-r-r ...about us, I mean." Mark squeezed her hand, like at the time of their very first walk together. He felt his enormous love growing even more at the memory of this fateful day.

"And after you told him about us, he asked you to call Platt?"

"Well, that's right. He wanted two extra liquid generators, just in case, and then, I called Platt, not that I like talking on the phone. You know me. I don't like it..."

"So you rang Platt and he agreed to the idea, despite the fact that your colleagues had already expressed their opinion on this and had told Timor that there was no real need for more generators?" Jennifer kept her gentle approach, searching for less painful finale of her story.

"Well, I did that, but what do you mean by all this? I don't understand…"

"Mark, what if I tell you that these generators are here and are presently fully operating?"

"Eh-r-r, well, Jennifer, this is impossible, because every state gets strictly their agreed quota. They are probably somewhere in storage. Well, I don't know for sure, but I could ask Timor if you would like me to, he will…"

"No, Mark. I know they are in use and I know where the energy is sent to. Timor is doing this secretly from Platt and he has obviously managed to fool you, as well."

"Well, no, he wouldn't do this to me, lie to me. Maybe, you are mistaken, or someone has given you wrong information or something…"

"I know that this is not a nice thing to hear, Mark, especially, coming from me! But Timor is lying!"

"Well, it can't be, Jennifer! You are wrong. Timor could not do this. He is not like this! It's probably a mistake, or you've misunderstood something from whomever you've heard all this!" Mark turned round, clearly offended and unwilling to listen to all this anymore. They stopped about 100 meters from the entry. Jennifer stood in front of him, prepared to prove her statement about the greedy liar Timor.

"Mark, please! Just listen to me. I don't tell you all this to hurt you. Please, hear me out!" She was telling him rather than pleading with him.

"Well, fine, go on! But I know for sure that Timor has not done anything that would compromise the project! I'm listening to you, though." Mark agreed to hear her out, mainly because he had no choice. He crossed his arms like some bouncer and frowned.

"If you want, Mark, don't believe me, but at least try to trust your own sense of logic. Answer me these questions." Jennifer asserted herself in her wish to put some sense in his views. She wanted to show him a different side to good old Timor, where he was simply a user and a selfish man.

"Eh-r-r, well, what questions, now…?"

"First, tell me how many liquid generators are required, according to the plan, in order to collect all the energy, produced by the six thousand reactors?"

"Well, Jennifer, you know, I've told you about the general energy distribution plan before. Don't you remember that we talked about it? You asked me, then, or I just started something about the subject and…"

"Mark, please! Just answer me straight." She snapped at him purely because they lacked time. If Mark took his time responding to her questions, the temperatures outside were going to become unbearable.

"Well, twenty, eh-r-r, initially, we thought we needed 18, but after we made some changes to the project, we decided on two more…"

"Right, this is my information, too. And what happens, once all the generators are filled up?"

"Well, then we send them to the designated countries, according to their level of participation in the project, and they just get their supply of energy."

"Could we send out twenty two generators? Is that possible?"

"Well, it is, but first, we'd have to produce more energy, which will take more time and the delivery will be delayed, and the schedule will be jeopardized. And no one needs more for now, anyway so I think…"

"Look, Mark." Jennifer paused, searching for the right words. She was going to ask him a few more introductory questions before directing him at the facts. But then, she changed her mind, getting a bit fed up with Mark's far too many ideals, which had nothing to do with reality. "Yesterday, I had to check the documentation, related to the number of generators, and according to the papers, we have received 22 in total. So far, nothing to worry about! I love my job and I try to be precise. When I called our colleagues to find out which 20 are in use

179

and which 2 are here on the ground, I was told that all generators have been sent under the orders of the chief coordinator and there's none, here, on the ground."

"Eh-r-r, well, where are the other two, then?" Mark asked confused.

"They are where they shouldn't be, Mark. I requested the schedule report from the military staff, responsible for the ballistic send-offs, and it appears that seven countries are getting more energy than they should, from the extra two generators that you have required. Timor is behind this..."

"Well, why would he be doing this, this should not be... but how?"

"Most probably, he's been offered money, and when he's realized that he can't pull this off on his own, he's used you, knowing that Platt trusts you. I just can't work out how the energy supply has not been delayed for the other countries, in order to fill the two extra generators." Jennifer was not very up on the nuclear energy subject, despite the fact that Mark had explained the process to her numerous times.

"Well, the 6000 reactors are designed to cover the needs of the world population, even if they work at 70-80% of the capacity. It was estimated that when the demand increases in a few years, then their full capacity will be used and a few more generators will be needed. I did not envisage this to be the case until another five-six years. We always say that the nuclear power plants can generate a surplus of energy, which is not put in use, right now. It's too early for that." Mark, in effect, answered Jennifer's question and gave her the missing piece of information. As usual, he did not realized, at first, what he had just done. His words proved that she was right and that Timor really had the opportunity to overstep the rules.

"Do you believe me now, Mark? We need to decide what to do. We can't allow this to carry on!"

"Eh-r-r, well, I don't know, I... but he..." Mark felt shaken. His best friend, the man he respected and admired for his sound character and great professionalism, was a conman. Jennifer's suggestion that his motive was possibly money was even more shocking. Timor had never suffered financial difficulties and according to Mark, the last thing he would do was to sell himself. Jennifer had no proof, but the logic was on her side: the obvious conclusion was that Timor had received a significant sum of money to do the clandestine favour. She had also noticed that the seven countries, involved, were some of the richest in the world.

"Mark, what are we going to do?" She repeated really worried.

"Well, I don't know, but how… how has no one noticed? It's impossible, but how?"

"I've been asking myself the same thing, until I got in touch with the militaries, last night. It's been actually quite easy, Mark. There is very little coordination between the departments. Everyone is doing their job, but no one cares what the others do." Jennifer had discovered the biggest weakness of the project. The staff worked independently from each other. The color-coordinated division by wearing different uniforms meant that no one cared about other people's business.

"Well, we are in this together, working together. There should be a good level of coordination and Timor's the chief coordinator, isn't he?"

"Yes, but what is he in charge of? He coordinates only the actual building process of the nuclear plants and their operation. He has no direct responsibilities over the militaries, the administrative department, over the maintenance people, nor the scientists. There is no coordination between any of the listed above, either. Have you ever seen any of the pilots, showing any interest in the actual process of energy production or what is happening in the tower?" Mark was smart enough to realize what Jennifer was pointing at. This was all true. He had no idea what was going on in the rest of the departments. If Timor was not his friend, he would not have probably set foot inside the tower more than a couple of times that year. The militaries had their own system of hierarchy and they guarded perfectly the security area of interest. None of them, however, needed to know why the liquid

181

generators were sent to such and such country, why today, but not next week. They knew nothing about the principle of work of the generator. They did not need this extra information, because they got their orders directly from Timor and his assistants and thus, there was a scope for misuse of powers. What if they were told that all energy had to be sent to one state? The change would be applied unquestionably, because they were not dressed in black and they were not competent to refute the orders. There were dozens of examples for poor coordination between the departments.

"Well, Jennifer, it looks that you are right and now, what are we going to do? I don't know… but I think to go and ask Timor and tell him to stop this, so everything becomes fair like at the beginning…"

"Mark, what are you going to say to him? <<Don't send the two extra generators>>, so everything goes back like it was before? This will never happen, especially if he's received money for it. There is no way back for him." Jennifer was led not only by the apparent injustice, but she was also feeling a personal resentment towards Timor. For her, he was simply her boyfriend's best friend and nothing more.

"Well, but if I… maybe…"

"You must call Platt, so Timor gets fired!"

"Eh-r-r… well, I think, first, I should talk to him and then, if he doesn't agree with me, I'll get in touch with Platt…"

"Are you out of your mind?" Jennifer snapped at him like that for the first time since they've started going out together. "He's been lying to you and now you want to negotiate with him? Just think about what would happen if any of the other countries found out and Timor was still employed in his position! Mark, we could be at the brink of another energy war, without even realizing it."

"Well, I can't quite believe this, but when I talk to Timor, we'll see what we're going to do. I'll call Platt, if he doesn't want to listen to me."

"Fine, but promise me that even if Timor stops sending on the two extra liquid generators, you are still going to let Platt know about what's been happening." Jennifer's ultimatum was actually going to lead to

Timor's removal from the project, irrelevant to whether Mark managed to convince him or not.

"Well, I promise, but now, I better go to the tower. Timor stays there until late and it's getting cold, here, outside."

Back, in the warm building, Jennifer went to her room to wait for Mark's return who finally realized the true character of his friend, full of greed.

The horizontal lift stopped a few meters from the vertical device that was leading to the "brains" of the entire base. Mark kept wondering about what exactly to say to Timor, so he would stop his illicit practice, using the two generators and the distribution of the energy went back to how it was supposed to be – just and fair. He could not think of the right words, on his way up, so at the end, he decided to simply ask Timor as a friend. Mark truly hoped that the malpractice could be stopped and time would just roll back to when everything was too good to be true.

Timor was very happy about earning his first two millions and could not stop thinking about the next two coming. In order to get it, he would need another two liquid generators, which his good friend Mark was going to provide. And soon after, the last pair was going to be ordered and he had no doubts about it. The chief coordinator had estimated that if all the reactors were working at their full capacity, he could be filling up another four generators with energy. He could, then, be able to get six millions, which would satisfy him completely. Timor, however, did not stop there. In his dreams, there was a lot more he could gain. He was going to ask for more money, every time he was about to send on another generator and the potential scope for competition between the seven richest states, was going to provide for him a serious opportunity to blackmail them. Whenever the metal container arrived back in the Base for yet another "portion" of energy, the bidding was going to resume. The simple calculation meant that if six generators made about 100 runs per year and if Timor took a minimum of 200 000 per run (he picked randomly this figure), then, he would get at least 20 million. The meagre 2 million, he had just earned, looked to him like a bad joke.

There was going to be a small problem soon, when the increased demand, worldwide, would lead to the necessity of employing the reserve capacities of the nuclear plants, carefully envisaged by Mark. This would be a difficult task, now that Timor would have used up everything. According to his narcissistic beliefs for the future, until the moment everyone found out, he would be so powerful thus, untouchable. Timor's intention was to privatize the entire project. He did not care about anything or anyone but himself.

Mark did not know that greed could be such a dangerous disease. He entered the control center and headed towards Timor's usual place of work. No one noticed his arrival. People had got used to his presence, as he would spend a lot of time there. The chief coordinator stood up from his chair to greet him. From a distance he noticed that his friend, who was going to make him a millionaire, was looking at him funny. The only light in the hall was coming from the different sized monitors, where staff watched the data indicators for all the nuclear power plants. For the ignorant, the graphics and diagrams looked like some chaotic jumble. Of course, it was a different story for the well-educated specialists, who were glued to screens, observing for the slightest negative change, about which the computers were going to indicate within less than a second.

The lack of normal lighting felt quite ridiculous, especially, because the hall was located in the center of the biggest energy producer. The reason for this was that the personnel lost their concentration easily, if the light was too bright. Their eyes got tired very quickly, which could lead to significant errors. Twilight ruled.

"Mark, what are you doing here at this time? I didn't expect you. I thought you usually go for a walk with your girl?" Timor asked quite surprised. His dark uniform made him look like some talking shadow of a man.

"Well, we just got back, as it became a bit cold and I know I did tell you that I was not coming over here this evening, but you and I need to talk about something, Timor."

"What's up? Did she dump you?"

"Well, no, we are fine, there's no problem between us… I just want to talk to you and…"

"Go on, then, talk. What's stopping you?"

"Well, Timor, let's go out for a minute, as it's not very suitable in here I think." Mark whispered, nodding at the exit.

"Just say it here. I don't feel like going anywhere!"

"Well, then. I want to ask you about the two liquid generators that you made me request from Platt, and I found out that they are in use at present and…"

"Come!" Timor grabbed Mark's arm just above the elbow and dragged him towards the door. The boss, physically very strong, had never applied force before over his scrawny employee. When they got on the well-lit landing, just outside the lift, Timor let go of him. The coordinator leaned menacingly towards Mark, leaving just ten centimeters between their faces and asked with open animosity:

"What do you know? Who's told you?"

"Well, Timor, I, eh-r-r, I just…" Stuttered Mark in fear. He had just learned two things for sure, which he never imagined that were possible. Firstly, that Timor was a liar and secondly, that he was not shy of any violent act towards him. It was clear who would be the winner.

"What do you know about this?" The chief coordinator said through clenched teeth, with his hands – clasped into strong fists.

"Well, I just want to talk, Timor, if you simply stop sending these two… and everything will go back to normal, but…"

"Who's told you?" The distance between him and his potential victim was diminished further by a few centimeters.

"Well, nobody has. I just found out, but things could be fixed, Timor…"

"So no one else knows, but you? Is that the case?" The question sounded less intimidating.

"Well, I haven't mentioned anything to anyone, because we could fix this and stop sending them. It's not fair and it's not nice to do such thing..." Jennifer's name was left out foresightedly.

"God, Mark, you really gave me the scares!" Timor's smile was a sign that his good old friend was back again. He gave Mark a friendly hug across his shoulder. "I nearly thought that you've spread the tale... and this would've been too bad! Look now, everything is under control and I can assure you that there's no infringement of any states' rights. All countries are equal. It's just that some are more equal than the others. We are just supplying those in greatest need with a bit more energy, because these states are developing faster than the rest of the world. All countries need energy, Mark, don't they? It was your idea!" Timor, as shrewd and clever as he was, believed that implying, what was right and what was wrong, was going to be an easy task. He always managed that in the past, but when Mark was still single and the good influence of Jennifer was not present.

"Eh-r-r, well, so, they have changed the schedule plan and that's why more energy is being produced, to fill the two extra liquid generators, which were going to be kept as a reserve? But I haven't heard about this change of plan..." The accountant naively tried, yet again, to see the obvious malpractice as something planned and in accordance with the Law.

"Mark, no one has changed anything. Listen to me now! Some countries need more energy? What's so wrong if we just send it to them by increasing the production capacity of the nuclear plants? The rest of the states don't need to know. It's none of their business, because they receive what they need!" Timor was not worried to reveal the truth, as he could not imagine that Mark would ever stand in his way. He expected that the accountant would agree with everything, unquestionably, and would stop bothering him with this in the future. For a second, Timor even thought about sharing some of his earnings with his weak-willed friend. The thought quickly vanished. Mark did not need money after all and there would be less for Timor.

"Well, Timor, you are right, but when I designed the project, I envisaged some sort of surplus, which had to be distributed evenly, amongst everyone. Now, seven states are in receipt of more energy than the rest and this is not fair, don't you think? It would be a different story, if you share this surplus with everyone, then…"

"Mark, what's up with you? Didn't you hear me? The smaller countries don't need more energy than they already get. That's why I'm sending it to the seven biggest. This is how it is and how it's going to be!" Timor uttered this, as if he was the sole owner of the nuclear facilities, of the energy and all, forgetting that he was just a regular employee at the Base.

"Well, so you're not going to stop this and just carry on?"

"There'll be no changes to the situation, until I say so, Mark! You are not going to talk about this to no one! Even if your colleagues start asking questions, just tell them that it's been done under Platt's orders." Timor was convinced that Mark was going to take his side and like a loyal servant, would simply fool the scientists, who could become rather curious at times.

"Well, Timor, if this is how you really think, I better go now!"

Mark felt rotten and almost tearful, as this became the breaking point of their friendship. Jennifer was right. Timor is a conman, who would never change, and he had to be eliminated from the Base at once. Mark removed himself snappily from his embrace, so that the coordinator's arm swung abruptly downwards. Then, the accountant quickly pressed the button to call the elevator.

Timor went back in his 'cloister', without noticing the sudden change in his friend. He was certain that Mark would not say a word to anyone and cowardly would remain passive about this matter. Well, he could not be further from the truth. Mark headed to Jennifer's room, so he could tell her about his meeting. His face was saying everything. When his observant girlfriend saw him, she immediately passed the phone to him. Mark made a phone call, which was one of the few he had ever made and then, felt good about it. Despite the badly uttered explanation, Platt understood that his interference was a must. A serious international conflict was at stake, especially now that the army had reappeared on the scene, so the effects of this could be really major.

Platt was prepared for this sort of events from the very beginning. His personal contacts and experience with most of the world leaders had taught him to mistrust them and their promises. He was always very diplomatic, when expressing his opinion. The richer states were 'arrogant'; whereas the poorer ones always 'moaned' that the others were exploiting them, even if this was not the case. Mark's utopia and credo that all were equal, a belief – integrated in his project as the real basis, actually could not withstand for long. Sooner or later, the powerful states would become the culprits for growing inequalities and the only question was how big and painful this division gap was going to be. Platt believed that if the transition of status quo was gradual and gentle and the new situation was slowly made legit, then everything would be alright at the end, especially if the smaller countries got reimbursed in some way. The important issue was how to make the small countries realize and agree that if their rich neighbours get more energy, they would benefit from this, too.

On the next morning, Mark went to breakfast alone. Jennifer was beginning to feel more apprehensive and fearful from the recent events, which affected her appetite slightly. She decided to go straight to work. Mark did not feel very good in the company of the chief coordinator. He felt as if he was in a strange place, sitting at a table opposite some bigheaded stranger, who had settled there without being invited. Neither of them said a word about their conversation last night, nor was Platt's name mentioned. Mark, the chatterbox, concentrated on his food and briefly answered the odd questions. No one knew how long this mental torture would go on for, but Platt. He had promised that he would visit the Base very soon, but having so many other important meetings and engagements around the world, it was hard to pin what his 'soon' really meant.

Jennifer had suggested they stopped seeing Timor until the problem was solved, but then she thought that he would notice this and it might make him more suspicious. Then, he might do something unpredictable if he realized that his greedy plan was coming to an end and he was about to lose his job. It was very possible that Timor would try to set them up in some tragic accident or he might even try to poison them! Yes, he could definitely organize something like this.

Jennifer, who had no reasons to imagine such scenarios, inadvertently passed her fears onto Mark. That day, they missed their regular walk by the wall, as it was the perfect location for some incident happening with no witnesses around. At meal times, he would be stirring and picking at his food, scrutinizing every piece, in the hope he would notice some trace of poison. Timor had his own explanation for their strange behaviour. Mark had gone a bit stiff about the whole issue, which was normal, and he was going to forget about it in a couple of days as usual. Jennifer, on the other hand, was simply pretending to be angry, because Mark was not letting on anything to her. Timor firmly believed that his friend would keep the secret and that he was still entirely under his influence and control.

The transportation helicopter landed on the especially designated platform. It did not look any different from the rest of the flying machines, so there was no inkling as to who was on board. About 200km before the chopper reached the Base the air control issued an enquiry, related to the purpose of the flight. The pilot lied that there was no one else on board and that he was coming to replace the machine with another helicopter, because this one needed some significant repair and maintenance. Again, the lack of decent coordination between departments came handy, so permission to land was granted straight away. Any helicopter that had just touched ground underwent a thorough check, including the pilots and the passengers. The level of security was extremely high.

Platt got off the helicopter and he was immediately approached by three heavily armed security guards, who kindly asked for his ID. The special stumpy visitor did not respond but ordered them to follow him. On their way to the 'nest' of the violator, he made the three soldiers phone their colleagues, who had to turn to the right place at once. The coup d'état had to take place as quick and painlessly as possible.

Platt was waiting for the lift in the cool landing and he was thinking that he could not wait to get rid of the chief coordinator. Going up, while the numbers, indicating each floor kept changing in an ascending order, he was wondering who should be the new replacement of Timor. Clearly, the post was very important and he should find someone skillful and conscientious, no doubt. He could not think of anyone. Mark was absolutely unsuitable for this position, but Platt did think of him as a possible substitute. He left this task for later. The unexpected visitor stood outside the control room and waited for the back-up security guys, who were climbing up the stairs. Finally it was time for the chairman of the Global Energy Project to apply the justice that the venture was so much lacking in recent months.

"Hi, Mr. Platt, what are you doing here?" Timor was standing a few meters from the door, listening to the night shift guard's report. Everything seemed to be in order. His face showed surprise, mixed with fear. Tall and fit, he was not really scared from Platt, but from the twenty soldiers behind him, who were, strangely, pointing their sub-machine guns at him.

"Sit down!" Platt ordered and pointed at the nearest chair. He pulled one for him, as well. The chairman got out one of his favourite cigars and lit it skillfully. His calm tone of voice did not give any sign that his visit was for some unpleasant reasons.

"But, Mr. Plat, why didn't you call first that you're coming? I would have met you personally, it's a great honour for me…" Timor started with his sweet talk, and at the same time, keeping an eye on the small army behind his guest.

"Sit down!"

"Right, Mr. Platt, if you insist. I just wanted to say that for me and my people, it's a great pleasure to…"

"Enough with this nonsense! I don't have time for this. Tell me who are you working for and how long the two extra generators have been in use? Be brief."

"I don't understand what you're talking about, Mr. Platt! Most probably you've been misled. The two generators have been in storage since they got delivered." Timor was trying to play the innocent. He just needed time, so he could conceal the breach and misappropriation. Once, Platt left, the malpractice was going to be reinstated, of course.

"Who are you working for and how long has this been going for?" It was hard to fool someone like Platt in such a naïve way. That's why he did not take in the story of the innocent misunderstanding. He did take in with great pleasure the aromatic smoke from his cigar.

"I'm telling you, Mr. Platt, there's nothing of the kind going on. It must be some mistake; someone has misled you, Mr. Platt! You've come all the way, here, in vain, although, I don't have a problem with this… You can come whenever you like but there is no…"

"Timor, nothing that you say will help you in this!"

"Has Mark been telling you stuff?" Cornered, the chief coordinator decided to change his tactic. If he could not lie about this, at least, he could blame it on someone else and belittle the incident as much as he could. "He has probably embellished things a bit. He does this a lot. You know what he's like, Mr. Platt! I can assure you that nothing wrong is going on!"

"Who are you working for and how long has it been going for? Timor, I don't like to repeat myself."

"What do you mean, Mr. Platt? With regards to the first part of the question – I've been working for you since you employed me more than a year ago to become the chief coordinator of this project…"

"Enough!" Platt uttered, remaining as calm as before. "Timor, you have jeopardized the entire project and I want to know how this has happened. If you tell me, you will go to prison for minimum of twenty years. If you continue to play the fool, you will be there until you rot."

"But I don't know anything about…"

"Of course, you may even get a death sentence if you don't start speaking this second."

"I don't want to end up in prison at all, Mr. Platt, and I will cooperate in every way and tell you all that I know." Clearly, the change of approach led to change of hearts and unlocked Timor's inner wish to collaborate. His fear overpowered his greed for money and power. His instinct for self-preservation 'spoke out'.

"Hmm, that's more like it, Timor. You are ready to bargain, which means you're ready to use your head."

"I don't want to go to prison." He repeated with slightly trembling voice.

"Who are you working for?" asked again Platt, knowing that this time he would receive an answer.

"Connor, it was Prof. Connor. He phoned me about five months ago. I couldn't possibly remember what day it was, but only that it was in the middle of the night. He told me that I was going to be replaced, once all the power plants were completed and that if I wanted to keep my job, I would need to start sending more energy to seven particular states." Timor consciously missed to inform Platt that together with the promise that he would stay in position, he was offered a substantial amount of money.

"And you agreed?"

"Yes, but Connor said that it is fine and the right way and that the surplus could be used without others knowing about it. I actually thought that you were aware of all this…"

"Has anyone else, apart from Connor, ever contacted you?"

"No, no one has. He actually called me just this one time. He was very clear and never said anything more. When you all came for the ceremony, I did not have the chance to talk to him."

Platt remained silent, not because he had nothing to say, but for a different, much more important reason. Timor visibly did not lie this time. His eyes gave him out immediately, when he tried to fool Platt to no avail, a little while ago. His unconscious way of drawing invisible figures in the air, the slight tapping of his right heel, as well as the spontaneous smile on his face, all this could not conceal the fact that he was lying, then. Whereas, all the signs were in support of him telling the truth and that he actually believed in what he was saying in these last few sentences. So if this was the case, then, it meant that Timor had received the order from someone, pretending to be Connor, which meant that the person behind this was unknown. Platt was certain that Connor could not possibly be part of this. The time that the mysterious phone call was made coincided with the time when the professor was in hospital. The car accident, caused by wet weather conditions, led to Prof. Connor spending almost a month under medical supervision, twenty days of which, he was in deep coma. It was a ridiculous suggestion that he could have been able to use the phone during this time.

"And what did you do after that?"

"Mr. Platt, I'm not going to prison, am I?" Timor could not read the face of the man opposite him, and this scared him even more. He found the carefree attitude of Platt very strange.

"You answer the questions and we shall see! What did you do after you accepted Connor's offer?"

"I tried to find two extra generators myself and when I couldn't, I asked Mark to call you. He did this and on the second year, since the project's been running, we started to send more energy to these seven states."

"So you've been doing this for how long, six weeks?"

"Yes, approximately for that long, Mr. Platt."

"Security, take the chief coordinator under arrest. We shall continue our conversation another time!"

"But… but you've said that you're not going to…" Timor jumped, ready to fight back against them taking away his freedom, but he was knocked down as quick and abruptly as when it happened to Mark at the 18th Conference. It took the professionally trained soldiers less than a minute to subdue the infringer and take him away. Platt ordered politely to be left alone and made everyone leave the room. The solution of the problem was not as easy as he wanted. The unknown factors were far too many and this made any sudden changes to the course of action extremely dangerous and unpredictable. One fact was clear – the man behind this was not Connor. Who was it then? It was logical that it must have been someone, connected to one of the seven states, as they were the beneficiaries in this. It was very possible that they all got together and selected a representative. Platt was quite prepared to believe that and just carried on thinking and trying to unravel the complex case.

The rich had been getting more energy in the last month or so and thus, breached the agreement they had signed. Well, they did not need it just yet, because their economies had just started to pick up, which meant that they had been storing it for the future. Platt liked to apply a sound logical approach, which led to the easily drawn conclusions. He usually avoided pondering too much in a heavy type of manner that led to convoluted answers. Now that Platt was convinced that his speculations were likely, the big question arose: what would the seven states do, when they stop getting the two liquid generators and equal energy distribution was reinstated? It was possible that they kept quiet, because no one knew about this, anyway. They had already managed to put some energy in reserve by fraudulence, so they were good. However, there was a more realistic scenario – the seven countries would demand immediately some changes to be made about the agreed quotas. They would reason and back their request with their fast-growing economies, which was leading to an increased need for energy. They would ignore the needs of the smaller and less affluent states and even if the proposal for amendment of the proportionally distributed

194

quotas did not get accepted, it was certain that the seven powerful and military sound countries would impose their will. Reaching the end of his predictions, Platt could not really say for sure, whether there would be a long and devastating war, where millions of innocent people would fall victims, or everything was going to evolve and conclude peacefully. Everything was possible.

What was the best solution? That was the next question. Platt believed that the state of uneven distribution had to be emplaced gradually, and not suddenly, overnight. First, he was going to punish the seven states for their clandestine games, and then, he would entice them to be gentler with the less powerful countries. So in the coming years, the rich would begin to get their quotas increased and everyone should be happy. Thus, any armed conflict or military enforcement would be avoided. Platt put this as a priority on his list of tasks. He believed unconditionally that he was going to succeed and that the bloodless approach was the right way. How further from the truth he was! Fate, if it existed, had chosen a different deadly ending to all this.

There were not any prison cells in the Base. Two rooms, next to the bedrooms, were designated for that purpose. They were called – temporary detention rooms. They were spacious and could accommodate minimum of 40 people, but so far, no more than 4 had been detained in there. Generally, the level of criminal activity in the Base was zero. However, some time in the second month from the start of the project, four maintenance workers decided to ignore the strict alcohol ban. After work, they drank a bottle of whiskey, which previous employees at the Base had left behind. The scrawniest of them got drunk very quickly, so he attracted the attention of the security. From there, the road to the detention rooms was rather short.

Timor was placed in the very same room. The guards had missed to remove his watch, so he was aware that he had been inside for three hours and 22 minutes. Starring at the door throughout the whole time, he kept thinking that Platt would come soon, so they could continue their conversation, as promised a little while ago. The former chief coordinator had thought of a few more arguments, proving his innocence and he could not wait to share them with the person, who literally had his life in his hands. Of course, he did not want to go to prison. This was his main wish. He did expect that he could go to prison for some years, if Platt decided so. Hopefully, it would not be for long, he mused. Timor thought that 2-3 years in prison was enough to atone for his sin before the global community, as long as it was not for any longer. And when he got out, he could still enjoy spending his concealed 2 millions and just have a new start. He was praying quietly.

The security alarm was set off a few seconds after the muffled thunder and the light shaking had passed. The staff, working underground, thought at first that this was an earthquake, as they felt as if the earth layers were moving. The rest of the workers, above ground, had full visibility, and this was definitely not an earthquake. The helicopter had taken off without a hitch and there was no sign or warning for what was about to happen – after just 100 meters in the air, the machine crashed back on the concrete. The device exploded in flames and the cause was electrical and not because of ignited fuel leak, like it used to be in the past. The energy batteries were fireproof. The firefighters appeared within a minute and put out the fire very quickly. There was nothing around that could have been in immediate danger. The concrete platform was very thick, so any damage to the tunnels underneath was simply impossible to happen.

The first witnesses were actually, the workers in the tower – Timor's former workplace. They first realized what they had just seen. They, in effect, granted the permission for take-off. On board, there were only the pilot and Platt. Everyone went in a flurry, asking each other about what they should do. The control center had no chief coordinator anymore, and the entire project was left 'headless', without Platt. The project had suddenly become an orphan. Confused, feeling the panic, several employees rushed to report the incident to the boss of security, who was naturally someone suitable to take charge of the situation. The militaries took the initiative, as they were best equipped for emergency circumstances like this. Their first order was, of course, that Platt's colleagues needed to be informed at once. The ball was in their court, so they should decide how to proceed from then on. Although the Global Energy Project had officially finished and Mark Eos's idea had turned into its successor, Connor, Merit and the rest had not stopped being active during the recent months. They had been working and assisting Platt in all his decisions.

A special team was going to investigate the crash and attempt to collect as much evidence as possible, until the arrival of qualified criminal investigators. The metal debris was cleared swiftly, so the sight did not disturb in any way the other pilots. No one wanted in further distractions, leading to more fatal errors. This was exactly what everyone believed that happened – the crash was most probably caused by a human error. The pilot had lost control of the machine, which had led to the tragic incident. In reality, the investigators were about to find out that the pilot had no chance when the two control systems had simply stopped functioning. It could have happened on any helicopter. The first few hours, after the tragedy, were the hardest. By the evening, all was under control and there was almost nothing that showed that Platt and one pilot had perished in the morning.

Timor learned the sad news from the young man, who was bringing his evening meal. Despite the strict ban for talking with the detained, the boy was very keen to share the news and enthusiastically described the crash, although he had not witnessed anything personally. Timor was over the moon. He even forgot about his empty stomach. Was this really happening? The only person, who could remove him from his post and put him in prison, was dead! The timing could not be more perfect! Timor was certain that as soon as he got out free, he would regain the control of the Base. He remembered that there were quite a few witnesses, when he admitted to Platt his illicit activities. The day shift personnel were present, but the chief coordinator did not worry about them – he knew how to deal with them. There were not courts, prosecutors, nor investigators on the territory of the Base, so even no one believed him, he was still safe and untouchable.

The militaries usually followed orders blindly, which meant that if the head of security believed his story, everything would work out perfectly. He had not heard Timor's self-confession, so it would be far too easy for him to fall into the webs of experienced liar like Timor. First things first - he had to find a way to leave this room, where he was held against his will. Actually, it was not hard for anyone, who was averagely intelligent, to do this, let along for Timor. He waited for the guard to do his regular check and nonchalantly got into a conversation with him. A few minutes later, after his soppy and emotional story about how he and Platt had just re-enacted a scenario, so they could catch out a corrupt employee from the Tower, who had threatened the entire project and how the chief coordinator was actually in the role of an undercover agent, he was let to go free to his workplace. The subsequent private talk, Timor had with the head of security, in effect, sealed and confirmed his superiority and power within the Base. The General could not be called naïve or weak-willed, however, he believed every lie he had been just subjected to. He proceeded this way, mostly because it suited him to transfer the responsibility over to someone else. He was afraid to be in charge in case another fatal incident happened, while he was at the top. After all, he was here to provide security for the Base, not manage it.

Timor, as rancorous as he was, had no doubts about who had betrayed him. He ordered Mark to be arrested immediately. He had no idea, yet, about what he would do with him, but one infinitely long walk in the desert, might well solve his problem for once and for all. The search for the accountant began around midnight. After all supposedly possible places were checked and the suspect was not found, the perimeter of the search area was expanded and more guards got involved. Jennifer was also on the hunt list, in case she had information on her boyfriend's whereabouts. There was no trace of her, either.

While the chief coordinator was detained, Mark and Jennifer got the opportunity to act. As soon as Mark heard of Platt's death, he promptly headed towards the administrative department. He could not remember exactly what he told Jennifer, but only how she dragged him to her room, squeezing painfully his hand with her nails. She was aware that Timor had been arrested earlier this morning and she wrongly connected the two events. Platt had got hold of Timor, and the latter must have caused the crash to eliminate Platt. Although this was not the truth behind all this, Jennifer knew that they had to leave the Base within seconds. Platt was a very good friend of Mark, and his biggest advocate. Without him, Mark became a very easy target. They packed all their belongings in a couple of rucksacks and were ready to go. Where to, though, Jennifer did not know? The only way to leave the Base was by helicopter and neither of them could fly one. Trekking through the merciless desert was the only thing she could come up with, before Mark showed her the right way for their escape. He from all people knew best how to get to it and use it.

Inconspicuous terrorism

Fight for justice is a permanent cause, which usually is doomed to failure. Good job that is, otherwise, if all was fair and equal, the world would be too peaceful, without conflicts, and that would be rather peculiar. Every country strived to achieve justice, and this was a never-ending process, as once reached, the very existence of the state would become meaningless. We would not need any state institutions to guarantee fairness and justice if injustice actually did not exist and everyone was equally happy. Justice was a relative notion, which opponents of the energy concept regarded how they knew best. They made every effort to achieve equality and fairness, but they also had different views on this. The majority and at the same time, less radical section of them, believed that energy corrupted people and it was just if people deserted the whole idea. The more people took the road to energy-free world, the more just the world would get. These people advocated for simple life in the countryside, where one devoted their days to primitive farming. Their view was that some electrical appliances were allowed to use, however, the list was pretty limited, excluding the most helpful and practical. There was a total ban for the use of energy batteries and this automatically made this group of people not very mobile. They only made use of some means of transport, when they had to go on one of their anti-energy protests. These demonstrations, which rarely turned into a proper civil unrest, were their only form of objection so that is why the authorities did not anticipate anything more serious on their part, like a deadly bomb attempt for example.

Only a few thousand people around the world, classed as the radicals, could go that far and actually get pleasure out of setting the odd explosion, here and there. These people were not so much against the energy, but they did not believe in nuclear power plants. Renewable sources were their credo. That was why Mark's project became an eyesore for them. Before the desert power plants project, their destructive attention was turned towards the existing nuclear sites. Of course, they also kept a close eye on the phony Global Energy Project. And although Platt and his colleagues really tried to solve the energy problem through clean and non-nuclear methods, as the ban, then, was still in place, their well informed objectors did not trust them in the slightest. Every move, undertaken after each conference, was severely criticized as being yet the next big lie, which only had one purpose – to conceal the truth about the inexhaustible natural energy resources, easily available to all.

Different processes in the core of our planet, as well as such above the surface, could unlock vast quantities of energy, as long as the right technology and approach were applied. The point, here, was not just to use the Sun, the water and the wind. Other natural sources included the numerous daily earthquakes, which released a lot of energy or the volcanoes that could be used for building new thermal power stations. It was not a secret that the undercurrents in the oceans could also generate energy, which was even more accessible than the first two methods. Of course, all these ideas were generally regarded as dreamlike and unfeasible. Never any direct and substantiating proof was presented in their support, so the serious explorers and scientists in the field rejected them out rightly. Earthquakes could not be predicted, although, after every powerful one, weaker tremors followed, so the energy released could have been harnessed. How exactly, no one knew, even those, who were behind the idea. It was the same story with the volcanoes, too. Their location made the concept of generating energy from them, pointless. The most active volcanoes were in effect, islands in the middle of nowhere, so it was impossible for any equipment to be built there. The scientists laughed out loud, when they tried to imagine a thermal power station, perched on the top of a volcano, which could erupt any moment. Even in sci-fi literature nothing of this kind had been ever described. The alternative idea for generating energy from the power of undercurrents in the ocean had its potential. The currents never slowed down and it was unlikely to do so in the future. The technology, related to this, had been well known for the last three decades. The idea was put into practice straight away and powerful underwater turbines were lowered deep into the ocean. However, only one year later, this project ceased to exist. It proved ineffective, after all. The currents changed direction too often and their location was also unpredictable. Even when the turbines followed and were placed in the heart of the powerful movement of water, they only managed to produce insignificant quantity of energy. The slow speed was the reason for the poor results. At the 9th Conference, the scientific research, related to generating energy from the undercurrents was renewed. The members of the conference voted in favour, simply because they wanted to subdue the rising pressure. Platt and the other five intended to pacify and fool the activists.

The main motive of the opponents against nuclear energy was actually their inner need to oppose of something, no matter what it was, and generally, their desire to be part of something big. This made some of them the ideal terrorists, because they had very low self-esteem, they were full of insecurities, so much that if they blew a bomb or engaged themselves in some sort of subversive activities, they simply waited for the <well done> tap on the back. Being praised about how great they were was more important to them than the actual ideas and principles that the fight against nuclear energy was based on. Often they engaged in unsolicited actions, in the hope to gain a greater recognition and not share it with anyone else. These people were absolute lunatics, but without them, the group could not have earned its radical status, nor would they have ever achieved anything for their cause. In reality, the energy terrorism had got into a futile trench war, since Mark's project began, and the sworn objectors had not managed to damage not one nuclear power plant or reactor.

The first attempts against were naturally directed towards the manufacturers of components, designated for the nuclear plants. To be precise, these were the factories that made the concrete platforms for the foundations. The heavy security managed to prevent a few terrorist troops in their attempt to slow down the production. The randomly thrown grenades and chaotic shootings from a great distance did not cause any damage. Instead, the attack achieved the protected area to expand, making meaningless any future attempts for a breakthrough.

Infiltration was the terrorist only chance for success, so they had to think of sending undercover in the Base one of their own people. They had the experience. One of the last attacks, which led to closing the nuclear facility, was done by an inside employee, who was actually an avid supporter of the radicals. He had patiently waited for the right time, when he could act and stop the use of this energy forever. Now the situation was different. They could not penetrate the Base, because experienced terrorists were hard to find and those, who were inexperienced, simply did not get a job at the nuclear facility or anywhere that was strategic for the project. It was not a bad idea if an attempt was made to get people into the service and maintenance sector of the Base, however, when the distribution base was established, the staff had been already hired. Moreover, the newly employed were thoroughly checked, so random malevolent individuals were not admitted into the system.

Looking at the map, in the same way Mark had been scanning it to pick the right place for his project the leaders of the three main terrorist organizations were cursing the large yellow spot, located slightly above the Equator, dividing the planet in two. The location, known as the Big Desert, was the largest uninhabited area for obvious reasons. Even before the start of the project, the radical groups were keen to sent in a few dozens of fanatical followers, all armed and well equipped, so they could cause some severe damage to the foundations and domes, once they were put in place. The whole idea was bad, if not very stupid, because the insurgents would have to cover at least 800km, deep into the desert, walking or driving. Naturally, this would have proved impossible. The best means of transport was the helicopter, but it was an easy target, so it would have been destroyed by the militaries, strictly guarding the building site. The missiles, responsible for making the surface flat, also appeared to be a direct threat, killing the entire idea, as they could have eliminate the terrorists within minutes, blowing them into little bloody pieces.

The radicals realized that they could not prevent the nuclear power plants of being completed, so a decision was made to find some weak points, when the first facilities were finished. They managed to get some inside information from the factories, where the dark titanium domes were made. Basically, the terrorists realized that unless they were fully armed with heavy weaponry, it was pointless to even think of attacking anything. Without missiles or something of the sort, nothing would happen. Here, the question about getting closer to the reactors was a major issue. Well, the terrorists had come up with another solution. There were a dozen former members of the landing troops amongst the terrorist organization. The idea was to perform a landing operation, so the men got near the nuclear plants with their parachutes, in the safest possible way. Whether they would land ten, twenty, or fifty kilometer away from their target, was something that no one could know for sure, until they tried. However, what would they be able to do, once they reached the base of the domes? How would they manage to cause any damage to the facility? The answer was simple – they could not do much. It was impossible. Standard grenades would just chip the concrete base a little, whereas the domes would not move an inch. The only entry to the nuclear plant was through the roof and although, the terrorists had a helicopter, it was unfeasible to think that the machine could get even near the place in one piece. The more information the radicals tried to gather in search for a weak spot in the defense, the more they realized how hard was to find a breakthrough point of the stronghold.

Before the terrorists lost their last hope that they could ever do it, a few volunteers amongst them decided to have a go and risk their lives, doing so. They jumped from a plane and landed around 37km away from the target, but managed to reach it after some strenuous efforts. The brave men had collapsed only a few meters from the nuclear power plant, prepared to give up, as they felt life was slipping away. Their bodies were going to rest in peace next to the most significant energy project in the world. They did not even bother set the grenades off, as they knew that the attempt would be futile, with the structure being so solid. The three guys were about to become the first unintended victims of Mark's project. The security system with the smithereens was not switched on, however, this did not leave the violators unnoticed. The daylight satellite images had pointed their exact location and a team was sent off to collect them. The injured received first aid, which really saved their lives and then they were taken to hospital, where they stayed for a good length of time, because of dehydration and bad injuries to their lower limbs. The militaries, which were in charge of dealing with this rare incident, had decided to keep it a secret from Timor, or any other personnel from the other departments of the Base. Their explanation of events was that the men just got lost, while hunting for camels, most possibly. The officers had come to this rather unwise conclusion, because they were dressed in clothing that was typical for the locals, who lived at the border regions of the Big Desert. And of course, all locals were into camels. The two guns that were discovered was the solid evidence for their interest in hunting. The bags, full of grenades were luckily buried by the desert wind, otherwise the story would have been quite different and the conclusions – not so stupid and naïve.

While still at hospital, the three heroes, who had failed at their mission, got a visit. Some of the high ranks of the terrorist group came to hear about the unfortunate adventures of the "lost cameleers", which confirmed that a break through was simply impossible.

When people could not have what they wanted, this made them rather stressed, to say the least. At the same time failure invoked people's ingenuity, which urged their brain to work harder in a situation of unpredictable conditions.

The days slipped by. The nuclear power plants proliferated in the heart of the Big Desert. They had to be exactly three thousand within a year. The facilities were impervious and invincible. This was the bitter pill, one had to swallow. The baddies also stopped showing any interest about the central distribution base. The seven meter-high wall as well as the much powerful sensors, which could indicate any movement from three kilometers away, made all future attempts of attack pointless. The guards, forming a true mini-army, additionally contributed to writing off the Base from the terrorist target list. Were there any loopholes and weak points in the project, so somehow damage could be done and nuclear energy production jeopardized? The incessant but totally fruitless search for an answer to this question was about to stop, once the smithereens system got activated. However, a light in the tunnel illuminated the way for the terrorists. Although, this was not so much of a brainwave, the radicals felt it was a rather good idea. They received some inside information, regarding a small unmindful error on Mark's part, which concerned the security around the water pipes.

The self-burying pipes project was an entirely separate process, about which not many people knew. Timor was the chief coordinator, but even he remained unaware of who was in charge of this operation. He had limited information – when everything was completed, the pipes had to be ready, too. The scientists also stayed out of this part of the project, although they had spent a significant amount of time on it, when modifications of Mark's plan were made before the start. In effect, the entire process of manufacturing, transportation and positioning of the pipes was assigned to a group of engineers, employees of the manufacturer. Each part of the long pipeline was designed with a view of its role – whether it would operate above or under the ground. The first section connected the ocean to dry land, and the rest were simply attached to one another, in the direction towards the Big Desert, until the line reached the nest of nuclear power plants. The two pipelines were built with a distance between each other that was equal to one tenth of their length together. It was allowed for the reserve pipe to be completed with a slight delay. The elements that were designated to operate above ground differed in length and respectively – in their number. This was because the terrain was not even everywhere, as well as the top layer was dense and hard in some areas, and soft – in other parts of the surface. Each element was covered with a protective steel sheet against the possible adverse effects of the weather. The pipe system that had to function out in the open was secured with armed guards, deployed there in their trailers and ready to act at once should anyone dare target the pipe.

Still, the terrorists were very pleased to find certain negligence in parts, which undermined the safety of the pipeline. They could not believe their luck! Everything else was well thought and perfectly secured, but there was one trivial mistake, which was going to be their big chance. According to the drawing plans, the pipe had two visible sections, 400 and 800 meters long, respectively, which were guarded by two trailers each. The trailers were positioned nearer to the center of the pipe segments, which inevitably allowed for some time, should anyone decide to get close to either end. The protective cover was strong, but still, the terrorists would have several minutes at their disposal, to act directly before being noticed. The best part was that even if the security guards called for back up, the helicopters would arrive no earlier than an hour time. So the terrorists would enjoy a window of opportunity to create a beauty of a hole, allowing for millions of liters of water to gush out.

Well motivated, the insurgents prepared for the attack. They anticipated a minimum of casualties on their part and a maximum of damage to the target. The shorter segment, which was 400m long, was situated near the ocean. This made the access an easy task, if one considered that trekking for 30km was easy.

The armed opponents of nuclear energy were about twenty, as they were aware that they would be confronted with eight security guards, at the most. One fourth of the terrorists had the difficult task to carry the heavy drilling machine, which was going to turn the pipe into yellow cheese. In the first cool hours after the beautiful sunset, the small terrorist group reached the right place, unchallenged and unnoticed. The plan involved them making a start with the drilling and when the security realized that something was up and arrived to check – they would be simply eliminated. The failed missions, so far, had boosted their lust for blood and the rebels really did not care whether they could avoid spilling it.

The silence in the desert, chilling at times, was broken by a strange noise. At first, the guards could not figure out what it was or where it came from, so they followed the instructions as usual. Back up was called on the radio and the armed soldiers just went to wait in the safety of the trailer. They could not possibly know that their cowardly decision had actually saved their life. Should they have gone to check the situation in person, they would have been met by loaded sub-machine guns.

While lurking in expectation of the military helicopters to arrive and solve the problem, they kept hearing the strange noise. They did not have to guess twice that someone was trying to drill through the pipe for real. Accepting the facts that, indeed, this was what that was happening, the eight young guards, who were lucky enough to have got this job in the middle of nowhere, suddenly burst into laughter. They tried to imagine how the faces of the idiots outside would look like once they realize that they had been drilling through a hollow, empty still not operational pipe, designed to be the back up of the one that actually delivered the water. None of the soldiers bothered to clock how long the pointless activity went for. Eventually, it did end. There was silence. An hour later, several helicopters, carrying about fifty soldiers, well prepared for battle, arrived on the spot. The sophisticated infrared equipment on board was used to scan the area above the pipe; however, the terrorists had clearly retreated sufficiently far. The state of emergency remained in force until dawn. It was evident that there was an attempt for a break-through, although, in reality, there was not even a hint of threat, even the hole was made in the pipe that was in use. The security guards could not believe how stupid the terrorists must have been in thinking that they could cause any damage. The hole was quite high. Elementary physics was probably not their strength – they had missed the fact that even if the pipe wasn't empty, the water, running through it, would not take more than three quarters of its volume. In this case, Mark had planned the water to take up about 60% of the pipe.

The lack of luck ultimately put off all the leading terrorist groups from any serious attempts to attack. They could just wait for a better opportunity to arise in the future than keep making fool of themselves over and over again. This last daring attempt showed the militaries their weak spots in the defense. The guards doubled and extra sophisticated technology was put to use, so as any intruder could be prevented from reaching the pipe. Timor was not informed about the case, nor did he hear about the new changes in security. It would have been a different story if the real pipe got attacked. Or maybe, not? The militaries in charge felt that this was their job and they did not seek any other person's opinion or help on this. They never interfered in civil matters, either. This event was yet another example for the lack of coordination between departments. However, the defense of the Base, of the nuclear plants and of the pipes, as well as, all matters, related to any terrorist activity was an exclusive priority of the militaries so it was pointless for them to involve in this the chief coordinator, Mark, or anyone else for what it was worth.

Escape

Mark and Jennifer had to change several horizontal elevators before they reached a dark tunnel, which was not like the others. There was no light and it rather looked more like an abandoned smelly cave, than a regular underground pathway in use. There was no one around, or any trace of anyone that had ever been there, like people from the maintenance team, or folks, who would wander about near the place, just out of curiosity. Jennifer had a rough idea where they were, despite the fact that she had never come to this part of the Base before. This, nevertheless, did not help her figure out why they had ended up there, nor how would they get out. Mark produced two torches out of his rucksack, switched them on and confidently stepped forward towards the dark hole.

"Mark, are we going in there?"

"Well, we are, we can get out of here, as there are no people and no one's guarding this place… So no one will see us." He replied briefly, as his mind was engaged with the more difficult part of finding an escape route.

"Wait, Mark, I'm not going anywhere until you share your plan with me! We need to get out of here, but I don't like the look of this tunnel. Is there another way?"

"Eh-r-r, well, Jennifer, I don't think so, or at least, I can't think of any other way…"

"So if this is the only way, do you know what's at the other end?" She pointed straight on with her right hand, and instinctively covered her nose with the other. The smell was bearable, but very unpleasant.

210

"Well, the exit will take us beyond the wall about ten kilometers from the Base. I'm pretty sure where about we'll end up, somewhere in the desert… Well, it's all a desert around us, isn't it?"

"And what are we going to do there? It's 50'C outside at this time."

"Well, I know, but the tunnel is long and by the time we reach the end, it won't be that hot, so we could carry on walking. We've got jackets, too, haven't we, when it gets cold?"

"Walk? Mark, where to?" Although, Jennifer was well used to his strange way of speaking, at this point she really hoped to get more sense out of his answers, instead of getting some, which posed further clarifying questions.

"Well, if we could get to the first line of nuclear power plants, we don't need to go any further." Mark noticed her sulky face, despite the weak light and hurried up to clarify the next question. "Well, Jennifer, there's an exit shaft at the end of the tunnel that we could use and then, reach the nearest nuclear plant, get in and escape this way."

"But if the tunnel is 10km long and the nearest nuclear power plant is 50km away, as far as I am aware, then, we'd have to walk 40km outside!" The primary school Math efforts only made her show her growing panic. "Mark, we'll never get out of here…! Timor will catch us and hang us on the spot! We are finished!"

"Eh-r-r, well, Jennifer, this won't happen. He doesn't know where we are and he'd never find out how we've managed to get out…"

"Mark, we're in such a mess! How did we end up here?" A few tears rolled down her face. She was fully aware that even if they got out unharmed, it was doubtful that they would ever have a bright future ahead of them. Who would ever dare to employ them or give them shelter, when everyone in the world knew who Mark Eos was! Where would they find refuge and feel safe? Mark had no idea about Jennifer's qualms, but it seemed he had found solution to all their problems.

"Well, Jennifer, calm down! You just follow me and I promise that everything will be all right. Now, we just have to go through this tunnel and get out. Come on, please!" She was still in despair, but felt she had to trust her sweetheart. She took the torch and lit the darkness ahead of her.

The tunnel was high and wide enough. It was dug by the same machine that had made all the other tunnels around the Base. Mark and Jennifer walked carefully in case there were objects and debris on the floor that they could trip over. They touched and rested on the damp mouldy walls only as a last resort. Their light uniforms had already become scruffy and grubby, especially around the sleeves. A few hundred meters in, they picked up their pace, advancing steadily towards the end of the smelly tunnel. Jennifer had overcome her little crisis and began to raise more questions about their escape plan.

"Mark, would you tell me exactly how we are going to reach the nuclear power plants? We have to cover 40km in the desert, where I feel exhausted just defeating these 10km. We won't make it!"

"Well, you are right, but it's actually about 38km on the outside, and we'll do them much faster than the distance in the tunnel." Mark kept illuminating the path in front of him and watched carefully where he stepped. He kicked a few times some invisible objects. He was certain that one of them was a tin and the other – a heavy stone, which made his big toe numb for a while.

"How are going to do this? You've said we have more walking to do!" Jennifer also made sure she lit every step of hers. She managed to avoid any obstacle ahead of her, because she was a meter behind Mark, who was deactivating all the "mines".

"Well, walking is probably not the right word. We'll do that for a bit, but in some parts of our journey we'll just make use of the terrain in the area and slide down the sand dunes, causing a sand avalanche, not that this term exists, really!"

"A sand avalanche?"

"Well, it's no different than the snow one, but in our case, we'll slide on the sand. Eh-r-r, when we are on the top, we'll just jump and our weight will cause the avalanche effect, so we could slide down…"

"Mark, what are we going to do when we get to the bottom? Also, we could end up buried under the sand?"

"Well, this won't happen! The density of the sand is different to that of the snow. One could easily fall through in the deep snow and suffocate under its weight, whereas we are out of danger, sliding down the sand, not that I have tried this before, but I'm pretty sure…"

"And then, we'll have to climb up the next dune and slide down, and then, climb up again and so forth? Mark, you've said it'll be much quicker!" Jennifer had a point, but only if one assumed that the desert was even throughout. In fact, it was not.

"Well, this is not the case. We'll only have to go up a hill once or twice I think. Our route involves only going down, because it includes a downward cascade of dunes, so it will be all very fast. The one that we need to overcome is not very high. It will all depend on how much sand the wind had piled up on top of it."

"This sounds incredible, I mean, to slide down the dunes like skiers." Jennifer had never skied before. This had been a childhood dream of hers and she could not wait to have a go. "Mark, wouldn't we need something of a device like a board or skis?"

"Well, I don't think so, it won't hurt if we had, but it's not a problem. I can't really ski… we'll just have to rely on our bodies…"

"How do you mean? Who's going to be on the left side and who – on the right?"

"Eh-r-r, well, I haven't thought about it. Maybe…"

"I'm only kidding, Mark!" Her light girlie laughter resonated far into the depth of the tunnel, so they stopped for a second, until Jennifer calmed down her chuckle.

"How far have we walked, do you think?" She asked, convinced that her own estimate would be definitely incorrect.

"Well, I can't say for certain, but probably, less than a kilometer. We are doing alright, especially as I feared that the tunnel could have been blocked by landslides. It seems it's not in good condition. Well, no one amongst the staff knew about its existence, I mean, when the Base was first built."

"Why it was kept secret?"

"Well, in case of an attack. The tunnel was going to be the escape route for the high ranks in the Base."

"This sounds terrible! So the ordinary workers would be left behind, to their fate?"

"Well, it's always been like this. Even if something bad happens now, it will be Timor and the department managers, who are going to get to safety first, using the emergency route, whereas the rest of the staff will be left to their own devices. Well, it doesn't sound fair, but that's the way, I suppose, because they are the most important employees..."

"Mark, how can you say this? Life is precious and some people are not more important than others."

"Well, that's right. I was just saying how it is, not that I actually believe that this is how it should be..."

"I'm sorry, Mark. I know you don't think in that way. I just think it is unfair people to be categorized as more important or less important. I want everyone to be equal, but unfortunately it seems that this is impossible! Mark, how are we getting in the nuclear power plant? You've told me many times that only the helicopters could access the interior, and the defense system outside with those metal particles is just ..."

"Well, I call those – smithereens."

"Yes, the smithereens, but they are charged with electricity. I just don't want to experience the sensation of..."

"Well, I don't, either, Jennifer, but we'll just have to do it. Don't worry too much, though, we won't get hurt. Anyway, if we are talking about getting in, we can only access the facilities in the first line, due to a technical weakness that..."

"Mark, I don't like the sound of this obstacle with the electricity. Isn't there a way we could avoid the security system somehow?"

Jennifer seemed to have only heard the dangerous part about the inevitable fate that awaited them, namely, being electrocuted.

"Well, we can stay away from the threat more or less, and we won't get hurt. You know, when I designed the system, then, my colleagues approved the plan, and we decided to charge the smithereens with electricity, enough to knock out someone or something, like an animal, of an average weight."

"I don't get you, Mark. Do you mean that we'll kind of faint or something for a bit and then, we will be alright again?"

"Well, it won't happen like that because there is an easy way for us to take the electric shock, designed to affect one person, together. This means that we won't get hurt as we'll act as one much heavier object."

"And how will we become bigger than we are? Our rucksacks won't make much difference to our weight!"

"Well, our rucksacks don't matter, really. We just need to hold our hands together and become one whole, when the electric current passes through us."

"So, it's that simple? If the terrorists get to know about this, then, the nuclear plants will be in big trouble!"

"Well, for them, it's not that simple, because they usually carry metal weapons and we don't! When the smithereens let out the electric current through a gun or something, then the person could be killed."

"Hmm, clever! And no one knows about this?" Jennifer was amazed yet again at how intelligent Mark was. She had, of course, met smart people before, but not in that way. With Mark, sometimes, she felt so intellectually inferior.

"Well, just me, the colleagues didn't really pay any attention to this and I didn't bother give them much details about it. They never asked, anyway, otherwise, they would have probably also known."

"This means that no one would think to look for us at the foot of the nuclear plants? Super! But, Mark, won't they send a team to check the signal?" Jennifer just about began to see a light in her imaginary tunnel, when her own logic threw some darkness over it again.

"Well, you are right, but not quite! They, actually, don't always check. There are camels in the area and often a small camel activates the alarm for real…"

"You mean we have to rely on our luck more or less?" She did not mind to be mistaken for an animal, if this was going to be of any help, but the question was what the likelihood was for all this to work out at the end!

"Well, you are right, but the point is that we'll be already inside, I hope, before the ground team manages to turn up."

"What about the staff under the dome? They will probably call the Base immediately and that will be the end of us! Mark, don't tell me you've thought about this, too!" Actually, this is what she wanted to hear.

"Well, Jennifer, and you know the answer to this as well. Do you remember how many people comprise the working force of each facility?"

"Three persons."

"Well, that's right – three! But they are in charge of more than one nuclear plant. The three employees have to check on four power plants via the short underground tunnels, which run parallel to the additional water supply pipe. The personnel only fill the reactors, check on things and charge the liquid generators. When we go in we'll be alone, because they won't be there."

"How do you know at what time they'll be in what facility?"

"Well, it's very simple, my colleagues and I have actually drawn up their shift timetable, so the idea is that we enter a facility that is free of any workers at the time. We'll wait if it happens for someone to be there."

"Mark, how are we going to get in? You mentioned, before, something about a small weak point in the technical side of things…"

"Well, the only thing is that it is not small and there are more than one! Eh-r-r, Jennifer, when the first concrete base blocks arrived, we realized that they were if not slightly faulty, they were unsuitable for our project. Nevertheless, after some discussions with my colleagues, we decided to use them, because we didn't want to admit we had some problems from the very start. Even Timor doesn't know about this."

"Do you mean we could gain entry through the foundations?"

"Well, that's our only access to the inside of the facility. The outer and even the inner elements, comprising the foundation, are quite weak. We will make a hole through the concrete, or a pathway, so to speak, and we'll manage to get in just under the main hall. The floor is made from metal slates, bolted together. So we only need to remove the odd bolt and here we go!"

"The guide" stopped talking, waiting for the next question. There was no such, however. He could not hear her steps behind him, which only meant that Jennifer is not moving. Her torch was pointing a bit higher than the one of Mark's. His lit the space of a few square meters in front of him. After 3km in, the underground passageway went lower by a meter and narrower. The height of the ceiling changed, because the tunnel was subsequently dug by a different type of machine, so from arched at the beginning, it went flat and low, the further in one went. The unpleasant slimy walls and nasty stench remained unchanged.

Naturally, there was no way that Jennifer could have known about these peculiarities of the tunnel. She was not very keen on being in confined places, but at the same time, she did not consider herself as someone, who had a serious problem with this, or being claustrophobic. But as the place was dark, stinky and unfamiliar, she began to feel like a trapped in a cage, scared animal. Her legs just froze and she could not make another step, even if she wanted to. She started to shiver with fear, rather than from the temperature. The tunnel was actually warmer by two degrees than normal. Jennifer noticed that the walls were not smooth and flat. Her frightened mind tried to find the right word to describe her environment and how she felt. Suddenly, the young administrative worker felt so terrified, like never before. A tomb. Jennifer was convinced that the way ahead led to some sacred sepulchre, where the dead had been laid there for centuries. Everyone knew that these vaults existed in the Big Desert. Well, it was true that the nearest one was flight hours away, by helicopter, but who knows, they might be some in there, too.

Usually, people, who fell in the same predicament as Jennifer, lost consciousness, when confined in a small dark place, unless they got out in the open or went into a well-lit spacious room, as soon as possible. Jennifer was heading towards this solution to her problems, until Mark's voice brought her back to the opening of the smaller tunnel, which was rather ordinary and free of any sacred meaning.

"Jennifer," Mark had uttered. "eh-r-r, well, now we'll have to take it easy, because here, it's getting quite narrow, Jennifer!"

Jennifer only heard her name. Her lack of response was taken by Mark as a silent agreement, so he carried on walking.

"Mark, stop, I can't, Mark..." Her unfounded fear had caused her to get an irregular heartbeat. It was hard to see, but the blood was severely drawn out of her rosy cheeks, turning her face chalk-white. Mark, who was standing at the entrance of the "tomb", went back to her, wondering about why they had stopped. Although, they had spent quite a bit of time together and those were the happiest times of his life, his progress about understanding women was not great. Jennifer still had to give him a subtle sign, when something was not right or if she needed some attention. In this case, he would have never realized her deteriorating condition, until she told him herself.

"Mark, I can't go in there. I'm scared! I feel dizzy... Mark, I feel sick..." She moaned. She was suffering quite badly.

"Well, what should I do, Jennifer?" Her pretty name was called out several more times, but she was already out. She fainted in his arms, as he instinctively caught her lifeless body. Mark was very knowledgeable on different subjects, despite the fact that he was not that academic and worked as an accountant. However, medicine was not his thing and he could not figure out what had provoked Jennifer's brain, so her physically fit body turned into breathing "corpse". The "switch-off", in

218

reality, happened due to the lack of sufficient oxygen in places, rather than her fear of confined places. Bad ventilation was the culprit and reason for high levels of carbon dioxide in spots. The combination between this and the prolonged walking, which required even more oxygen, ultimately led to the predictable result. Mark was safe in this sense, because, by the time his body got worn out, he would have reached the end of the tunnel. He placed Jennifer on the ground as delicately and gently as possible. He used her rucksack instead of a pillow and held her head in place. Mark was thinking hard what to do. It was an extraordinary situation. It was one of those moments, when one knew they were there, but could not quite believe it, and time froze suddenly. Quietly helpless, he switched off the torches and tried to find the right solution in the dark. Sitting at the entry of the narrow tunnel, it took Mark some time to realize that he simply had to continue walking. Not just him, of course, but carrying Jennifer to the end of the tunnel and towards the beginning of their long and peaceful life together. From the minute he had met her, he often dreamed of their future together, which made him feel extraordinarily happy.

Mark got out the most essential things from her rucksack, put them in his and picked her floppy body. He was not physically strong, and he had never pretended that he was, however, Jennifer felt as light as a feather. The narrow tunnel forced him to walk sideways, so he did not accidentally knocked her head into the walls. Mark felt a significant change in the quality of the air, during the last stretch of a few hundred meters. It was far too pleasant to breathe. More oxygen meant a better circulation in the brain. Jennifer felt the change, despite still being unconscious. The first signs of awakening were the few mimics that ran over her face involuntarily, followed by a couple of movements of her hands. Mark sensed that in a few moments, she would be back with him on their road to escape, so he hurried up towards the end of the tunnel. He feared that if she regained consciousness while still in that narrow place, she might faint for a second time. He reached the exit shaft and she was still asleep. He opened the heavy metal hatch to let some fresh air in, but he did not get out immediately. He rested on the wall next to the two-meter high ladder. He placed her head on his lap and began to wait for her to come round. Not long after she inevitably did.

The cold was openly unfriendly and warned for their unpleasant journey ahead. However, their extra warm jackets were designed to withstand this sort of temperatures and keep their body heat intact, aided by the big hood. Mark was feeling slightly tired from the 10km-marathon in the tunnel and his right arm ached quite a bit from carrying Jennifer. She, on the other hand, felt fresh and walked energetically by his side. Their trip in the desert was going to prove rather short, because in half an hour they reached the first cascade of dunes, they were about to 'ski' down. Thanks to the powerful moonlight this night, Jennifer managed to see from afar what Mark had been trying to describe about the whole sliding venture to her. It was clear to her now, how they were going to do this and that it was totally possible. They spotted the first dune that they had to overcome, concealing from them the thousands of nuclear power plants, spread ahead in the distance. The sand hill was not very high. They reached the top, feeling the heaviness in their legs, where the two runaways got ready to jump down the steep hill, hand in hand, taking in the risk of a minor injury or the odd bruise. The screams were their natural way of counteracting the fear. They screamed from the top of their voices. The speed they reached was nearly 40km/h, which meant that they would cover the distance much quicker than what it took them to go through the tunnel. The feeling was indescribable and their adrenalin levels went up through the roof. No doubt, this was the most memorable experience in their life. The fugitives overcame the second cluster of dunes and this ended the series of their exciting sliding. It was time for the next stage of their venture to begin. The couple had to walk a few kilometres and break in the empty nuclear power plant and hopefully get warm. Mark had not let go of her hand throughout the whole time they skied down the dunes and he did not intend to let go of it soon.

They were approaching the range of the electric security system and in order for them to continue their journey they had to take on the electric charge together. Jennifer had not forgotten his words. She felt nervous and looked around fearfully. The young woman anticipated the inevitable electrical threat. Her beau, and companion, was also worried and tense, very well aware what was awaiting them.

Mark tried to compare the feeling of being gently electrocuted for a second with something like a strange quiver, as if being pricked rapidly with a needle on the back many times. Jennifer clearly had too much from the experience with the desert avalanches, so she thought of the strange security system as being like as if one had three double coffees without sugar, one after another. It was good that both of them were in great physical shape, so they could carry on.

The 3 000 nuclear facilities were "planted" in lines as much as it was possible. The missiles that had to flatten the surface could not always fall into target so the long rows were not completely straight. Mark did not consider this to be a big deal. When they reached the nearest nuclear plant, he carefully looked at the cracks in the concrete, aided by his torch. The accountant discovered one that was quite big. Amazingly, he managed to pull a large piece that weighed at least 100 kilos, just with his two strong fingers. Underneath, they noticed that the entire structure of the concrete block was full of cracks. Mark and Jennifer succeeded in creating a huge hole, through which they could manage to go in, under the titanium dome. So far, it all went according to plan and they soon got inside, after removing a loose floor metal plate. Mark was not really interested in the interior of the spacious hall, but Jennifer, who had never been in a place like this before found everything to be rather strange. She expected much more, so she was surprised to see that there were only two reactors at each end of the hall, very little equipment next to them and just one large platform, where the deliveries were lowered down through the hatch in the dome. There was also something like a container, which was the workers' designated area for coffee breaks. Actually, the mere fact that the nuclear facilities' design was very simple, had allowed for building such a huge number of them.

The man, responsible for every detail of the power plants, so well thought and precisely executed, pulled Jennifer to the right of reactor number one. They stopped, when they were inches from the black titanium wall. Mark stroke the surface with his hand, which, to say the least, looked rather weird. Obviously, there was some hidden purpose in this gesture, unknown to the uninformed observer. He repeated the same movement a couple of meters away from this spot, along the wall. It worked this time. He pressed into the wall, which gave in, revealing a secret escape passage, created for emergency situations, when danger was upon the staff. The idea behind this was simple, as much as it could be, considering the high-tech project that it was, and at the same time it was brilliant. In every dome, there was a cavity, through which one could reach the life-capsules. Mark wanted them to be like sub-water motorbikes, but at the end, the decision was to re-use space capsules, after their slight modification. Once the endangered workers lay down in the pod, they had to choose from three options, in order to make their leave. The best of them was going to expel the oval metal pod straight into the ocean via the water supply pipe. This was where the two fugitives had to end up. The device was one-seated and Jennifer felt apprehensive at the thought of going in such a confined place. At least, there was no risk of fainting again for her, as the air inside was enriched with oxygen. She understood clearly Mark's instructions. The last thing he did before losing her out of his sight was to kiss her. He did this without any unnecessary dramatic emotion, because both of them knew that everything was going to be alright. He set the timer of the release-mechanism and waited. Ten seconds later, the capsules touched the water and quietly took their course, with the gentle sound of the engine.

Jennifer wondered about what they were going to do when they arrive. This was the last thing she thought of before falling asleep. She wanted to know Mark's ideas about this, when they were still walking through the tunnel but her fainting, then, prevented her from asking him. Mark was sleeping sound in the other capsule. The ocean was their refuge. Or to be precise – certain dry-land formations in the ocean, which had a special political status and which, according to the map, were not located far. These islands were not any further than 100 sea miles from the pipe; however, no one had ever mentioned them. The fact that people did not talk about them did not change anything like their geographical location and this was what the fugitives counted on, heading in their direction.

New World Order

The scrutinized search did not produce any leads, regarding the 'how' and the 'when' the two individuals had made their escape, nor was there a trace of their current whereabouts. This forced the chief coordinator to cease the hunt exactly a week after it began. Timor did not doubt that the militaries were capable professionals, especially when the action zone was a closed-off and isolated area. However, he did not forget, at the same time, what Mark Eos actually was about. The odd accountant would think of something clever and unusual to escape and would never approach any situation in a mainstream way. The word 'mainstream' or 'standard' did not go well together with Mark's persona.

Although, it was discovered on the third day of the search which horizontal elevator had been used by the two runaways, this information, in effect, had no practical value. Mark and Jennifer had won in this unequal intelligence contest with the 'dictator' of the Base, where the latter could not even figure out how he had lost it. On one hand, Timor wanted to catch him and punish him, but on the other – he would have been happy if Mark managed to escape and he never saw him again. Perhaps, this was the best for both of them.

The end of the search operation actually deleted Mark's name from the mind of the chief coordinator. He had to concentrate on solving far more important issues for him. If successful in doing so, he was going to become not only profanely rich, but also – extremely powerful. Timor believed he was the new Platt, his unauthorized successor, especially, when he realized how weak and indecisive his colleagues from the Global Energy Project were. When Alex Rice and the others heard the tragic news, they headed towards the place of event. None of them strived for the newly vacant position. Quite, the opposite, they asked Timor for his opinion and views about the future. Feeling rather tired of everything, the scientists happily headed towards retirement from the project, especially now that the nuclear power plants had become a reality. The only reason they did not do this earlier was Platt. It was not a secret that their leader, who perished in a nonsensical accident, could have managed the job alone. However, none of them, even the mouthy Rice, showed any signs that they wanted to withdraw. Timor got all the power unobstructed and this became a turning point in the project, which subsequently led to the establishment of a new world order. Once he had realized the vast resources of power in his hands, he took immediate measures to strengthen his positions.

The four new liquid generators arrived, ready to be sent to the seven richest states, and thus deepen further the gulf of inequality in the world. High ranked representatives of these countries visited the Base in person. They finally came out of the shadow of the strange voice on the phone, which pretended to be that of Prof. Connor. The delegates wanted to thank Timor for the good job done and to negotiate his financial demands. The requested sum of money was logically increased, surpassing the initial measly one million per generator. The generous guests accepted the higher price and did not even try to haggle. They were capable of eliminating the greedy blackmailer but they soon realized that he really was the master of the Base. Replacing the chief coordinator with one of their man would have probably had a negative effect on the entire process. That's why Timor was left in place and free to feel and play like god. The high profile visit could not remain a secret, so soon it was followed by delegations from the smaller countries, whose representatives were fooled that everything was alright. Timor felt that they were trying to control him in this way but he always managed to come out clean,

225

presenting the world through tainted glasses as if it was just and fair for all concerned. The delegates had no way to find out about the illegitimate deliveries so they could be regarded as harmless visitors, if not tourists.

All the leaders of the countries that took part in the crazy project of building nuclear power plants amidst the desert did not miss to send their sincere condolences. The seven most developed states did not want Platt's death, either. What was important for them was to establish control over the energy resources, with the help of Timor and his notorious greed. They would have acted on the sly, without Platt knowing anything. He would have been simply fooled that everything was absolutely normal. At a later stage, of course, these countries were going to strive for even more energy, well deserved. When the premature death became a fact, these states decided to act in a direction of change much earlier than they had planned.

Two months after the fatal tragedy, the seven countries got involved in their first ever operation together. They founded their own Energy Union and did not allow any other members. Their excuse was simple and made sense, however, it could not conceal their motives. The common borders, the natural geographical proximity, had pressed on for establishing such an alliance. Should any energy-related problems occur, all members would act and help each other. Well, this reasoning could not be any far from reality. The real purpose was to create an exclusive organization against all other states. They could not rely on any collaboration with the seven states, regarding energy, and in that way they would inevitably have a weaker position.

The small players decided to act upon and make a stance against the obvious energy aggression. So they formed their own alliance. This was a natural decision and it was easily predictable, as well. It was clear to everyone involved that such project was doomed from the start. The reasons: the vast number of states that became members of this new union, each of them – having their own demands and agenda, was going to make it rather hard for any of them achieving an agreement on something. The weak union was no match the alliance of the seven. Basically, some of the smaller countries were badly dependant politically and economically on some of the rich states so any confrontation with them was equal to self-destruction. This correlation was becoming even more obvious now that the energy problem was solved and the rich and developed states had sufficient resources to produce artefacts that the rest of the world so desperately needed.

The second step that the Seven Great undertook was clearly predicted by Platt. He had not envisaged its scale, however. The military industry was not only profitable for the great margin and added value, but it also had another significant purpose in a capitalist sense. In the era of energy shortage, the army stayed still, as it was a luxury to charge the energy batteries on a regular basis. The difference between then and now was clearly noticeable. Hundreds of military factories worked around the clock, not only to fulfill the interior market of the seven countries, but also they produced for export. The stock did not clog the warehouses no more, like in the past. Quite the opposite, the goods were ferried to and from across territories that needed strict security. Army trainings, performed together by the seven states, involving large quantities of equipment, illustrated the powers of the day in the most conspicuous way. It was clear what would happen if anyone dared to rise against them. At the same time, these very countries were trying to sweet-talk their smaller pals, so they could siphon as much cash from them, by selling them weapons.

It is a historical fact that the possession of weapons is the main requirement for the start of a military conflict. Although, the best-armed states had always declared that they would use military force only when provoked, it was well known that usually, they produced the first shot.

Being significantly in a superior position in a military and economic sense, the seven states took actions towards the third stage of their plan for establishing a new world order. It involved a "fair" use of the energy, generated by Mark Eos's nuclear power plants. At the end of the first year, after the project had been completed, these countries prepared a small surprise for the rest of the world, making all other states energy dependant slaves. In a heartfelt declaration, their leaders proclaimed the new distribution quotas of the energy, produced in the desert. The emphasis in the document laid on the fact that the seven had been receiving unfairly less energy than they would need in the future. That's why from then on, there was going to be a new system of allocation, according to which the seven would enjoy 80% of all energy produced, whereas the rest of the countries would have to evenly share the meagre remnant. And that was not all. Anyone, who did not agree with the new just and fair resolution, should clearly declare their stance and be prepared to take the unseemly consequences for disregarding the principles of equality. In short, this was clear war threat, a war that the seven undoubtedly were going to win.

Timor assisted in the quick change over of the Base security guards, who were replaced by union soldiers. Two hundred helicopters arrived in a day and they were clearly military. The long barrels, attached to their elongated snouts, made them the best airborne guards, supported unexpectedly by sixty tanks on the ground. Their job was restricted to the enclosed area of the Base, where they had to stop anyone, who would dare attack it on land. The unnecessary military pile-up achieved its threatening purpose, so evident from all the heads looking down. There was not going to be a war and the smaller states had accepted their secondary role. The last nail in the coffin of the old democratic world was placed, when on the second year after Platt's death it was announced that another thousand of nuclear power plants were going be built. There was enough titanium for this project. The mining operations had established that there was also sufficient uranium to last in by the end of the century. It was not hard to guess who was going to benefit from all this extra energy.

The political changes in the world led to some major social change, too, a huge surprise to even the most pessimistic sociologists and researchers. Unseen ever before hatred towards the population of the seven states was born, which very quickly transformed into a new ground for terrorism. The futile fight against the nuclear plants project diverted the forces of the most avid activists towards anyone, who was born in the wrong place, namely – on the territory of the energy union. Quiet and friendly people suddenly joined terrorist organizations in attempt to resume the old energy status quo of fairness. The protests and demonstrations outside the foreign embassies of the seven states quickly grew into riots, which the local police forces had no intentions to interfere with. Those diplomats, who managed to escape back to the safety of their homeland, did not want to ever return and appear in the way of the crazy mob. Gradually, these events became bloodier and bloodier, so that all diplomatic missions of the seven across the globe were closed. Not only official representatives were aimed at, but also the ordinary folk, whose only unforgivable sin was their birthplace, noted in their IDs. The towns and cities were now full of gangs that were trying to catch every national of the energy conqueror and kill them. Publicly, spectacle-like and retaliatory, barbarity was coming back in full swing. The police and the army presumably were expected to stop the outrages and enforce order in situations like this. However, they found some weak excuses that they could not confront such powerful dominance of people. The officers stood with a smile, observing the situation and often even helped the rebels by informing them on the whereabouts of the misfortunate nationals of the seven states, so they could be caught and executed.

In effect, people had taken the law into their hands and this could not be ignored by the union countries. The rich knew that there were two sides of the solution of the problem. Nevertheless, they had to find the right balance. On one side, if they killed everyone, who was against them, the population of the world was going to be reduced significantly. They could not afford to lose their markets. The smaller countries guaranteed them a long lasting economic control. On the other hand, these low and primitive emotional outbursts had to be treated with merciless and as primitive means. Mass bombardments had followed as the first such act of violence since the last energy war. This had an exemplifying purpose, so as to show the local leaders that it would be a good idea if they calm down their pathetic citizens. The "wrongly" hit and destructed state buildings clearly showed that it would not be difficult for the powers of the day to destroy the entire country. The terrorists received a hard lesson within less than a month. They realized that this would be yet another war, which they were going to lose at the end so it would be best if they went into hiding, in order to save the innocent life. The temporary retreat was going to give the activists some time for thought. They had to come up with ideas of how to harm the seven great without provoking their own defeat again.

Emotions calmed down, but this did not affect the imperial ambitions of the seven, nor did it change the subordinate position for the rest of the world. It was quite the opposite. The seven powerful countries issued an order for allocation of only 10% of all generated energy to reach the smaller nations, which was in effect much less than it was promised to them. Naturally, this resumed the power restriction mode, especially in the big cities. Almost all attacks on the so hated foreigners that followed just after the announcement of the new restrictive measure stopped overnight. The reason: declaration according to which if a citizen of a country member of the Energy Union loses his life anywhere in the world because of actions of the locals, energy supply would be cut off for a week. Some people did not take the threat in the declaration seriously and executed publicly several nationals of the seven states. Immediately the liquid generators were diverted away from this country for a week. So any actions against the seven finally ceased, however, this did not make them any less hated by the rest of the nations.

Time was passing, the rich became richer, and the poor – poorer. Hatred had gripped people's hearts like never before. The citizens of the seven states also hated the rest of the world, perhaps, not as much, but still – enough! People did not dare travel anywhere but only to member-states, from fear they could get killed. On the other hand, those, who wished to move to the union-countries, were millions. Of course, they hated every local resident, but the foreigners sought better conditions and standard of living. The random bombing had destroyed tens of thousands of homes and the reduced energy supplies had increased the level of unemployment, hence people were willing to immigrate to the enemy's states. Half way through the third year since Platt's era had demised, all seven states forced their governments to act accordingly – a dividing wall was about to get built. The majority of people in the privileged countries would have been more than happy if the unwanted visitors were eliminated like some cockroaches. However, the more humane solution prevailed and that was erecting a wall. Those, who made entry illegally were locked up for life or extradited, so the problem was solved for once and for all. Unless the visitor had a special work permit, no one could come and disturb the comfortable life of the people, living in the empire, who existed with no sense of solidarity and equality, as it was removed from their system of values. The minority, who believed in acting as the Good Samaritan, had to revise their credo very quickly.

Timor knew about the wall. He knew about the cruelty, about the bombings, about everything. None of these events, which had changed the world forever, made any impression to him. His permanent residence was the Base and what happened outside of it, was just something interesting, but of no concern to him. As long as his bank had not been bombed, all was alright. Timor's greed and egotistical side thrived. Year after year, he wanted more and more money and it felt he cared less about anyone else but himself. His beloved Jess had joined the man, who she really loved for about two months since he rose to his throne. Very soon she found an arrogant dictator, who tried to control her life, too – a man that had nothing in common with the person she first met. Later on, when yet another argument between them ended with a smack across her face, Jess left the 'devil's den' in tears. She did not want to see him ever again. After a few months had passed, when her small country, which was not a member of the energy union, got hit heavily by missiles, Jess lost her mother. She blamed Timor for this and felt such hatred towards him that she had never experienced before. Two years later she lost her job and like many of her friends, she decided to go to the Promised Land. They did not let her in, so Timor was the one, who she cursed again.

The changes took place in the space of a few years. This time, no one ever blamed the New World Order on the energy batteries. No one actually understood the crux of the problem, concealed in the fast development that everyone strived for so eagerly. No one was careful, when they made a wish in the past, blinded by the very desire and now, so many were going to suffer for a very long time.

Tumor

The eight-hour journey in the pipe was sufficient for them to regain all their energy back. Lying down, they could not get the chance to move their limbs more than a few inches in each direction. Their mental rest also helped them feel much better, and the fact that Timor and the Base had remained miles away, added to their pleasant feeling of safety.

Jennifer woke up first. She did not know whether they had arrived, nor where they were supposed to get to. She was certain about one thing - the small engine had stopped its monotonous work. The darkness did not allow her to see anything. She began to feel the ceiling of the capsule, in attempt to find some mechanism, which could help her open and lift the hatch. She did not find such device, which was good, as she could still feel the swaying movement of the pod. This only meant that she was in the water and if she had managed to open the capsule, water might have gone in and... Jennifer stopped her imagination from creating a scenario, where she, as the main character, was drowning. She simply decided to wait for Mark to appear from somewhere. She counted on him coming any moment to open the hatch, tell her that everything was alright and kiss her. Waiting for the so desired salvation, she began to wonder about where they were going. She could see, in her dreams, the best possible place for them both – a safe and secure location, but most of all peaceful. Without a doubt, this was the country of the small and jolly people in the Far East. It was well known fact that there was still a certain level of power restrictions, because the country did not sign the agreement for building Mark's nuclear plants. Well, Mark and Jennifer might be suffering a bit without electricity, living amongst some small strangers, but at least they were going to be left in peace - without Timor after them. The country that Prof. Alex Rice detested was far away and they could not get there by any means. A dream was just a dream. Jennifer would have happily lived in another impossible for them place – her home country, in her hometown. Her reasons for this unrealistic wish were down actually to the people, who lived there. Her parents would have definitely liked Mark, they would learn to love him and accept him as their own son. Jennifer also dreamed about marrying her strange boyfriend in the presence of her dear family. She felt saddened by her illusions and a few tears ran down her face. Crying quietly in the small and confined place, she was waiting for Mark.

It was such a rare opportunity for one to experience traveling in a space capsule, but to spend eight hours in one, under water – this had really not happened ever to anybody. Well, it was not such a great deal in comparison to the roller coaster of emotions they had, when setting off the desert avalanches. Avalanche was the best way to describe the rolling movement of the sand, really. Mark also felt incredible, sliding down with the sand grit, but this was down to person's hand he was holding tight. The water journey had separated his hand from hers for a painfully long time that was why, when Mark woke up, he could not wait to return to the old happy situation before. The most difficult part of their journey was over. It was hard to believe, but floating in their metal coffins, in the middle of the ocean, meant that they were about to get through the easy stage of their arrival to the final destination. Now they only had to wait still in open water, for the sunrise.

Mark knew a lot about these capsules. While he was working on his Moon base project, he came across some very interesting information on the subject. He could not figure out how the third issue of "Space view" happened to be in the library, especially because exactly this one was banned for sale. He had discovered something on page twenty-seven and that was really significant. There he found a detailed plan of the space capsules, which were going to be used in emergency situations. The article was written by anonymous author, however, the news spread fast that he was one of the scientist from the engineering team, who had revealed classified information to the public. Mark wanted to take the valuable magazine home for a month, so when he was granted permission; he spent his entire time to copy all its content. He had managed to memorize every technical detail of device structure, and this now was what he relied on, in order to realize his escape with Jennifer successfully.

The capsules were made from some very special alloy that could withstand the very high temperatures that occurred, when the device entered the atmosphere at high speed. They could also endure big pressures like in the great depths of the ocean. Nevertheless, these good characteristics, remembered so well by Mark, were not of much help to him now. He was relying on all the complex data stored in his head that related to the capsule's intelligent control system. Thanks to the scarce energy that was sending radio signals about their exact location, they managed to travel the whole distance of the pipe without a hitch. The devices had run out of energy, however. It was a good job that the smart machines had their own solution to the energy shortage. The rescue pods could still generate power via the silicon cells, located on top. So the devices could be perpetually in motion, as long as there was a strong and constant sunlight. A red indicator in the top part of the machine noted that there was sufficient energy and the capsule was all set to go again. There was no need for setting the coordinates, nor had one to control the driving. The autopilot system did not need human interference.

Once the emergency capsules dropped down, the clever engineers had designed them in such a way, so they preserved precious time for their passengers until the rescue teams arrived. The satellite system made sure the machines always fell into the water. The sufficient oxygen, enough to last a few days, also made the capsules buoyant.

Nevertheless, it was not a very good idea to leave the machines stay still in the water and do nothing. When Mark was thinking hard about the last stage of their escape, the design of the engine had suddenly appeared before his eyes. He remembered precisely the shiny page of the magazine with the basic characteristics of the engine. The complexity of the control system block was actually rather simple. It consisted of an electric motor, which was powered by the panels, attached to the body. There was also a compass at hand. The compass always positioned the capsule in a North-South direction, and as long as there was enough power, the device just went southwards. Of course, the machine had many faults, but the biggest of all, was the fact that by always going south, it could inadvertently take its passengers further away from their rescuers and make their work harder.

The metal "torpedoes", with Mark and Jennifer inside, ploughed steadily the salty waves of the ocean. Jennifer's capsule got stuck first into the sand on the beach, resembling a baby-whale, committing suicide. Mark's vehicle crashed, almost at the same time, but twenty meters away, as if to show that although separated, they always moved in a tandem. They were very lucky that they got onto the short curve of a sandy beach and did not hit the cliffs, which predominantly surrounded the island on the north side. They had reached their final destination and now, they simply had to wait for someone to open their caskets. The capsule could be open from the inside only if they were not half submerged in water, and this was the case this time. There was a real risk for them to get killed when the hatch was lifted. Well, who knew what would actually happen?

The fishing sailing boat had a crew of ten people and none of them was the captain. This did not cause any chaos on the ship. On the contrary, everyone was going about their duties and minded their own business. The only exception to this rule was, when someone needed assistance. For instance, three people had to lower the heavy nets down in the water. That regular working day, which had started at dawn, was rather different, because of the interesting live discovery they made.

The shouting immediately attracted the fishermen's attention and they rushed towards the screaming man, imagining the worse. When they reach him and saw that he was safe and sound, the old fishermen followed the raised arm. They noticed the two odd elongated objects and straight away headed in that direction, according to the local laws. Someone suggested that these were some strange type of fish, which they had never caught in their nets before. The metallic reflection refuted the theory about the animal origin and directed the general opinion towards the idea that this was simply some scrap. The ocean regularly delivered some strange objects, all different in shape and size, which had to be collected and destroyed, if found, in accordance with the local directives. Nothing alien that was coming from outside should be allowed to contaminate the Tumors. Uncompromised isolation was what everyone wanted – as paradoxical as it might sound!

The fishermen got on shore, just a few meters from the waste. They were scratching their heads about how to lift the object with their strong ropes and move it onto the boat. They were going to take the refuse to the main port of the island, where the objects would get re-cast and turned into a lot of fishing hooks and other useful tackle. The second capsule was destined to the same fate. Before doing anything, however, the fishermen had to estimate their weight. The empirical approach of calculating the objects' mass was rather crude, but it did the job. Those, who were standing nearest to the capsule, kicked it a few times and judging by the distance that it moved, they tried to conclude how heavy it was. If the object did not move at all, then this meant that it was very heavy. Nevertheless, if the pod budged a bit, after a moderate kick, then the conclusion was that they would not need any ropes and they could manage carry the capsule by hands.

Mark had not heard when they came near, but he felt the kicks. In respond, he, too, began to hit and kick the rubber lining of the capsule's interior. The light noise he had created was enough to freak out the fishermen, who jumped back in alert. Two of them pointed their harpoons, trying to imagine what possibly could appear from the inside. The hectic waiting for something to happen lasted for about an hour. The sailors were certain that they had heard the noise at least several times. They stood still in one place, waiting for the creature to come out voluntarily. Mark expected that the locals would get a bit scared at the sight of the capsule; however, he yearned for their curiosity to prevail and make them try to open it. His wish came true, when one fisherman got tired of just staring at the scrap and confidently went near the pod to find out what was inside. He got hold of the handle, attached to the body of the machine and pulled slowly it with his hand. With the other, he held tight onto his harpoon. When the hatch went up open, Mark smiled with his eyes closed, due to the strong sunlight that entered his darkness suddenly and began to shout from the top of his voice the same phrase over and over again. The smile was there to show he was coming with peace and the sentence he uttered repeatedly was an old proverb that originated a long time ago in 'tumor'-land. The closest translation went like this: "The fish would never kill a man if it could, but no man was a fish…" or vice versa. The men laughed out loud at the accent of this stranger, who hardly spoke their language. They at once realized that in front of them, there was this harmless man, who was most probably thrown out of one of the large ships in the ocean. They helped him get out of the small corpus of the pod and then, they headed towards the second capsule, where it was certain, there must be another stranger, also cast away from some ship. Mark reached it first and went on to lift the hatch. When he saw Jennifer, who was still a bit sleepy, he quickly pecked on the lips, as discretely as possible, knowing it was in public. He got her out of the capsule and introduced his new friends to her, despite the fact that he was not aware of their names - he could not understand what they were saying to him. Somehow he knew that they would become their new friends. The fishermen loaded the now much lighter capsules and got aboard of the small boat, together with their two extra passengers. The sails took advantage of the gusty wind, making the wooden shell move, and headed towards the main council of the island. The fishermen were taking them there, where the five members of the council had to decide on their fate.

Mark was holding her hand again, and this time, he had no intention of letting do. The feeling was incredible. They were told to stay away from the railing, but Jennifer wanted to watch the fish, swimming in the shallow crystal clear waters. She did lean over, way too much, a couple of times. Despite the language barrier between them, she realized that it was better if she followed their orders, so she agreed to the well-meaning reprimand. It took the ship about half an hour to go around the north rocky coast, in order to reach its final destination. The uninvited visitors realized that the island was significantly populated, when they got to the right side. The entire southern hill was covered with the same wooden shacks, built as much in a chaotic order, as they were actually spread around, following some sort of pre-thought architectural plan. Mark found it interesting that so few children that he just noticed, were playing on the beach. He did not think that it was normal, at this time of the day, all kids to be at school. Those, running around on the beach, were too young and 'fresh' into this world to have their heads filled with knowledge. What the educational facility looked like was just another interesting detail. From where they stood, on the ship, the "school" could not be seen. Actually, the place was hidden from all angles. It was a cave, the entrance of which was concealed by lush greenery at the top of the hill. There were dozens of caves on the island and the locals cleverly used their natural advantages for a better standard of living. The health station was also situated in one underground gallery. The same applied for the main fish storerooms. The fish was kept alive, by just being dropped in one of the manmade salty cave lakes, where it could swim illusorily in peace, until its time was up and ready for its consumption.

Jennifer's eyes were all over the place, too. She did not find anything strange about the cone like-shaped island, especially its southern half. The entire side was covered in grass and low-ride bushes around the houses. There was a very pretty forest around the top,

239

which looked like a hat. When Jennifer stepped on hard land, she found herself amazed not at the natural beauty or the building-side of the island, but at the fact that she did not see even one female around. She could see a figure, about 200 meters away that looked like a women, but Jennifer was not certain. Amongst the kids, there were little girls playing, which was a good sign. Her limited experience as an administrator and the general lack of information prevented Jennifer from guessing that perhaps, the fishermen's wives had work of their own, which obviously did not take place out in the open. In effect they took care of the kids' education, attended to the injured fishermen at the health station, and just tried to get over and done with all the never-ending chores and errands, waiting for them in their wooden shacks. The patriarch in the house did not act extreme and the women were not in a subordinate position in any way or form. They just did what they thought was their duty. Besides, this philosophy of living was followed by all islanders, and it was irrelevant what sex they belonged to, how old they were, or which island they inhabited.

Jennifer first noticed that on the top, where the unfamiliar type of trees formed a thick forest, there was a very different kind of roof, sticking amidst the foliage. It was much bigger than these of the rest of the buildings. She rightfully thought that there must reside the governing body of the island. And this was where the two fishermen, who got down with them on dry land, were taking them. The boat that brought them ashore left quickly, now that it felt much lighter. Just because Mark Eos had arrived, it did not mean that the fish would jump in the nets by itself.

After an hour of cross-country trekking, the winding path took them almost to the top. Right in front of the gates of the large house, Mark and Jennifer did not know what to expect, but whatever there was hiding inside, it could not have been any worse than if they had to go back to the Base and Timor. Mark opened the heavy and squeaky door, urged by their silent companions, who did not go in with them, but instead – headed down the same path. A very civilized welcome, accompanied by an expressive bow, performed by the elderly host, calmed down the newcomers that everything was going to be alright. In the center, four men were sitting around a medium-sized round wooden table. Judging by their clean clothes, which were free of any fishy smell, it was clear that men hardly ever had to go out at sea. Mark and Jennifer kept quiet, waiting for some sort of a sign from the man, who took them on. The others briefly looked at them and then, just carried on talking in their undecipherable language, without showing much interest. The fifth person joined them, leaving the visitors stood awkwardly, a couple of meters from door.

They could have come nearer to the table and greet the group, but Mark's vocabulary was limited to that proverb he kept uttering, when he was trying to get out of the capsule. Jennifer also felt a bit silly, standing there as if she was being punished unfairly. She decided to attract their attention, as long as she was not simply waiting. She shouted almost from the top of her voice one word and this looked rather rude. As she did not know anything to say in their language, she uttered the one word, which sounded the same in any language – her own name. Mark felt worried that her actions could be regarded as total disrespect. However, he was surprised by what followed. The five islanders got up slowly from their wooden chairs, dragging them back a few inches. The men formed a line and marched towards the guests. So far, nothing extraordinary, but when they invited them in understandable words to join them at the table and then apologized for making them waiting, Mark was in a real shock. His presumption that no one could speak their language was wrong. He had not taken into account that according to the island's history, before the disaffiliation of the Tumors from the rest of the world, their language was widely used for a long time. All the overseas traders had spoken it. The age of the five men suggested that in those days they were old enough to learn the foreign tongue.

The conversation that followed was short and clear, and did not leave any open questions. An hour later, Mark and Jennifer headed down the path towards the designated wooden house, which they would call home for the rest of their lives.

The Tumors were twenty-one. Those without population were not counted in; otherwise, the number of the islands was ten times greater, including those with the developed mines on their territory. Every tumor was governed by a council of five elderly men. They made sure that the population strictly observed the policy of restrictions, after their voluntary disaffiliation. The councillors were also judges in the rare occasions of some sort of a dispute between the islanders. If any person dared talking about the outside world, or hinted at the idea that there were other people and other countries out there, at once the council interfered and took over. The guilty person had to go in the large house, where he was told in detail that he was wrong and if he continued to be stubborn, he would be sent down in the mines. Talking to and convincing the culprit was the credo, the council stuck to, instead of throwing around threats about physical punishment. Their noble age was important, because from a very young age, kids were taught to respect and listen to the elderly, but mostly those, who resided at the top, in the big house. Over the years, keeping the propaganda became easier and easier. Those who still remembered the time in the past before the isolation were either dead now, or kept quiet, knowing what was awaiting them in the mines.

It was only a problem, when some lost foreigner appeared from nowhere and began telling fantastical stories about other countries and places, situated on a big continent and not on some island. Mark and Jennifer were not the first strangers. In the first years of the separation, quite a few boats, mainly with some sick adventurers on board, appeared from the ocean and stopped around the Tumors' shores. Despite that this was forbidden, the visitors knew that the local population was not hostile, and despite knowing that eventually they would be sent away, there was a chance they could be allowed to stay for a few days. The soft approach did not last long. The General Council of the islands, which included one representative of each tumor, decided that if they wanted to stop the curiosity of the foreigners once and for all, they had to be treated with hostility. Sending the visitors down in the mines was not a solution, because there, they would tell about their world, and this should be not allowed – no local resident should hear about this ever! So they began to kill them. They caught them as soon as the foreigners reached the coast, then they were taken on a ship, which would get freed from the unnecessary load somewhere deep in the ocean. The barbaric approached worked, and for more than two decades now, no one uninvited ever came near – until this day, when Mark and Jennifer arrived. They were not going to get drown not because they were very likeable, but because the new isolated society, created on the Tumors, wanted to part with the violence of the near past. They offered integration to the newcomers. They could effortlessly become part of this re-invented society, to which the world was presented erroneously (if one knew the truth), or the world was seen as it was by those, who were ignorant and oblivious to the truth. Should the guests refuse to follow the rules, this inevitably would have led them to the bottom of the ocean, although no councillor had actually expressed this aloud.

The small wooden house had a strong smell of fresh wood. The rest of the houses suffered from the same characteristic and the only way to live in one of them was to get used to it. The new residents liked the simplicity of their first new home together. There was one room with a table in the middle and a bed in one of the corners. On the opposite wall, there was an improvised kitchen with a sink. The water that ran from the tap was ice-cold, despite the fact that the climate on the island was mellow and warm during the day. The temperatures at night were also bearable. Mark wondered why the water was so cold. He even tried to find the answer from a scientific point of view, but to no avail, until he was shown the caves. That was why the houses were built below them, so the gravity worked its way and brought the water down to the residents. There were no worries that the water would ever

243

run out, because the daily summer rainfall made it sure that the hidden freshwater reservoirs were topped up.

Another convenient feature of the houses was that they had electricity. For a small quantity of fish, the residents could purchase their light bulbs from the big ships in the ocean. Hardly any power they used, especially when compared to what a liquid generator required. The energy was generated mainly from solar panels and a few half-working underwater generators. Those were a legacy from before the separation. They were trying to catch the waves in the moment they broke into the shores, as this was when the most energy was released. Both methods were a waste of time, because they were not that efficient, but this was good enough for the island. The runaways landed on a tumor, which did not have wind generators on the beach. Well, their efficiency was dubious, too, as they mainly killed dozens of birds every day. The low demand and the lack of energy batteries made the ineffective facilities well efficient.

Put aside the interior of the house, which had water supply and electricity, Mark noted the lack of variety when it came down to the food. It took him a week to realize that fish and everything made from fish was the only thing the locals ate. There were not any of the popular agricultural crops, growing on the island. There was no wheat, corn, let along potatoes or anything of the sort. Only a few types of unknown fruit added to the diversity of the daily menu. The bright red, which were the juiciest, were Jennifer's favourite. She was regularly given those for a payment of a juicy kiss. There were also two kinds of root vegetables that tasted like reddish. Mark did not like them that much.

The Tumors lacked money and this was one of their many peculiarities. Before the isolation period, money was used, but after that it was decided that it was better to rely on barter economy. Actually, it was too strong of a word to call this an economy. People simply exchanged goods – what they had for what they needed. The lack of money almost eradicated the sense of greed. If one ever decided to commemorate this human quality by building a monument, surely the face of Timor should have been placed on top of it. There were, of course, some insecure folks that wanted to have more, but their greed was harnessed in a positive way, because they purely tried to catch more fish, which, nevertheless, was shared equally amongst everyone later. Helping each other was something that guaranteed that no one was ever left hungry or thirsty. Everyone had clothes and all kids were able to go to school. Homeless people did not exist, because everyone lived in their smelly house. The properties belonged to all and every primary need was satisfied.

Mark noticed that some small differences between people existed. The fishermen fished with handmade fishing nets, which differed from each other by their pattern. They took a long time to be made. Their boats followed the same design, but the sails were always different. The same thing applied to the women. On the island, there were not any clothes shops and designer boutiques, but every woman made the effort to add a small detail to her attire, so she felt different from the rest, although their clothes were made from the same material. An example of this was the different colourful brochette, which held their long hair in place. This was how every female islander emphasized her individuality, and when the wooden needle was not placed in the hair, it could be noticed, attached somewhere on her clothing. Something so minute could make all the difference and turn the unified mass into individuals. Mark, who never used to notice in the past how people dressed, nor did he observed the human behaviour, now the new environment had provoked in him the desire to analyze the ever so slight differences in people. Clearly for these people, who had been put to live in far from privileged conditions, this was a way for them to express their inner desire for progress and development. They developed what they were allowed to. However, Mark was certain that if they were given more freedom and more information, they could easily become part of the rest of the world again, within less of a decade. Well, maybe, the way it was now seemed better for them.

Mark and Jennifer learned every day about the peculiarities of the new place and its people. The lack of any law enforcing institutions, in the normal world, it would be the cause of chaos and crimes. There was nothing of this sort on the island. If someone breached the rules, they went down to the mines. There was no written law to abide to. No one could escape their punishment or hide somewhere, because of the size and proximity between all Tumors. Besides, your fellow citizens would grass on you straight away, as they would know your whereabouts. Their duty was to follow the council's orders, as well as their sense of justice, which was an intrinsic part of their life. The offender was taken forcibly by the fishermen and not some armed men, who did not exist on the islands. The worse crime was usually a theft of fish. It was committed from stupidity rather than from real need. The consequences for the stupid folks were usually moral. They were banned from going fishing for a few days and this affected badly their reputation.

The Tumors had no armies. They did not need them. They had no enemies in the world, where Timor believed he was great. After the disaffiliation took place such a long time ago, no one cared about the islands, apart from the neighbouring continental state, which traded with them. Basically, the ships of this country often crossed paths with their sailing boats. Also, the islands could not boast with anything valuable like precious stones or other resources of this kind. They had small deposits of ore, which did not attract any interest.

The newcomers did not get their house as a gift. In exchange for a roof over their heads, they had to deserve the right of living in it by following strictly the all rules that their wise leaders shared with them. Their integration was impossible until they learned to speak the language. So, their first duty, starting on the next day, was to go back up to the main house, where the five councillors would take them to school. In the spacious cave, there was surely a place for two more grown up kids, who were going to take as much time as they needed and learn to speak, until they felt at ease communicating with the islanders. After this stage was over, they would join the adults in their real working responsibilities. Mark had to make the hard decision on what occupation to choose. There were two options – a fisherman, or being a carpenter and a black smith at the same time. These were man's jobs – to provide the food or to make sure that their homes and boats were well maintained.

Jennifer had on offer much more pleasant and safe opportunities. She could help at the school or at the health station, and later in the evening, like the rest of the women – spend some time, doing the household chores and attend to her husband. On their arrival, no one asked them if their relationship was in any way official. According to the conservative beliefs on the island a man held his woman's hand, only if she was his woman officially. Mark and Jennifer never let go of each other hands, perhaps, they were holding them even when asleep.

Each day on the island was a repetition of the day before. Work finished at sunset. The fishing boats were tied along both sides of the long wooden pier and the tired crew went back home. There, the women and children were waiting for them. The wives cooked some dinner and the kids played outside after school until daddy got back. The family would gather around the dinner table and after the meal, lights went out and everyone went to sleep. These synchronized actions applied to all islanders and no one ever dared to breach the unison. One house did not join in the harmony for the first few days. Mark and his non-official wife stayed until later at night, because they did not feel tired. All day long, they had to listen during their lessons to different teachers in the big cool cave. The tutors changed every half an hour, but still, the couple did not grasp anything that was said to them. The system of education was as primitive as everything else. It relied on the students' ability to concentrate and memorize the content through numerous repetitions. As a consequence of this parrot-like torture of approach, there was no one that did not remember everything by heart. All graduates left school with elementary skills in Math and some basic knowledge in the main subjects. The percentage of high marks was unprecedented, in comparison to the rest of the world.

Silence during school time was obligatory, especially because any noise made in the cave was highly irritating. Mark and Jennifer had to catch up in the evenings for not speaking all day. Usually they discussed yet another oddity of the locals they had encountered during the day and hardly ever talked about their previous energy dependant old life. Despite all the novelties they had to adopt and adapt to, both of them did not feel isolated in any way. It was true that their neighbours appeared to be sulking, but there was a reason for this, which they figured out a month later. People expressed their disagreement with something that they did not like the other person do, by sulking and frowning. Verbal reprimands were not customary; hence personal conflicts did not exist. The frowning was to say that they should turn out the lights at the same time as everyone else. And because the unwise newcomers did not speak the language and could not read people's minds, they failed to correct their innocent mistake sooner.

The kids at the cave-school also treated them nicely. They did not sulk. The warm welcome was typical for the Tumors, but not for any other place in the world. The locals did not hate Mark and Jennifer, nor did they judge them for being foreigners. They simply had no reasons to do this. The strangers did not cross paths with their fishing and they were no threat to them in any way. On the contrary, the locals found them interesting. They might be like an alien body, which had appeared suddenly in their lives, but if the council had allowed them to stay, it meant that this was the right thing to do. None of them asked the question about where they had come from. There could be one possible answer to this, anyhow. If they had not come from any other island that was part from the tumor alliance and that represented their entire world, they must have come, then, from one of the big ships, far in the ocean, which bartered with the islanders. Full stop.

Mark and Jennifer were now able to communicate on a simple level with the locals in their language, as long as people spoke slowly and listened carefully to what they had to say. Jennifer was the better student and the braver one, too, so she let herself speak more often than Mark. Her attempts were regularly met with laughter, because she produced some meaningless phrases that only she made sense out of them. After the language barrier was not an issue anymore, Mark realized that the locals were so limited that there was nothing to talk about with them. This was not because he had nothing to tell them, but because the council had put a condition that they could share nothing about the outside world. Mark and Jennifer were not interested in the topics, the locals liked to discuss. They always, without an exception, talked about fish or about something, connected to fishing. Besides, they spoke in short and simple sentences and this felt as if they were not really willing to communicate for long. So despite being amongst people, they did not feel as being part of the island community. This feeling did not leave them even when they started work and the school period, which lasted for more than a year, had finished. They dreamed to see the sunset after work and could not wait get back together to their wooden house. This was when their day started. In the darkness, so they did not annoy their neighbours, they talked until the late hours of the night about their life on the island and about their life in the future. They knew that they could not escape, but this did not worry them. Despite the fact that they had nothing in common with the locals, they felt self-sufficient in their happiness. During one of their long walks – an old habit, left from their time in the Base, Mark decided that he wanted to share something very important with Jennifer. He was the man, who had solved the energy shortage in the world outside the Tumors, by building thousands of nuclear power plants in the desert, and now, he was an ordinary resident of an island, full of blind fishermen and their blind families, yes, now, he had a new project to take on. The scientist in him had woken up, motivated and provoked by simple logic.

Walking bare foot along the beach, Mark and Jennifer enjoyed the bright moon, which had created a shiny pathway on the surface of the ocean, reaching to the end of the horizon. They did not take this path. They stuck to their traditional route, in the same way, when in the Base they chose exit Number 7. The waves were coming and going, softly stroking their feet. The water produced a calming sound. Their steps in the wet sand lasted for less than a few seconds, when the beach resumed its smooth surface straight away. The dead fish, cast ashore, was the only obstacle and they carefully jumped over them. Their hands were, as usual, inseparable.

Another boring working day, amongst uninteresting people, had finished and now, it was their time, when they could talk freely about anything they wanted.

"What's the matter, Mark? Are you very tired?" Jennifer noticed that he was unusually quiet at dinnertime. She thought he must have had a lot of work that day at the woodwork shop.

"I'm alright. I was just thinking about things and that it is so quiet, I find it rather pleasant. Other than that, I was making these wooden boxes today, for two of the boats, because all theirs have gone a bit damp, and they needed some new. I will have to finish them tomorrow. And how was your day, anything interesting?"

These days, this was how Mark – the Islander started his sentences. He had managed to forget about his typical "Well". The reason for this was that there was not such word in the newly adopted language he used now every day. His speech was not that improved by this and there were moments that one still struggled to understand him, but at least it was not so irritating.

"It was the same as usual!" His darling woman sighed, remembering her mundane and boring working day. Her responsibility was to mind the kids in the big cave and make sure they behaved and kept the noise down. She also helped serving lunch for them, when they had to go to the other cave next door, and together with their teachers they charged the batteries before the afternoon lessons started. She did not have much work to do and this made her feel undervalued.

"You are right. Everything here seems to have stopped, as if time has frozen."

"Mark, this deep freeze is getting to me sometimes. These elders up at the top, they'd never realize that this is not the way forward, would they?"

"They are not heading anywhere, nor would they decide to do something about it soon. You know that this is how it is and we have discussed it before."

"Yes, I know, they just like it like this. Everyone is crazy around here and they'll never change!" Her words were strong, but Jennifer did not hate the locals. She could not forget the priceless gesture they had made for her and Mark – the uninvited runaways.

"Still, we could learn something from the way these people live. I mean, the rest of the world could, although the folks, here, have no idea that other countries exist, really!"

"Our world to learn something from the Tumors? That's impossible! They can't teach us anything, but fish. They're so retarded, they haven't heard about real science! Everything is so primitive here. There's a light bulb in every house and that's it! These are your words, Mark, not mine!"

"I know, I have expressed such an opinion and I still stand by my words. I'm not talking about this but about their way of life."

"And you call this "life"? Mark, do not exaggerate, please!" She appealed for him to be more serious and she meant it.

"Not everything is perfect here, but Jennifer, we have a greater chance for a future, being part of this made-up society, than if we went back to Timor, or even to our home country…"

"Mark, that's ridiculous! Don't talk nonsense!"

"It's not nonsense, not at all! I haven't told you actually… and I just found out… Hmm, I'm not sure how to tell you this, really… but…"

"What haven't you told me?" Jennifer knew him too well and she believed that he could not keep secrets from her. The thought that this was not the case truly worried her. Ugly wrinkles appeared on her white face, lit by the moonlight, giving out her inner feelings and thoughts.

"Eh-r-r, it's…"

"Mark!" She pierced him with her eyes. She demanded an answer at once and a second later.

"The nuclear power plants could not really solve the energy problem. I know for sure that in the near future, the energy crisis will return, but the people, here, would carry on living as before and nothing will change for them."

"What do you mean? What will happen to the nuclear power plants? They've got a dome, the security system is good and you've thought about everything, so they are safe and protected!"

"They really are, the project in its essence is perfect and the only problem is finding more nuclear fuel – uranium, which will prolong the production, but I'm not certain that they'll discover more resources to last centuries ahead."

"Then, I don't understand you, Mark! How come the power plants cannot solve the problem, when in effect it has been already solved?"

"For how long, though? Jennifer, within just several decades of functioning, they will be completely destroyed. I'm certain of this and then, the world will go back to the dark ages again, but this time, there won't be any light at the end of the tunnel! No one will be able to find another source of energy, which could be easy to get and that could last forever. Such source simply doesn't exist. There isn't one and that's it!" Mark had slowed down. He clearly talked under the influence of powerful emotions.

"Who will destroy them? The terrorists? But I thought that this was impossible!"

"They could not get even near the facilities. Even if they did, the terrorists can't cause any real damage to them."

"Then, who? Who?" Fretted she asked.

"Jennifer, when at the beginning of all I visited the neighbouring country to explain my ideas, I had to present a solution to the possible

252

threat of natural disasters that could affect the nuclear power plants. I said, then, that the structure is strong and solid enough to withstand everything, no matter what."

"Yes, you've told me about that, when we were still living at the Base. Wasn't this the first ever meeting between you and the six scientists from the Global Energy Project?"

"That's right! Then I told them that they should not worry about earthquakes, because the next one in the desert will happen after half a century, and it won't be that destructive, anyhow. A few days ago my theory fell apart." Mark looked down in guilt and continued rather moved. "I was totally wrong! It will happen much sooner and it will be more powerful than I've thought. It will destroy everything there, amidst the sand and the entire work of the international community will end up being all in vain. The worse is that this will be the end of nuclear energy production. Never again will be there a chance for it!"

"But how did you come to a conclusion that you've been wrong? Why now?" Amazed and bewildered, Jennifer asked. She could not figure out how Mark, who was always faultless in her eyes, had managed to allow such significant imperfection to occur in otherwise the most perfect project-plan of his!

"It was very simple, actually! Two days ago, when we got on board of one of the boats to replace a section of the deck, the ship started to sway. The feeling is like when there is an earthquake, but the waters were calm and there weren't any waves. The motion was simply provoked by the fact that all of us have stood on one side of the ship and we were heavy. So later when some of us got off, the boat again tried to adapt to the changes in the weight on board and started swaying. Well, the ship is in the water, let's not forget, not on dry land…"

"Mark, I can't make sense of anything you've just said!"

"What I mean, Jennifer, is that the tectonic plates of the Earth also move and when I thought that there won't be a strong earthquake in the desert, I didn't take into consideration the weight on top of that plate. After we had loaded millions of tons right in the center, this inevitably would change the weight, the speed and even the direction of movement." A dramatic pause followed as if to emphasize the next important words coming. "The extra weight creates a bigger pressure under the plate and this increases the speed of movement, as the underground energy needs to be released quicker and that is why, the earthquake will be so powerful and destructive."

"Mark, these things are absolutely unpredictable!" Her attempt to downplay the risk was not successful.

"That's not true! They are easily predictable if you know the size of the tectonic plate and I know it, then, you need to know its speed of movement in the last few centuries, and I am aware of this figure, too. In addition, one needs to know where the plate meets with the other tectonic plates. The earthquake will be perhaps, one of the most powerful the world has ever seen."

"And you are sure about this? This will happen and everything will go to hell?" Jennifer stopped still all of a sudden. She did not let go of Mark's hand and thus, made him stop as well. She turned around and looked at him with tears in her eyes. She was not going to make another step until she received a clear answer.

In this moment, she thought about her family, about her friends and about all the people in the world, she never met. What kind of future they were going to have, or their children and grandchildren, after the end of the desert nuclear power plants, when darkness came to reign again. They were doomed. Dark future was no future. Jennifer believed like almost all ordinary people that the project of the accountant Mark Eos would make the world a better place, by providing enough energy for all. That was why she saw the picture, depicting a total destruction of the nuclear park in the desert, as a true apocalypse in its very worse.

"I am certain and even if I am wrong by 10-20 years, the end will be the same and it's inevitable. I'm sorry, Jennifer!" he said in a mollifying voice.

"So nothing could be done? Mark, you could think of something! No one is more experienced in this than you! We'll get out of here and we'll warn everyone! They'll take some measures, fortify the domes, so they could withstand the earthquake and the people will still have the energy that you secured for them and it will…"

"No, Jennifer, that's impossible and we can't leave the Tumors, either. Even if we manage to go on board unnoticed, on one of the ships, it will never take us to the continent! It's too far. You know that we are banned from visiting even the other islands."

"Are you really going to leave everything that you've fought for to just simply vanish?" She could not believe that Mark was giving up so easily. There should be some solution in his strange mind. There was always something there that he could come up with! Always!

"None of us can do anything to stop this earthquake. And even if we all knew about the danger, again, nothing could be done to avoid it…"

"But can't we at least… at least, somehow to… can't we do something?"

"No, Jennifer, there's no way we could transport the nuclear plants elsewhere and we could not make them any stronger. Even if my idea about activating some powerful electromagnets, integrated in the foundation, and which would have helped the facilities stay up by being drawn to the Earth's core, went ahead, even then, it would have not changed anything. The return of darkness is inevitable!"

"I can't believe it! There must be a way, Mark! There must be – it's simple as that!" Shouted Jennifer hysterically.

"What can be done and what I actually wanted to share with you this evening is that, after the end, there will be a new beginning, and I think I know what it should look like! This was the reason I told you before that we could learn something from the way the islanders live their life. The merging of the two kinds of worlds could help us build a society, without the negative sides of each of them, if they existed separately. A society, where people are not so heavily dependent on energy, no matter what was the source for it! A society, where people will know that the world does not consist of a few islands and that there's other food but fish."

Jennifer did not hear the last sentence. She let go of his hand and went near the ocean. She waited for the next wave and when it broke into the shore, she kicked it angrily, splashing the water high above her head. She turned around towards Mark again and uttered a little calmer:

"What is going to happen after the earthquake?"

"Our tumor will stay the same. Even if we get big waves as a result, they will be stopped by the cliffs on the northern side of the island. So I doubt we'd even feel anything. As far as I am aware, the other islands will be safe, too. Some sailing boats may get affected, but they are quite strong, so I don't think any of them would sink…"

"I don't care about the bloody islands! What will happen to the real world?"

"I imagine, everything will change, Jennifer. The power restrictions will be even more severe than before my project came to light. As you know, all sustainable energy resources were harnessed and diverted towards the desert and nothing new of this kind has been employed for a very long time. And the nuclear energy will be dead in the same way the petrol era ended. The conclusion is that the world will has to use transport as little as possible, because there would be no way to charge many energy batteries. We would turn back to agriculture and the industries would be wiped out almost entirely and from this follows that…"

"The whole world will become Tumor Number 22?" Jennifer concluded his sentence in great disgust.

"You could say this, but this is not so important. When the nuclear power plants get destroyed, people will begin to ask themselves about what to do, what's next and then, I think I could give them the answer, because they've never set foot on this island and they'll start all over again, repeating their mistakes."

"No one comes here, because there's no point, Mark!"

"May be so, but when nuclear energy is not a solution to our energy problem anymore, and when there are no other alternatives at hand, then, what can we do, but try to change ourselves by changing our old way of living and replacing it with something new that is not dependant on energy and just makes us happy. Have you noticed how happy the people here are? Their life does not depend on energy. There are no arguments and conflicts, and it's so very unlikely that there could be ever a war between any of the islands. Also, you know that you and I are the only foreigners, living on the Tumors, don't you?"

"Yes, and?" Jennifer followed his words, but could not follow his train of thought.

"This means that we are the only people, who had access to a different type of society. We realized at the beginning that it is rather primitive, but at the same time, the population has managed to overcome, in an extraordinary way, problems that our society, as it is now, could never dream of solving, unless we all see the ready answer here."

"Mark, I don't get it. What do you mean?"

"I mean that people could learn from the principles, the Tumors are governed by, and use them to build a new beginning after the earthquake. If people do not try to adopt some new ways from here, the world we used to live before will become a terrible place, I think, because we would all go back to the same old mistakes and pursue the same old ways."

"And why do you think that this will be the case?" Jennifer was still confused.

"I just think so. Since we got here, what I see every day is how happy our simple neighbours and their families have been! They are content with what they've got. They do not seem to have the same problems, which the rest of the world have…"

"You are forgetting all the negative sides we have to cope with on a daily basis here. We have to constantly hide and lie, when we mention the other places, we've been to. This is a farce, Mark, and we are simply puppets, but at least we realize this, where the rest don't."

"I know, but that's why I've told you that the Tumors could teach us about certain things, not everything. If I could compile the best from here and the best from the old world that I know so well, and present it to someone like Platt, who would put it into practice, after the energy era has gone for good, then, it could all become a reality!"

"He's dead, Mark, and we are prisoners for life. Even if you draw some rules and principles for the people to follow after the earthquake, so they could live happily ever after and in peace, no one would ever see these notes or hear about your idea!" Jennifer "stuck the knife right in the heart." This time, her logic was sound.

"I know."

"So this won't work, Mark. Let's go home and we'll talk again tomorrow. What you told me today really upset me. I want to go to bed now."

"Alright."

Mark took her hand again and they headed back. Jennifer did not notice that he had answered her twice in one word. He had never been so succinct before.

The former accountant was gazing at the only natural satellite of our planet and the idea that came into his head shook him. Jennifer was right. Even if he drew a detailed plan, step by step, about what the leaders around the world should do after the quake, so there were no more wars, and the ordinary person did not strive for owning something in a quantity that could go around to millions of people, but instead, was content with what there was, enough for him and his family and everyone was happy – the historical memory remained! The Tumors were deprived from such memory, mainly because of their small size and minute population. Nevertheless, this was difficult to happen with the rest of the world. People could not forget their past, which formed their views about the future. The only way for Mark's idea to work was if it was started from the beginning, in another place, and in a different time. The Moon, which very soon was going to be the target of space missions, could easily become the new home of the first perfect and happy human society, or almost!

On the following day, Mark was very excited to make a start of his new scientific project. He was aware, of course, that when finished, there was no one he could present it to. He was also aware that once the nuclear power plants were gone for good, there would not be enough energy around to send people on the Moon, either. What mattered to him was the idea to be kept alive. Nothing more!

Neither Mark, nor Jennifer had any idea about the new world order that had come, after Platt's death. They did not know about the occupied Base and the nuclear power plants controlled by the seven states. They could also not imagine the dividing wall, preventing millions of people from going, where there was light. All this did not matter, because the forthcoming earthquake was going to change everything, making the existence of the young empire rather short. The new beginning, no matter what it would be, was inevitable.